JOURNEY OF FATE - BOOK TWO

FATE
OF THE
REDEEMED

"Be prepared to reevaluate what you think you know about angels, demons, and spiritual warfare! Author Chad Pettit tackles this important subject in a fictional work which combines scriptural truth, imagination, and artistic license to present a picture of what this heavenly battle could look like. You just might find your preconceived notions not only challenged but perhaps even thrown out the window."
—Phyllis Helton,
Book Reviewer, Among the Reads

"*Fate of the Redeemed* is honestly the most exciting, edge-of-my-seat expression of spiritual warfare I've read to date. Our Redeemer is brilliantly glorified in this riveting story full of trials, faith, love, and, of course, war. A must-read for everyone. And I do mean everyone."
—J. Reese Bradley

"For fans of interaction with the supernatural realm, it's definitely worth the read. The interplay between the physical realm and the spiritual realm was intriguing."
—Marlene Rempel,
Book Reviewer

"*Fate of the Redeemed* is an eye opening, page turning whirlwind of a story. The characters become dear to you as they face with full humanity the supernatural forces tearing their world apart. Read it for the story. Read it to let its disturbing glimpse of the unseen spiritual war around us settle into your daily thoughts. Fans of hard-hitting spiritual warfare and suspense need to read Fate of the Redeemed."
—Brett Armstrong,
Author of *The Quest of Fire Series*

JOURNEY OF FATE - BOOK TWO

FATE
OF THE
REDEEMED

CHAD PETTIT

AMBASSADOR INTERNATIONAL
GREENVILLE, SOUTH CAROLINA & BELFAST, NORTHERN IRELAND
www.ambassador-international.com

Fate of the Redeemed

Journey of Fate, Book 2

© 2019 by Chad Pettit

ISBN: 978-1-62020-973-8
eISBN: 978-1-62020-989-9
Library of Congress Control Number: 2019949737

This is a work of fiction. Names, characters, and incidents are all products of the author's imagination or are used for fictional purposes. Any resemblance to actual events or persons, living or dead, is entirely coincidental. Any mentioned brand names, places, and trademarks remain the property of their respective owners, bear no association with the author or the publisher, and are used for fictional purposes only.

Scripture taken from the King James Version, The Authorized Version. Public Domain.

Cover Design & Typesetting by Hannah Nichols
Edited by Katie Cruice Smith

AMBASSADOR INTERNATIONAL
Emerald House
411 University Ridge, Suite B14
Greenville, SC 29601, USA
www.ambassador-international.com

AMBASSADOR BOOKS
The Mount
2 Woodstock Link
Belfast, BT6 8DD, Northern Ireland, UK
www.ambassadormedia.co.uk

The colophon is a trademark of Ambassador, a Christian publishing company.

Dedicated to persecuted
Christians everywhere
and
to all those facing a trial.

"But he knoweth the way that I take: when he hath
tried me, I shall come forth as gold" (Job 23:10).

FROM THE AUTHOR

The following continues the story of Lester Sharp and his angelic guide, Draven. In *Fate of the Watchman*, Lester was a callous, indifferent workaholic. He was the final result of true apathy, a man who saw nothing but his own life. Lester was not so different than all of us. But unlike us, Lester was given the rare opportunity to see the world in a new light, one that would forever haunt him.

When time froze, Lester realized that he alone was still moving. Left with no choice, he was forced to step into the lives of others, guided by an unlikely angel, though it is never explicitly stated that Draven is among the heavenly host. Lester saw what most of us are afraid to see and things few of us could handle. The truth of what really takes place in the span of a single moment of time uprooted Lester's view of the world, but I won't spoil that here. If you haven't read the first book, I highly recommend that you do so before proceeding with this book. Although both can be enjoyed separately, they do build upon one another.

Fate of the Redeemed looks beyond the veil of spiritual warfare that *Fate of the Watchman* merely pulled back. Loosely based on the spirit world revealed in passages from the books of Job, Daniel, Ezekiel, 2 Kings, and others, I have tried to create a depiction of some of the spiritual wickedness in high places we are called to be aware of and armed against. Please understand that I have taken some creative license. The following is a work of fantasy fiction. Please treat it as such. The towns, cities, and locations are fictional. However, Lester's situation, for the most part, is highly plausible.

On a practical action level, my heart is burdened for my brothers and sisters in Christ suffering persecution in places like Somalia. I have tried to raise awareness in hopes that you will be moved with compassion just as our Lord Jesus was. Our persecuted family needs prayer, and organizations bringing them aid need our support. By purchasing this book, you have contributed to The Voice of the Martyrs, an organization founded by Richard Wurmbrand to assist the persecuted church around the world. I encourage you to pray about supporting them further—or groups like them, such as International Christian Concern.

I pray this story entertains you, but I also pray it enlightens you and drives you to the Scriptures. I have provided questions for individual or group study at the end, as well as information to help you find more resources in your righteous battle as a soldier for Christ. May they bless and strengthen you.

I feel obligated to warn readers that this book contains depictions of violence and graphic descriptions of situations that may be difficult for younger audiences. However, these are done to further the story, and nothing is done gratuitously. All of this has been in good taste, but I respect the rights of my readers to be able to choose what they are exposed to.

In His service,

Chad

PART ONE

WITHOUT DEATH, NEW LIFE CANNOT begin. This is declared in the heavens and proven in nature, yet man is far too often willfully ignorant of the inescapable cycle of death and life.

Night must die for day to live. The moon has no light of its own; it only reflects the light of the sun. Every season must die, fading into days gone by, for a new season to be brought forth. With the dying of summer comes the changing of leaves. The fall. The old leaf withers, dries up, and falls to the earth to be replaced by new and vibrant leaves saturated by the energy of the sun. That same energy resides in the plants eaten by the animals that depend on the death of the plant to live. The energy of the plant becomes the animal's until the hunter takes the animal.

The hunter needs the animal to live and goes on, living on the energy that came to him through death. He never turns his eyes to the sun, never acknowledges that it alone brings life. But the heavens know the truth held in their choreographed dance, for they have rehearsed the rise and fall since their inception.

They foretold of One who would come forth as a tender plant and then be devoured by the animal that is man. His life would transfer to the man, and death would bring new life. Yet man would still not see that in receiving this new life, the old life would be null and void. And so, man would return to the hunt, seeking the fleeting energy of animals that fed on second-hand life, grown from the burning light that is but a picture of the undying light.

Hence pain. Hence heartache. Man suffers because he does not realize the freedom found in the new life and shackles himself to the bondage of a dead, material life. A life filled with nothing that lasts, nothing that fills. Until man learns that new life resides in him, and access to the true power of that new life resides in releasing the old life, suffering will endure.

That was the life I lived. The life of self. The life of routine and repetition, seeking satisfaction in that which can never satisfy. It is a life I do not wish to return to, for it is a grave, and I now walk among the living.

- Lester Sharp

PRELUDE

Town of Olympia, Eastern United States

THE WATCHER STOOD SILENTLY, ENSHROUDED by the ageless camouflage of the spirit realm. It is the place of no place, a tangible reality only to the immortal and supernatural players on a timeless battlefield for the souls of mankind. It is where "bumps in the night" are born, where unanticipated tempests of raging lightning and rain lash out on a fallen Earth as the elemental warriors dance their cosmic melee of undying death.

The watcher smiled. Comfortably. Peacefully. Transitioning from his human form of dark skin and long dreadlocks, he kept his immortal gaze fixed on the quiet house, which he had just left and where a newly reformed soul now comforted a man snatched from the claws of death. A single light in the living room of the house remained on, its faint yellow glow piercing the night like a beacon atop a lone lighthouse faithfully guiding lost ships to its reassuring shores.

He sighed and let down his guard to complete the transition.

Dark brown, sinewy arms began to turn into thicker, but still slender, arms that blended into the shades of myriad colors surrounding him. He shifted his attention to this, enjoying the spell of the ever-changing skin tones. Dark green and shadow like the grass at his feet. Yellow, glowing like the light from the house. He turned his hand so the palm was facing him and wiggled his fingers in order to watch them rapidly change between the mixtures of color and light.

His pleasure at the sight was intense but unmatched by the elation of the night's victory. Centuries behind this invisible curtain, decade after decade watching unaware mortals go through their endless loop of birth and death, killing and being killed, starving and warring. Years passed like seconds to Draven, the watcher for so long, but tonight had been different. He had been allowed to go to one of them, to show his power in the presence of a mortal and be a part of the reclamation of a soul.

He looked up from his transparent hand to the house. A part of him wanted to go to the man, Lester Sharp, to listen to a redeemed soul as he spoke to Wayne Burmeister, the same man whom Lester had saved with what he thought to be futile life-saving measures. Lester, though he was about to experience a tragedy like none other, had been given the triumph of a second chance. Draven was bound, however, and could not go. But he had shown one. One mortal had finally seen the truth. The light in the house went out. The watcher's chance to experience humanity was over.

He heard a vacuum of wind before the hit connected with his head, felt its searing bite before a burst of light, like smoldering electricity, crashed into his temple. He was on the ground then, his half-mortal, half-immortal head slamming into the dirt with another burst of white light. Powerful hands pulled him to his right and then onto his back. He stared through the darkness into the ebony eyes of a towering figure. Lightning sparked and danced in his eyes.

Morane.

He was a head and shoulders taller than Draven and half a foot wider. Electricity danced along his body and sparked at the end of his enormous claws. The haze in Draven's vision cleared enough for him to make out the details of the demon's enormous, inhuman face. Draven's supernatural vision clearly saw his nemesis, even though the oily black skin of the demon blended perfectly into the night. He smiled with a hiss, revealing razor sharp teeth that were so brilliantly white, they could stand in as lights in a cave. Their glow temporarily drowned out Morane's face.

"Quite a show, Draven," Morane said in a rasping whisper. "A pity you won't be able to see the unhappy ending."

Draven clenched his teeth and tried to get to his feet. He was weakened by the blow and not able to transition into his true form without getting away from the demon. The giant, clawed hand grabbing him by the throat tightened. He swung his arms, saw them pass through Morane's thick, black hide and mentally berated himself for taking so long to transform.

"Caught off-guard, watcher?" Morane laughed, then slammed his head into Draven's. The force of the demon's square head cracking into his forehead nearly made Draven black out, but he didn't have time to assess the damage or pain, for a series of righthand punches pummeled into his face in rapid succession. He swooned, felt his throat nearly collapsing under the pressure of Morane's grip, and then was on the ground again. He felt the impact as if in a distant tunnel, as if the force of the impact was delayed, and he realized he was losing consciousness.

"You won't win, Morane," he said, croaking. The words sounded pathetic, tiny and echoing from the far end of a long tunnel.

Morane picked him up by the chest and legs, lifted him high, and then slammed him onto the ground. Draven heard his breath blast out in a gust with a groan that may have been his. He felt something splatter on his face, something cold and wet. His blood. Again, he was lifted; again, he was slammed down. More blood sprayed. More air blasted out. He could no longer breathe, but a distant memory of something important called to him, willed him to stand. He turned his head, caught a glimpse of a dark house on a pleasant lawn at night. He wondered whose home it was. His jaw was hit from one side, and the other slammed into the ground with a sickening crack.

The rebound of the blow forced his eyes skyward. Lightning surged above him, then into him. His body lifted involuntarily with a wicked jolt. He clenched his teeth and grimaced in pain. The lightning stopped, and he collapsed. He registered a thousand nerve endings all firing at once. He was numb, and everything felt distant. He heard a voice above him, telling him the human would never survive what was coming. It said the Dark Lord was ready to rise. He wondered who the human was, what the Dark Lord meant. There was another surge of electricity. This time, there was no strength in him to clench his teeth or grimace. His body was suspended until the electricity left, and he understood that, somewhere, his body had collapsed.

He was in the air then—up at first, then soaring. He heard wind. Through the hazy black cloud, he saw the night fade to day. He felt something on his back, hard at first, and then he was sliding through a hot, gritty substance. Above him, there was a blackened sun and a sky that should have been bright. It faded to onyx as he slipped into a sleep like none he had known before.

CHAPTER ONE

THE DEMON, MORANE, TURNED TO face the quiet house of Lester Sharp as he allowed his lightning to return to its dormant state at his core until he called upon it. He grinned, feeling his sharp teeth fold over his thin, bottom lip. Bringing his hands up toward his face, he placed his hand over the scars on the opposite wrist and massaged the skin. The burning sensation caused by a century in chains was nearly unbearable, but he relished in the victory over the one who had put him in those chains.

Years. He scoffed. A century?

The blink of an eye to the mighty Morane, lieutenant to Lucifer himself. He had waited patiently, mentally ticking away the years like seconds on a clock while he plotted his revenge. This was their way. He had lost to Draven before. The puny watcher was nothing compared to Morane in open combat, but the tiny warrior had prowess and cunning. Morane marveled that Draven had been so easily caught off his guard. Apparently, the soft-hearted angel had been so engrossed in the reformation of this mortal that he had forgotten the dangers lurking all about him.

Morane smiled again. How fortunate for him. He suffered none of Draven's weaknesses. In fact, he allowed none of the hindrances that so often crippled those still loyal to Jehovah. Obedience, loyalty, compassion—these were the marks of a fool and had no place on the battlefield of true warriors. Among titans, mercy meant death.

He marveled that any of the princes still served Heaven. Hearing how Draven had spent time with one of the mortals, showing him the ills of mankind in efforts to reform him, nearly made Morane wretch. Mortals were all the same. Show them the error of their ways, and they would change for a time, but only if it was in their best interest. It took so little to tempt them and turn them back to the dark side. This mortal, this Lester Sharp, would be like all the rest.

"Time for you to show the world who you really are, Lester," he said.

He purred as he crept toward the window of the house. The night was still. No sounds, no movement. The demon slipped from the spirit realm and gingerly pressed his hands against the window. The room inside was dimly illuminated by a faint glow from another room. To the left, several feet away, a pale-skinned human with tousled hair slept in a reclining chair. A cup was in his lap, atop a thin blanket. The human stirred, restless, and appeared to be breathing hard.

Morane laughed to himself. "Your redemption did not come without consequences, human." He stepped back and licked his teeth with his serpentine tongue. "Perhaps I should allow the nightmares of what he has witnessed torture this weakling."

He shook his head and chuckled. "But what would be the fun in that, Morane?" He rolled his head, relishing as it cracked and popped. He let a spark of lightning escape his fingertips. "Enjoy the nightmares, human. Tomorrow, the fun begins."

Outside the village of Khufia, Somalia

He heard voices.

Someone was shouting. No, not someone. Many voices. Men shouting. Close and coming closer.

He heard them, tried to discern their words. He was only able to pick out one: *sahir.*

The word meant nothing to him, but the anger in their voices told him it did not mean "friend."

He scrambled to his feet, swooned, and fell to his knees. A cough spasmed its way out of his throat, and blood splattered onto the sand.

Sand?

He looked up and instantly had to shield his eyes as he inadvertently looked into the sun. His mind told him it was supposed to be night. He saw a flash of darkness in his mind, a small house on a well-manicured lawn, but that had to be wrong. He was on his knees in the sand. A desert. There were no lawns there, wherever *there* was.

The voices were too close, but he could not get his bearings to figure out where to run because he was still being blinded by the white hot sun rays. He noticed, for the first time, that he was looking directly through his arm. The sun shone through it, and he saw the faint, clear silhouette of a sinewy arm. He lowered his head and lifted his left arm in front of his face. Dark skin began to appear, chasing the transparent skin away. He let out a gasp and fell to his back. The sand was hot and burned his skin, so he sprang up and got to his feet.

He ached all over, and the close proximity of the voices made his heart pound; but he was distracted by his own appearance. He forced his chin as close to his chest as he could and saw scorch marks tracing across it. He reached to touch his cheek bone and winced as soon as his fingertip made contact with the swollen bulge. He pulled his hand away. It was solid, and his fingertips were covered in blood.

He turned to his left, realizing for the first time that his left eye was nearly swollen shut. Five men in dark clothes and wrapped faces were running toward him, rifles in their hands.

He gasped as he realized they were not as close as he had thought. They were still far in the distance, but he saw them as if they were in front of him. They were too far to hear, yet their voices were clear.

How? he thought.

A building burned behind them, and he saw a woman hanging from a tree next to the building. He blinked, and the woman came into focus. The decapitated body of a man lay at her feet, intermittently shaded by her body as it swung back and forth. He concentrated on the woman. She was thin. Her skin was dark and smooth but bloated. She was familiar, but his mind was helpless to name her.

He heard whimpering.

His head ticked in the direction of the sound. Quiet and muffled. He rolled onto his hands and knees and crawled quickly toward the sound. It was feminine and young. He located the sound, letting his ears guide him while he kept his good eye squinted against the sun. He crawled toward a thicket of dry brush. As he crawled around it, he found a girl huddled there, lying on the ground with her arms clutched about her head. She was young. His mind instantly told him five. Then a name came to him.

"Yara?"

He spoke her name before he understood how he knew it belonged to her. The whimpering stopped, but only for a second. He rushed toward her, still on his hands and knees, and reached out. She moved her arms from her head quickly and turned her face so that she was looking directly at him. She screamed, and he crawled back in panic.

The voices behind him were very loud now, and he heard shots being fired. The girl jumped up. He leapt to his feet, grimacing in pain, and ran to her as another volley of shots rang out. Something stung his back and legs; then he felt the same stinging in his nearly transparent arm. He looked down and watched it passing through, mesmerized that he could see it as if it was moving in slow motion. The girl screamed. He looked away from his arm and saw blood explode from her shoulder. Her head was so far back that her face was to the sky, and she wailed.

Without thinking, he reached into her shoulder. It took him a moment to fish around; but his fingers quickly gripped the bullet, and he yanked it out. Another volley erupted. He heard the bullets ripping through the brush and moved his body in front of hers. The bullet fell from his fingers as he dropped his weight on top of her.

He closed his eyes and wished she was not there. He spoke her name again in a whisper, tried to calm her. Then he felt weightless and slammed into the ground. His face and chest crunched against sand. He pushed himself up and looked beneath him. She was gone. Yara was gone. He looked left and right. She was not there; but when he looked to his right, he saw the black boots of the first man. He sprang to his feet and faced them. Five men, larger than he and armed with rifles. All of them pointed and shouted the same word he had heard before: *sahir.*

He steeled his muscles, stretching to stand squarely before them. He felt the muscles in his back stretch and flex. Felt the hot bullets push their way out of his back. Nausea washed over him, and he fell to his knees. They yelled and rushed toward him. The first man pulled up at the last second and slammed the butt of his rifle into his face. He saw stars bursting through an explosion of red and felt his head twist to the side. Spit flew from his mouth as he fell. As he struck the sand, darkness descended; and his mind told him what the word meant.

Sorcerer.

Ibrahim Dualeh set the heavy, ceramic water pot on the ground with a thud. Cool water sloshed out and spilled over the curved rim, and he grunted angrily. A few drops had splashed onto his sunburned hand, which was still on the lip of the pot. He stood and leaned back, feeling and hearing his brittle spine crack several times, and then used the coolness and dampness of the water on the back of his hand to wipe sweat from his forehead. He felt the odd mixture of cool and hot moisture tingling in the wrinkled skin beneath his damp kofia.

He looked around, making sure no one else had come in from the fields early to witness his inability to carry a simple water pot from the well to his home. Satisfied that he was still alone, he walked over to the small, square house he had built himself, turned, and let his back rest against the mud wall. He sighed, immediately grateful for the cool sensation of the clay bricks and the two-foot-wide shade provided by the thatched roof.

"You are too lazy, old man," he said. He chuckled and wiped his forehead again, this time with his arm. "The water will be no good if you leave it out here." The sun was nearing its apex, the heat of the day approaching its punishing climax. Beneath the shade, squinting out toward the field, Ibrahim continued to talk to himself.

"Too old for the heat, Ibrahim?" he said in a high-pitched tone.

"No, no. I am not well. I will be back in the fields tomorrow. A full day." This he said in his normal voice.

"Bah, you are lying, old man," he said, again high-pitched.

"You will see," he said in his regular voice. "I will outwork all of you. You are too young to know how to work like a man."

"And you are too old to remember where you are supposed to be to do the work."

He nodded. "Perhaps you are right. Perhaps I am speaking to myself because I am an old man who has lost his mind. But who is in the field, sweating his backside off, and who is home with a fresh pot of cool water?" He smiled, knowing he had won, then frowned, realizing the ramifications of winning an argument against oneself.

With a resigned sigh, he pushed off the wall, groaning, and readied himself to walk back to the water pot. Before he could take his first step, a flash of light forced him to turn his head to the right and shield his eyes with both arms. A rush of scorching hot wind blew around him, making his shawl flap in the breeze and cling to his thin body. He was hesitant to move his arms and look to see what the source of the strange light was, but a scream of pain and terror eliminated that fear and replaced it with another.

Slowly, he lowered his arms and stood up straight. Standing in front of a line of small shrubs was his granddaughter, Yara. She was dirty from head to toe. Her black hair was matted down on one side of her face and knotted all over. Her clothes were torn, and she had fresh blood smeared on her face and body.

Ignoring his aches, weariness forgotten, Ibrahim ran to her. He knelt before her when he was close enough, letting his kameez sink into the hot sand. He clutched at her arms, then snatched his hand back when he saw the fresh blood up close. He touched her arms, gingerly this time, and then began to reach up to her teary, bloody, and dirt-stained cheeks. She wailed and took a step back, hugging herself and hunching over. Ibrahim scooted toward her on his knees, keeping his hands stretched out to her.

"What is it, Yara?" he asked as soothingly as he could manage over his own panic. "Where are your mama and papa?"

She replied with another blood-curdling scream and dropped to her bottom in the sand. Her back scraped against one of the brown, prickly shrubs, but she didn't seem to notice. She reached down to her right side and scooped up a fistful of sand, then let it pour over her head. She did not move her left arm, which seemed limp. As Ibrahim watched the grains of sand stick to the blood on her face, Yara reached for another handful; and the implications made him stop crawling to her.

"Nala?" he whispered as he watched the young girl pouring sand over her head and kick her feet. She began to pound the sand with her right fist and continued to scream. "Guleed?" His son's name seemed to fall from his lips.

He remembered the secret meeting Guleed had organized on the outskirts of the village. An argument over whether they should continue to hold the services in their homes, in silence, or build a place to worship outside the village. Guleed calling him a coward over his shoulder, then slamming the door. Searching the village but not finding Yara and cursing his son for endangering the girl. It all came in a flash as he fell to his hands and then crawled on all fours to his granddaughter.

He paused, remembering that she had just appeared in front of his hut with a flash of light. He looked around, worried. Her screams had not attracted anyone yet, but they would. But where had she come from? What was that light? He lifted his head toward the fields. The path leading to them was still empty, and he could not hear any voices.

"Yara!" he whispered harshly. He raised a finger to his lips and shushed her. She paused, turned to look at him, but then let out another scream. "Enough, Yara!" he shouted. "No more screams. Listen to your opa." She stopped screaming and whimpered, drawing her knees to her chest and placing her forehead between them. Ibrahim crawled the rest of the way to her and then placed his hand on her head. She looked up but then dropped her head back down, overwhelmed by her emotions.

"Yara, where did you come from?" He spoke so fast that his words strung together. "What was that light?" She did not answer, but she did look up. He could not take the sight of her puffy eyes. Yara reached out to wrap her arms around his neck; but he was afraid of her injuries, so he moved away, instinctively. Her hand touched the side of his head, and he was again struck by another flash of brilliant light, this time in his mind.

He was no longer on the ground in front of his screaming granddaughter. He was hiding in the bushes, staring through them. A couple hundred meters away, a building was being drenched in gasoline by men whose faces were wrapped. In front of the building, men with weapons were standing in front of a group of men and women on their knees. Beside the building was a small tree, the same tree that he had planted with his wife years ago. His daughter-in-law, Nala, swayed back and forth on a rope wrapped in a noose around her deformed neck. Her face bulged. At her feet lay the body of his son, Guleed, his head severed.

He felt a sinking in his stomach and heard short, panicked breaths. He looked into the bush and down to his body. What he saw nearly made him scream and tumble backward. He did not see his own thinning body. There was no shawl or kameez. He saw the tattered, blue shirt of a young girl. The body was not his but Yara's. Blood-soaked hands that were not his covered his eyes. He forced them down, amazed that he could do that, and looked through the shrubs again.

He saw a man on the other side, but this was not like any man he had ever seen. He was dark-skinned with long dreadlocks, but half of him was transparent. One of his arms and half of his face blended in with the environment around him. He was inspecting himself, and Ibrahim saw that he was covered in blood and burn marks. A power emanated from the man that filled Ibrahim with fear like nothing he had ever known. It took him a moment to realize that he was not feeling his own fear. These were Yara's emotions.

A whimper escaped his lips. Her lips. The man's head jerked in their direction. They rolled themselves into a ball and covered their head with her arms. A few moments later, guided by the girl's whimpers, the man began to move around the brush toward them. Ibrahim heard Yara's name being called, which nearly made him sit up. He heard the scraping of sand, and then something touched them. They pulled their arms away and saw the man up close. His eyes were like flames of fire, and his hair like living water, flowing but never receding.

They screamed, and the man, or whatever it was, crawled back. They heard screams. Someone shouting "sorcerer" and running toward them. Gunshots followed, and they jumped to their feet. The creature was to its feet then and moving.

Standing.

In front of them before they could see it move. Its body jerked and twisted as they heard more shots being fired. They felt a searing hot pain in their shoulder and screamed. It put its hand into their shoulder, making the pain of the bullet ten times worse. There were still shouts, closer now.

Like the sound of a foot being pulled from thick mud, its hand came out of their shoulder, and its fingers dropped a bullet to the ground. It looked down at them, wrapped them in its arms, and fell forward. They were falling. Falling.

Ibrahim snapped out of the vision with a gasp and scrambled backward, pushing Yara's hand away from his head. He gulped rather than swallowed. He was frozen with fear, staring at the whimpering girl. Finally, he saw it. The blood on her shoulder. He heard shouts coming down the path. *Get up!* he told himself. The shouts were growing louder, getting closer. They were confused, searching.

He got to his feet and hurried to her scooped her up in his arms, and then turned. He ran, Yara screaming and struggling against him. He fell into the water pot, and they all tumbled over. Water cascaded out in front of him, but he ignored it. He picked her up again, feeling every bone cracking, and then he ran as fast as his tired legs would carry him into the brush.

CHAPTER TWO

LESTER SHARP OPENED HIS EYES and peered through a haze of bright, fluorescent light. He inhaled sharply, and the sound echoed. Using his elbows, he lifted himself to a sitting position. Cracked vinyl squeaked beneath his elbows and forearms as he pushed up. His neck muscles strained as he scanned from left to right.

He swiveled on the bench and swung his feet out and down until they rested on the grated metal. There was another bench across from him. It was green and well-worn, long enough to seat ten average adults. There were double sliding doors to the left and another set of similar doors across the aisle, next to the other bench. To the left of the doors was another row of benches. Silver poles were lined up in front of the benches, bolted to the floor. He braced himself by gripping his palms on the edge of the seat and exhaled. His breath was visible, billowing from his mouth, silhouetted by orange light that had somehow found its way through the smudged windows behind the benches.

He stood and walked to his left. There was a single sliding door with a rusted exit sign above it, lit with square, green letters. He paused, turned slowly. There was another door at the other end. It was identical, except the sign designated it as the entrance. No, he realized. Not identical. He squinted to see closer, assuming the distance was causing an illusion of depth, but the door to that side seemed slightly narrower than the exit. Confused but unwilling to stay in that eerie silence, he took a step toward the narrow door.

An eardrum-piercing hiss from outside made him stop mid-step. An unexpected swaying of the floor caused him to throw his arms straight out to the sides and drop into a half-squat. The hissing dissipated, giving way to a metallic squeal, like metal scraping over more rusted metal. The floor seemed to shift. He looked out the dirty windows and saw the incandescent lights begin to pass by. He swallowed, took a shaky breath, and was about to run toward the exit sign when everything lurched.

I'm back on the subway, he thought.

He opened his mouth to scream in protest, but he was thrown to the floor and landed on his chest. His face went chin first to the ridged floor. He groaned through the impact. He pushed himself up enough to crawl to the green bench to his right and pulled himself up. With his legs still sprawled out on the floor and his arms folded on top of the cracked seat, he managed a brief glimpse up at the window. They were clear now, the smudges completely gone. The orange lights began to streak past so quickly that he could not tell when one stopped and another started. The light began to bend and stretch until it became almost solid, fixed on the window.

The motion of the train stabilized, and he found his footing. He held the cold, metal pole next to him to pull himself up and then continued to hold for balance, all the while looking out at the lights that had become like a movie projected through an unfocused lens. Images began to appear in the light of that living, shifting screen.

He heard himself gasp and felt his mouth gaping open as soon as he discerned what the images were. A man lying on the stained carpet of a living room floor, surrounded by beer and pill bottles. A dead man in a pool of his own blood lying prostrate in a jail cell. A dead, bloody woman next to a baby who would never see life and the killer, down the block, sliced open. A boy covered in blood and bruises, alone in the shadows of a park. The images came and went too fast for him to focus on, and his head began to throb as his eyes strained to keep up with the rapid passing of horrifying scenes.

Two lines of people shouting at one another appeared on the screen. A moment later, they disappeared, replaced by the skin and bones apparitions of men, women, and children. Their eyes bulged, looking directly at Lester, through him. Past him. Then the apparitions faded, and a headless body filled the screen. The image zoomed out, slowly, and a line of men and women on their knees with another line of masked men holding rifles came into view. Lester's heart sank. The images were so intense that he began to wretch.

A sharp ringing sound worked its way through the subway car, but Lester noticed it only as something in the background. The images were different now, almost live yet clearly frozen in time. An aerial view panned dried-up fields and sparse vegetation. There was an inverted tear drop shaped monument. An ancient temple near a gray, faded asphalt road. The view came to ground level and rushed toward a convoy of tan, armored trucks. The image slowed, stilled, and Lester saw the soldiers. His heart pounded, and he gripped the pole so tightly that his knuckles popped. The ringing sound intensified, but he ignored it. He squinted and put his hands to his ears. The image on the screen darkened as his eyes narrowed, but there was no escaping the familiar face of Dillon. His brother.

The ringing got so loud that it forced him to look down and turn his head to the side. He shifted to his right and nearly went to his knees. He leaned his chest into the pole but kept his hands over his ears; still, the ringing would not be silenced. It pierced his hands and bored into his mind. He closed his eyes, squeezed them, and pressed his palms over his ears. He felt the train slow, heard the sound of hot brakes scraping and squealing. The braking was normal at first, gentle, but then the car lurched and came to a stop so suddenly that he opened his eyes and wrapped his arms around the pole.

Clutching the cold metal to his chest, Lester nearly let go and fell over when he saw him.

Draven.

He saw him through the thin windows of the sliding subway doors at first, but then the doors opened. The slender, dark-skinned man stood comfortably, hands in his pockets. His long dreadlocks draped his narrow face. His eyes were the color of the ocean and glowing. Lester released his death grip on the pole and let out a relieved sigh. He slid his hand from the pole and took a step toward his guide.

Draven shook his head.

Lester paused, considering. The ringing hadn't stopped. Draven reached into a pocket and then held out a phone. Lester's phone. The screen was lit up, but he could not read what it said. The ringing was not loud or high-pitched as he had thought. It was just a ring. Lester looked at Draven, again wondering exactly what, or who, he was. The guide who had taken him on a terrifying journey on a subway car similar to this one. The guide who, the night before, had showed him the images of the movie but in reality, not on a screen.

Draven nodded toward the phone. Lester shook his head. "No."

Draven nodded again.

Lester growled and walked forward, reaching out and then taking the phone.

When he answered, Draven was gone.

Olympia

Lester sat up and instinctively pushed his hands down to brace himself. He felt the soft arms of his recliner and looked down. An empty mug rested lopsided between his legs, which were extended out on the leg rest of the recliner. A single drop of dark brown liquid rolled up the side of the mug and then trickled back to the center, carving a wet streak in the premature stain of the night's old coffee.

Still reeling from the dream, Lester shuddered and let out a deep breath, then let his back and head nestle into the soft cushion of the chair. The images still flashed through his mind. He closed his eyes and saw them all clearly. Not images, he remembered. Memories. He glanced across the room at the man curled up beneath a thin, gray blanket on his couch. Lester tilted his head to regard the man, searching his mind for his name and how he had gotten there.

Wayne. Wayne Burmeister.

Draven had told him the man was dead. "Wayne Burmeister is definitely dead," he'd said. The knock on the door a few hours ago had been a surprise. It was not often a dead man came back to life and showed up on his doorstep. After getting over his initial shock, Lester had invited the man in, and they had talked late into the night. Well past midnight—a time Lester would be wary of for a long time.

Wayne was going through a divorce, had not seen his wife or child in weeks, and his work had declined. The loss of his job had been his breaking point, and Wayne had decided to take his own life. Unwilling to directly and physically hurt himself, an overdose of pain medication and alcohol became his weapon of choice.

During the night, listening to the story, Lester had nodded and reserved judgment the best he could, but he had often drifted between two thoughts: How was this man alive? And had Dillon survived the explosion? He had nearly missed the answer to the first question while dwelling on the second when he heard Wayne talking about vomiting.

"Woke up and just went to pukin'," Wayne had said. Lester's only reply had been a confused "huh?" to which Wayne had nodded and continued. "Craziest thing ever. Stuff comin' up blacker'n anything I've ever seen from a man's gut. Chest hurt, too, like someone had been just a poundin' on it."

Lester had simply nodded in silence. He had seen Wayne's light on, gone into his living room, found him lying on the floor with no pulse, and administered CPR. It had been only the night before, but Lester remembered it as if it was years ago. Sitting back in the recliner, he felt warmth on his cheek and glanced to his right. A trail of dust was captured in a thin wall of light between the gap in the curtain and his chair. Frozen in time.

A shrill noise pierced his thoughts, and he nearly sprang from the recliner. He looked left, looked right, shuffled with his clothes and the coffee mug, and then finally found his phone. Uncoordinated fingers grabbed, dropped, and finally gripped the phone and brought it close enough to his face for him to read the caller I.D.

Harold Sharp.

Lester sighed, ignoring the incessant ringing. He contemplated not answering. He pressed the volume button on the left side of the phone to silence the ringer and glanced up at Wayne. The man was oblivious and sleeping so soundly that Lester feared he had not thrown up enough of the medication from the night before. He dismissed that thought and answered.

"Hello."

"Hello?" The gruff reply was instantly accusatory. "Seven calls, and all you have to say is *hello?*"

Lester closed his eyes and breathed in through his nose. He let the air out slowly and silently before responding. "Is *hey* better?"

A pause. "I should fly out there and knock you out."

Lester shook his head. "What do you want, Dad?"

"Your brother is dead."

Lester lowered the phone with a lifeless hand until it rested in his lap. He turned and looked at the trail of dust, no longer captive in the moment but falling. He had been bracing for those words all night, yet they still took him by surprise. Hours before, he had been standing on a broken road in Iraq, pounding on the door to his brother Dillon's armored vehicle. Hours before, he had stood there, helpless, with the knowledge that his brother—and closest friend—was about to drive over a bomb.

Muffled shouts pulled him from that moment, drawing his eyes from the swirling dust and back to the phone. Lifting it to his ear once more, Lester wondered if any of that had actually happened or if he had just fallen asleep from exhaustion and dreamed that time had stood still all over the world. Dreamed that a mysterious man named Draven had come to him, forcing him to see the gruesome images that would not leave his mind. That was a lie, and he knew it. The proof was a man, risen from the dead, lying on his couch.

Why did he get to live?

"What?" he asked as he silently scolded himself for wishing Wayne had died in place of his brother.

"Dillon is dead," Harold said, obviously repeating, based on the agitated tone of his voice.

"How do you know?" Lester asked.

"They came this morning. Two men in uniform. They told us he died yesterday in some kind of explosion."

"Did anyone else die?" Lester asked the question and immediately wondered what had prompted him to do so. In his mind, he could see the driver of Dillon's vehicle and the gunner standing in the turret.

"How would I know?" was followed by, "and why would I care?" Harold didn't give him time to respond. "They're flying the body back to the States as soon as they get everything in order. We don't have a funeral date yet, but you should probably start looking into flights now."

Lester swallowed and squeezed his eyes shut. He definitely wanted to catch a flight. Wanted to fly all the way to Huron and end this feud once and for all. Though they were several months apart, every phone call was more painful than the last. He was sick of it; but in that moment, he did not have the strength. In that moment, he wanted Draven to come back. To take him back to Abu Ghraib and do something, anything, to save his brother.

"You are planning on coming, aren't you?"

His father's sarcasm practically dripped through the phone. Lester thrust his legs downward, slamming the leg rest back into the recliner, and sprang to his feet. He felt the mug leave his lap and vaguely heard it hit the floor with a dull thud.

"You listen to me, old man," he began and then had to shout "shut up" when Harold tried to tell him not to speak to him that way. "You don't get to call me after six months of the silent treatment and accuse me of not caring about Dillon." He felt himself shaking but could not calm down. "You just make sure you call me and tell me when the funeral is, so I can come pay my respects to my brother."

Harold interrupted. "You better watch it, Lester," he started to say, but Lester interrupted.

"As far as I'm concerned, we don't have to talk anymore. You can text the information to me or send it in a stupid email. But don't you ever call me like this again. Matter of fact, when this is all over, never bother calling me again. Period."

He heard Harold shouting something as he hung up. His breath was coming out in bursts through his nostrils, and his hands trembled. He looked up from the phone and saw Wayne sitting up, looking at him with wide eyes. Lester opened his mouth to say something but turned instead and picked up his coffee mug. He set it, along with his phone, on a small table next to the recliner and then turned around.

"I'm sorry, Lester," Wayne said, looking down.

"Not your fault."

"About your brother."

Lester nodded and forced out "thank you" in a whisper.

"Man oughta have some time to himself when he hears that kind of news."

Lester chewed on his bottom lip. "I don't think it would help any, Wayne."

Wayne nodded. "Nah." He sniffed and stood slowly. "I don't guess it would." He stared at his feet for a few moments and then looked directly at Lester. "That your old man?"

Lester nodded. "I'd rather not talk about it, y'know."

Wayne nodded once. "Yessir." He chuckled and held up his hands. "Hey, I'm the last person to judge."

Lester laughed, despite himself. "Aren't we a pair?"

The other man wiped moisture from his eye with his thumb and laughed. "Yeah, I'd say so."

"Listen, Wayne," Lester said as he walked over and put his hand on Wayne's shoulder. "How about I pick you up on Sunday morning, and we go to church together?"

Wayne hesitated for a moment, then nodded. "Ain't got much to wear. You think jeans'd be alright?"

"Just don't come naked," Lester said and forced a smile.

Wayne grinned and sniffled. "You got a deal. What time?"

"Pick you up at ten-thirty."

They shook hands, sealing the deal, and Lester walked him to the door, Wayne thanking him again for listening and giving him a place to crash for the night and Lester telling him "of course" before opening the door. There was another handshake; then Wayne was on the doorstep. A wave. And Lester was behind a closed door again without realizing he had shut it.

Outside the house, Morane smiled. He marveled at his good fortune as he turned his head and watched the skinny man named Wayne emerge from the house. He thought about how he could use the nightmares and the phone call Lester had just received to his advantage as he watched Wayne walk across the yard toward his own home.

Although Morane wanted to get busy torturing Lester right away, the possibilities looming before him were nearly irresistible. *Church on Sunday?* he thought. He wondered what would drive a man like Wayne to a house of religion. Moreover, what would drive any man to the home of Lester Sharp?

Turning his head back to the house, the demon decided that pursuing those thoughts would have to wait for another time. Lester was the key. Though grieving the loss of his brother, the human clearly had experienced change. Morane slipped into the house, through the wall, and stood before Lester. The pale human was unaware, going about the business of straightening his living area. Among the items he picked up was a red shirt with the words THE WATCHMEN written across the front.

Yes, Lester had "seen the light." He was different, a redeemed man. Morane snarled, unheard. A redeemed man was far more dangerous than a hopeless man, for the redeemed can lead the hopeless to the light. Morane slipped away, vowing as he went to cast his dark shadow over that redemptive path.

CHAPTER THREE

LESTER PULLED HIS PHONE FROM his back pocket and looked at the caller I.D. He groaned when he saw the name. Dave. Again. Lester had not missed a day or been late to work since he had purchased his automotive repair shop. The general manager he had hired, Dave, was probably in full panic mode, judging by two missed calls and one text asking Lester where he was. He pressed the decline call icon and looked to the end of the road, scanning past the stop sign while flicking a bee away with his free hand.

He felt bad for ignoring Dave. The glimpse from the previous night had made Lester feel bad about a lot of things. Remembering a particular moment when he and Draven were on the subway, Lester was haunted by the revelation that his abusive approach to business had inflicted a great deal of damage on his employees. Dave, in particular, had been sleeping on his couch and not speaking to his wife because of the amount of hours he worked. Those demands were Lester's, which meant the damage at home was partially his fault. Now here he was, late for work and no intention of showing up there anytime soon.

He checked the time before blacking the screen out and sliding the phone into his left back pocket. He tapped the tip of his right foot on the gravel at his feet a couple of times. Folded his arms. Unfolded, folded again. Leaning against the house on one shoulder, his body was angled toward the stop sign. He unwittingly glanced right of it to Wayne's house. An image of the man lying face down on a carpet littered with empty bottles flashed through his mind. He looked away from the house to the ground. As he was looking at his feet, the pressing of the siding of his house against his shoulder reminded him of the end of the glimpse. Pushing both hands against the siding. Then pounding on it with his fists. He growled and pushed himself away from the wall.

"Where is this guy?" he said. His teeth were clenched, and he realized he had been tugging at the bottom of his t-shirt.

He tucked his chin in and looked down. Ran his hand down the white letters on the red shirt. After his rushed shower, the shirt had been the first thing he had seen, so he'd pulled it on, along with an old pair of jeans and some running shoes. They were gray. He looked past the shirt to the tapping toe of his right foot. He was contemplating going back into the house to change the shirt when a red Honda Accord pulled onto his street. He turned his head with the car, tracking its progress up the still, quiet street, and he saw a Wheel Share sticker in the back window. The sticker bore the logo of the local rideshare company, an alternative to traditional taxis.

He started down the short driveway, waving to the driver, and they met halfway. Lester nodded to the portly man behind the wheel as he walked to the rear, passenger side. The driver was pasty white with Coke bottle glasses and wisps of gray-blonde hair combed over a bald head. He gripped the steering wheel at exactly ten and two with meaty hands.

Lester climbed in and pulled the door shut, offering a grunt of a hello as he slid and scraped his way into the stained, cloth seats. He smelled stale french fries and not-quite-fresh coffee, saw the source of the former, and suppressed a gag as he looked up and saw the driver taking a drink of the latter with a slurp. The paper cup holding the obviously burned coffee stood no chance in the devouring clutch of the driver's hand. Lester fumbled through fastening his seatbelt as the man turned his head and gave Lester a crooked, stained smile.

"Where to, dude?" A vein stood out on the man's forehead, which was turning red from the strain of such a large man turning in the confines of the Honda.

Lester cleared his throat. "City hall."

The driver nodded. Slowly. Awkwardly. "Going to jail, dude?" He winked, and then his face lit up with amusement, and drops of coffee coughed their way out of his throat to splash onto his lips as he wheezed through a laugh. It was the tar-scarred lung outburst of a man who'd never been told his laugh was hideous, and Lester found himself wondering how pleasant it would be to hear nails being dragged across a chalkboard.

"Um." Lester waited for the laughter, or wheezing, to end, which happened with a violent series of coughs. "Picking up my car."

"Just messing, dude," the driver said through spasmodic coughs. "Getcha there'n about ten, K?"

Without waiting for Lester's response, the driver turned, coughed two more times, and went through the painful motions of setting his coffee down, switching gears to reverse, and backing down the driveway. Lester kept his hands on his lap and the heels of his feet off the carpet. He tried not to think about the shirt he was wearing and looked out the window to his right to avoid looking at the man, wishing the glimpse would have at least ended back at his car. He sighed and settled in for the short ride to the Olympia police station.

Lester had hoped to ride in silence, but those hopes were dashed as soon as they passed Wayne's silver pickup. The driver, who announced that he went by the name Duck, was a lifelong citizen of Olympia and was glad to make Lester's acquaintance. Lester smiled and offered up a weak "you, too" as they pulled away from the stop sign. By the time they merged onto the highway, Lester had already learned that Duck lived with his mother by choice and had never married because all the women he'd met were too clingy. The rideshare job apparently allowed Duck to work on getting the magazine he and his good friend, Goober, had initially launched in their sophomore year of high school. Regular jobs, after all, didn't allow Duck and Goober the flexibility creative entrepreneurs needed.

"That's a nice shirt," Duck said before slurping away at his coffee.

Lester turned his head and looked away from the other cars. "Huh? Oh, thanks," he said. He looked out the left window and found himself staring at the driver of a white Corolla. The driver, a woman around thirty, looked back and forth between him and out her windshield with quick head jerks before accelerating past them. Lester was amazed to see cars in motion. The night before, driving on the same road, all of the other cars had been at a standstill. *Or had they?* Lester wondered.

He was beginning to wonder if any of it had been real. Time at a standstill, images in a dream. Which was reality? Was Dillon really dead? Maybe he had somehow anticipated that Dillon was going to die, and his mind had created a scenario that made it easier for him to cope with it. Maybe, he thought, his mind had retroactively created the scenario; and the glimpse, the dream, and the phone call from Harold were all something that happened after hearing about Dillon's death. It was possible. The mind is powerful, and memory cannot be trusted.

" . . . often?" Duck was asking.

Lester cleared his throat and turned to the front. The driver was looking at him in the rearview mirror. "I'm sorry, what?"

Duck laughed. "You alright, dude? I was asking if you and the other people from your church go out often?"

Lester looked down and touched the W of the word Watchman on the front of the shirt. "No. I mean, yeah. I don't really know. I don't really go anymore."

Duck grunted. "But you used to?"

Lester nodded. "Yeah. I, uh, I haven't been out there in a long time."

"Don't they go out on Fridays?"

"Not always. I mean, at least not before. It was usually on a Friday, but they'd go on Saturdays or different days of the week, sometimes."

"That right?"

Lester nodded. "Yep."

"So, why are you wearing it?"

Lester took a deep breath and looked at his hands. They were folded in his lap. "I don't really know, Duck. I guess maybe I might start going again." He turned and looked out the window again. Duck didn't respond, at first.

"Right on, dude." He pointed at the rearview mirror. "This town needs it. Not just Olympia, either. You dudes should go to Hudson. That place is a cesspool of activity."

Lester nodded, thrown off by the "activity" comment. He brushed it off and thought about his supernatural trip that had led him to the subway of Hudson the night before. Neighboring Olympia, Hudson was one of the smallest cities in the country; but the growth in both population and crime was comparable to most. The addition of a subway a few years ago was evidence of that. Within two years of the "state-of-the-art" transportation making its debut, it had become a meeting place for drug lords and pimps and was the battleground of gangs looking to settle turf wars. For Lester, the subway led him to thoughts of something other than crime.

He had traveled in a subway car that did not need tracks, above ground and even under water. He drowned out whatever Duck was saying and looked into the distant skyline of the city. His mind traveled to the places the supernaturally powered subway had taken him. He smiled, remembering the frozen eye of the giant whale. The smile faded when he remembered the executed pastor in a field in Somalia. Starving men digging for snakes in the side of a mountain in North Korea. Dillon, on a broken road outside Abu Ghraib, Iraq.

When Duck turned in to the parking lot of the police station, it was a much different scene than the one Lester remembered from the night before. Nearly every parking space was taken. Several black and white cruisers and sport utility vehicles were backed into parking spaces. To the right, the parking spaces extended past the front of the building and toward the two-story city hall building at the back of the lot. Everything from motorcycles to four-wheel drive trucks were parked, some taking up more than one space. Lester quickly scanned the entire parking lot but did not see his sedan.

Duck stopped the car in the middle of the lot. "Here you go, dude." He started to go through the awkward jerks and gyrations it took him to turn partially around and speak to Lester but settled for getting his head far enough around to give Lester a sideways glance.

"You mind waiting a few minutes?" Lester asked.

Duck narrowed his eyes and nodded slowly. "Oh, I see." He sniffed and pointed at Lester. "Want me to flip this baby around and keep the engine running?" He shifted so that more of him was facing Lester. "She looks slow, but she'll get you outta here before the boys in blue even know you're runnin'."

Lester blinked, opened his mouth to respond, but shook his head. "No, Duck. I—" he started but cut himself off. "Yes, flip around, and keep the door unlocked."

Duck grinned. "Knew it, dude."

Lester got out quickly, hoping his own car was in the back and he wouldn't have to spend more time on the graham cracker dusted seats of Duck's "getaway car." Shutting the door behind him without looking, he started toward the steps leading into the police station. Memories of Draven standing on those steps in the dark came back to him, and he paused. The previous night continued to haunt him, mocking his hopes that it had all been a dream. He had to talk to someone, and he found himself oddly wishing that Draven would appear. As terrified as he was at the thought of seeing the strange man again and being whisked away on another nightmare trip, he needed to talk about what he had seen.

He shook his head and sighed, then trudged up the steps and entered the police station. Like the parking lot, the scene inside the station was much different than the night before. The same desk was just inside the entrance, but it was spotless, the wrappers and cups having been cleaned up. The police officer behind the desk looked every bit the part of an officer on duty. A crisp, freshly pressed uniform fit perfectly over her body builder frame. She was average height, Latino, and had to be the most intimidating woman Lester had ever seen. He looked toward the full waiting area past the desk and to the right. Uniformed officers and people in business attire moved about the large area below an open balcony that could be reached from a set of metal stairs at the back of the room.

"May I help you, sir?"

Lester turned back to the officer. She smiled brightly, revealing teeth that could have been on a billboard advertising a dentist's office.

"Yes, ma'am." Lester walked up and then placed his hands on the edge of the counter but refrained from leaning his chest into it. He also did his best not to stare too deeply into the officer's chestnut-colored eyes. "I left my car here last night, but it's not in the parking lot."

The officer made no immediate response. She finally frowned and placed her hands on the keyboard in front of her. The monitor was against the edge of the desk, beneath the countertop. "Make and model?"

"Lincoln MKZ."

"License plate number?" She looked up at him as she finished typing.

He gave her the letters and numbers, and the officer, whose name plate read Arroyo, entered the information. He watched her eyes glance up and down, and then she nodded.

"Yes, sir. It was impounded a few hours ago."

Lester leaned back and gripped the counter tightly. "What?"

"Illegally parked." She looked up and shrugged. "No one answered when contacted."

"I didn't get any—" he paused. "Wait." He pulled his phone out of his pocket and turned the screen on. There was another missed call from Dave, along with a text message. He opened up his call log and saw that there were two calls from an unknown number. He sighed and let his shoulders droop.

He slid the phone back into his pocket. "When can I pick it up?"

Officer Arroyo stepped away from the computer. "Actually, you'll have to answer some questions before we can discuss that." She stopped and looked over Lester's shoulder. Her eyes widened, and her jaw dropped.

"My client won't be answering any questions today, Officer Arroyo."

Lester turned at the sound of the deep voice. Behind him, standing head and shoulders taller than him, was a slender man whose pale skin was accentuated by a black suit and navy blue tie. The man's head was bald, but he was not old. His eyes were impossibly dark, a color Lester had never seen in anyone's eyes before. His thin lips were pressed firmly together as he looked down and gave Lester a sideways nod.

"The vehicle was parked there under emergency circumstances," the man said.

Lester's eyes darted back and forth between the stranger and Officer Arroyo.

"This is clearly the case, given the fact that my client was unable to answer his phone calls this morning. It is not for me to disclose his personal affairs, but Mr. Sharp is experiencing extreme difficulties in his immediate family."

Lester nearly gasped out loud. He looked up at the man and felt himself pressing his back into the edge of the desk. The stranger made no move to acknowledge Lester or his fear. His face was set like stone, eyes fixed on the officer. Lester felt a lump in his throat and tried, with great effort, to swallow it down. Forcing himself to remain calm, he turned. Officer Arroyo had stepped back from the counter, and the color had drained from her face. After a moment, she stammered through a reply.

"I just need to know why the car was parked there last night, and tell there is a fine for illegal parking." She took a deep breath, and Lester saw her trembling. He turned toward the stranger.

"Perfectly reasonable," the man said. "All of your questions will be answered with this." He reached into his suit pocket and removed a slip of paper and handed it to her.

She reached for it gingerly and took it in her trembling fingers. Lester could hear the paper rustling. As she read it, he watched the color drain from her face, shocked there was any left. She gasped, eyes open so wide, he thought they might pop out of her head. After a moment, she lowered the paper and looked up at Lester. She swallowed several times before saying anything.

"This has all been a misunderstanding, Mr. Sharp," she said, barely above a whisper. She grabbed a card from a stack on the desk in front of her and reached it toward him, nearly dropping it. "You'll find your car there, sir, and I'll call ahead to make sure you don't experience any further trouble."

"That's it?" Lester grabbed the card. "No fine?"

Officer Arroyo shook her head. "I . . . I'm truly sorry for the trouble you're facing, Mr. Sharp. My apologies for adding to your distress."

"Distress?"

Lester felt a strong hand on his shoulder and turned his head. Looking up, he saw the stranger leaning over him. "Time to go, Lester."

A feather could have knocked him over. The man's voice was low, nearly a thunderous rumble. Electricity sparked in the man's onyx eyes, and Lester nearly screamed. The grip on his shoulder tightened, and Lester heard himself grimacing.

"Time to go," the man said again. Lester nodded, and the grip loosened. He stood to his full height again and smiled to Officer Arroyo. "Thank you for your understanding, officer. Have a pleasant day."

He then put his hand behind Lester's back, between the shoulders, and turned him toward the door. He led him out of the police station forcefully, relaxing his grip only once they got outside. Standing on the steps in front of the entrance, he took his hand away from Lester's back and looked down at him with his menacing eyes.

"Don't be afraid, Lester." He smiled, which was more terrifying to Lester than his normal look. "I am a friend of Draven's. All is taken care of."

Lester was immediately skeptical but did his best to hide his emotions. He remembered Draven's last words and the way the strange guide had simply vanished. Fear for Draven crept up his spine like a spider. He couldn't move or think straight. He wanted to know what had been on that note, but the man's eyes held him captive.

"Go, Lester."

He took a deep breath. "Where's Draven?" he asked through trembling lips.

The stranger leaned down and got within an inch of Lester's face. "That is not your concern. I suggest you go on your way, or the rest of your day may not be so pleasant."

Lester took a step back, and his foot slipped but found the next one before he could fall. He glanced back and saw his foot on the edge, let out a sigh of relief, and then turned back. The man was gone. Lester gasped and looked in every direction. The stranger had vanished. He turned in a circle on the middle step, looking around frantically, but all he saw was Duck, staring at him from the driver's seat and a few officers gawking.

Lester took the remaining two steps in one leap and rushed to the car. He yanked the door open and nearly jumped in. He slammed the door and was about to tell Duck to go when the car sank for a moment and then took off with a surprisingly smooth and powerful burst of acceleration. Lester screamed at him to slow down, that he wasn't running, as his face slammed into the back of the front passenger's seat. The car slowed, slamming him back into his seat, and he fumbled with his seatbelt.

"Are you crazy?" he shouted at Duck when he got the seat belt buckled.

"Hey, sorry. You came out of there, talking to yourself on the steps, looking around all crazy; and then you run to the car and jump in. What was I supposed to think?"

"What are you talking about?" Lester rubbed his face. "I wasn't talking to myself."

Duck made a scoffing sound. "Look, dude, when I see a guy standing by himself and moving his mouth, I call that talking to himself."

"Are you serious? Did you not see that giant in the dark blue suit?"

Duck was silent at first, and then reached down and took a dramatic sip of his seemingly bottomless cup of coffee.

"Is everybody at your church this crazy?"

Lester looked up and saw Duck's eyes in the rearview mirror. "What?"

"'Cause, dude, if they are, I'm there."

Lester ignored him and looked out the window. Though there were plenty of buildings, people, and cars, all Lester could see were the eyes of the stranger boring into his mind.

"Where to, man?"

Lester didn't bother looking at the driver when he responded. "Allman's Towing."

"Car got impounded, huh?" Duck sipped his coffee again, and Lester cringed. "The plot thickens."

As Duck made a righthand turn at the next intersection, Lester thought about Duck's question. Lester closed his eyes and thought it might be a good idea to stop by the church and see if the one man he knew would still listen had not succumbed to the madness that had taken over his life.

CHAPTER FOUR

HE GETS TO HIS FEET, fighting the pain, and looks around. The men with the rifles are gone. He squeezes his eyes shut and breathes in deeply. Hears himself wheezing. Hears a faint whisper. He opens his eyes and drops into a low crouch. His fists are clenched, but where is the enemy? Who is the enemy?

He turns and hears the slow dragging of his foot through sand. The desert. That's right, but how? The whimper is louder this time. He sees a bush, goes to it. Pulls it aside. Covered in tattered rags and huddled is the girl. Her name is Yara, but he does not know how he knows this.

The wind grows cold, and the sky turns dark. Lightning dances across the sky, and thunder booms loudly enough to shake the ground. He remembers the house. Someone important is inside the house, but someone dangerous is outside the house. With him. Darkness and lightning.

The dark man.

He lifts the girl into his arms and looks around with wide eyes. His eyes see through the darkness. They see for miles. There is a train, one he knows should be under the ground and not in the desert. The train makes him think of the house, and his mind wants to remember the person inside the house; but the dark man is coming. He runs, carrying the girl. Carrying Yara.

Thunder booms. Lightning strikes ahead, and they fall. The ground splits. Another flash of lightning blinds him. He screams, but then there is silence. He stands, pushing with his hands off of the metal of the train. He pauses and looks down. He is inside the train. Alone.

The girl is gone. Yara is gone.

He is blinded by a powerful, bright light, and there is pain. So much pain. His eyes clear, and the dark man is there, holding the girl and laughing. He is not a man. He is a monster. The monster's mouth opens as he turns his head toward the girl in his arms. She screams. He yells at the monster, and there is darkness.

Khufia

The man tried to spring to his feet, tried to save the girl, but he was yanked back to the ground. His back slammed into something solid and cold. His mind took too long to register that it was the ground. Hard, but not metal. He was not on a subway. That was what the train had been—not just a train. This made no sense to the man, but he was on the ground, lying on his back. The smell of urine and feces overpowered his other senses.

Above him, silver beams of light came through small windows, streamed across the room he was in, and were stopped by a wall to his right. The silver moonlight trickled through a cloud of dust and cast a hazy light on the chains bound to both of his outstretched arms. He followed the chains from the wide, metal cuffs on his wrists to the walls of the box.

He shifted and twisted himself enough to get his feet behind him and rise to his knees. The effort was exhausting, and his body ached in every place. He looked at his arms and saw burn marks running down them. When he pulled against the chains, the cuffs sliced into the paper-thin skin on the inside of his wrists. He tucked his chin to his chest and looked down at his body. Bruises and scorch marks covered him. As if on cue, he felt the pain caused by each mark.

He closed his eyes and breathed in through his nose. Held it. Exhaled slowly out of his mouth. He listened to the escaping air and wondered what the dream had meant. Was it a dream? Was the girl safe? Was he safe? Who was he? He heard a metallic sound, a scraping in front of him. Straining his neck forward, he peered into the darkness but saw nothing. His mind told him he should be able to see more, but there was only darkness.

A door opened, and someone entered, silhouetted by dim light from the outside. He could not see the details of the shadowed figure, but it was walking toward him. It carried something—something long and metal. Then the figure was over him. He could see it wore something around its face, and he thought it was a man. The shadowed figure held the metal object up and then brought it down on the man's head.

Pain and a burst of light exploded in his mind. He fell to the wood floor. It seemed like he was falling through it into darkness.

"It is a demon, Ibrahim."

Ibrahim rolled his eyes and shook his head. His sister, Nasteexo, was staring at him with her arms folded. Younger than him by three years, she was still wiser, but her reaction to his account from that afternoon was not her most mature moment.

"Would a demon have saved Yara?"

Nasteexo unfolded her arms and tugged at the waist of her guntiino. Her graying hair shook in her face, and she pushed it behind her ears. "Would a man shapeshift?"

"No," Ibrahim said, shaking his head. "It was not a man, but it was not a demon."

"If it was even real."

Ibrahim exhaled and let his shoulders slump. He and Nasteexo had been going back and forth over the source of his vision for nearly half an hour. He looked to the corner of the room where Yara was curled up on a mat, asleep. Although Nasteexo's home in Khufiana was nicer than any home in Khufia, it was still small. There were two rooms in the back, but Ibrahim wanted to keep his granddaughter in sight.

"Why do you doubt me, sister?"

She stepped forward and touched his face. "I do not doubt you, brother. Nala and Guleed are dead. You were in the field too long. Your mind could not take it."

He pushed her hand away and scoffed. "Bah! You think I imagined it?"

"I think grief and the sun played tricks on your mind. But if what you saw is real, it is a demon and should be destroyed."

He looked at her and shook his head. "He saved Yara. How could you say that?"

She waved her hands in the air and walked away. "It does not matter. You ran before you could verify any of this. With hope, Nala and Guleed are fine, but they are worried and will come looking for Yara."

He grunted. "Yara, who is covered in blood that is not her own? Who is wounded in her shoulder from a bullet that was somehow removed?"

Nasteexo put her hand on the edge of the counter and turned toward him. "We don't know what happened. She has not spoken, and we have only what you think you saw when she touched you."

He turned his head and walked over to Yara. "No. We have more than that."

"You have not told me everything?"

He shook his head. "I did not want suspicions to be raised, so I took Yara into the woods. I hid her among the bushes and told her to stay until I returned. She was frightened, but she listened." He closed his eyes and steadied himself with a slow breath. "I got back to my water pot just as the workers came in from the fields. They were too frantic to care why I had spilled it."

"Why?" Nasteexo asked from the other side of the room.

"Yusef and his men were dragging the man, whatever he is."

"Dragging him?"

He nodded. "They took him to the center of the village. Everyone gathered to see. Yusef told us that they had found the secret church. He looked at me, walked over after his men dropped the man in the sand, and got so close I could smell the blood on him. He told me that my son was the pastor of the church and asked me if I knew."

Nasteexo's voice was close. "And you are still alive, so you—"

"Please, Nasteexo," he interrupted. "I cannot bear my own shame."

Nasteexo was in front of him then. She blinked several times, and moisture rimmed her blue eyes. A tear squeezed its way out and streaked down her cheek. She reached out as the memory of Yusef standing in front of him came back in full force. The memory of what he had told the man who had killed his son. Nasteexo embraced him.

He sobbed on her shoulder, looking at Yara all the while and feeling very much like a coward. "I waited until nightfall and then brought her to you."

"She is safe." He felt her patting his back. He squeezed her waist. "You are safe here. Both of you."

Ibrahim pushed her to arm's length and looked at her. "No. We are not."

"You cannot go back, Ibrahim."

He turned and walked back to where he had been standing a few minutes ago. "There will be suspicions if I do not return to Khufia."

"There will be more death if you do."

"No, Yeshua has sent us help."

He heard her snort. "Fool."

He spun to face her. "I am no fool, and I know what I saw. You say this man is a demon, but the only demons in Khufia are Yusef and his men."

"So, you will go to this mystery man? He is still alive?"

He nodded. "I do not know why, but I do not think he can be killed with their guns. He is being held."

"And you think you are going to sneak past Yusef's men? Al-Shabaab? They are the terror of the entire coastline, Ibrahim."

Ibrahim balled his fists at his waist and clenched his teeth. "I will not continue to hide, Nasteexo. I dishonored my God and my son today. I lied to that monster and betrayed my Savior."

"And you think that will go away because you commit suicide by trying to free this man?"

He waved his hands in the air and started walking to the door. "This is a waste of time."

"Ibrahim!"

He reached the door and grabbed the handle. He paused before turning the latch and looked at Nasteexo over his shoulder. "You know me, sister. I have never been a man of resolve. I have hid, been a coward.

If not for that cowardice, I would have been among those who died with Guleed today."

"Then I thank God for your cowardice." She wiped her face and then folded her arms. "Stay here, and be a coward. A living, breathing coward who can be here for his granddaughter who just lost both parents."

He shook his head. "If we deny Him before men, Yeshua will deny us before the Father."

She rolled her eyes. "How convenient to quote your precious book now. What about protecting His people? Isn't that in your sacred Scriptures?"

"No," he said. "He told us we would suffer for His name's sake."

"Finally, it's true. I don't want to serve your God if this is what living for Him means."

"I do not think I can even say I know what it means to live for Him." Ibrahim turned his head and opened the door. Behind him, he heard Nasteexo.

"Well, you will soon know what it means to die for Him."

He took a deep breath and nodded. "So be it." Trembling, he stepped into the night.

Olympia

Lost in emotions and racing thoughts, Lester was confused by the sound of Duck yelling in the front seat. It was a distant sound, an echo bouncing its way through the nightmare consuming his mind, but he eventually focused on it enough to be pulled from that place of horror. From memory and anticipation.

When he finally turned away from the window to face the front, he saw that Duck had managed to get enough of his large torso turned around in the driver's seat to look at him squarely. There was almost a serious look on Duck's face. His skin was red and bulging from the strain of being twisted around in the too-small seat. His eyes were narrowed, and his brow furrowed. The methodical insertion of a Little Debbie oatmeal cookie into his mouth by a nearly robotic hand discredited the seriousness, however, and Lester found himself fully immersed back into the present reality.

"You gonna need me anymore, dude?" Duck asked while chewing on the snack. Bits of cookie fell out of his mouth. "I'm late for a little online rendezvous with my business partners." He swallowed the remainder of the cookie and looked like he was about to choke.

Lester assumed "online rendezvous with business partners" meant playing video games and shook his head. "No, I'm good from here." He pulled two twenty dollar bills from his wallet and handed them to Duck, who took them without so much as flinching from the narrow-eyed stare he'd affixed to Lester.

After shoving the money into the row lidless coffee cup in the center console, Duck nodded. "Be in good health, Lester Sharp."

Lester blinked several times. 'Thank you, Duck." He got out of the car as quickly as he could. He looked up at the oddly immaculate sign above the street that told him he was at Allman's Towing and sighed.

The building in front of him was isolated from the rest of the shops on the street, set apart by nearly a hundred yards. It was a brick structure with large windows that made it seem much classier and fitting for a downtown venue than the salvage yard behind it. Any illusion was quickly dispelled by the high fence on either side with barbed wire at the top and a wide, padlocked gate to the left of the building. While the office looked nothing like a typical towing company, the rows of cars behind the fence fit the bill quite appropriately, as did the black, oil-stained asphalt.

He took his phone out of his pocket, checked to see if there were any messages from Harold with information about Dillon's funeral, and then turned up the ringer volume. He tried to push thoughts of Dillon away, and anger threatened to rise at the memory of his callous father's voice. He felt a rumbling in the pit of his stomach and thought it was a manifestation of his fury before realizing it wasn't emotional at all. He had not eaten.

He scanned up the sidewalk, to the right of the impound lot. There were various, old storefront-style shops, including a walk-up coffee and breakfast stand not far away. Though he was in a daze over thoughts of Dillon, the smell of fresh coffee allowed him to focus on the present. He decided the car wasn't going anywhere and took the short walk. When he arrived, there was already a short line. Lester exchanged nods with an elderly man but was ignored by the rest—a college-aged guy with one side of his head shaved and a woman in a business suit whose eyes were fixed to whatever was on her phone.

Lester tried to occupy himself while waiting, but the line seemed to be completely frozen. He wondered if any time had passed at all; and as he looked ahead of the line to the ordering window, he began to feel anxious.

Not again. Did it ever really end? His thoughts drifted from the cafe, away from Olympia, and across an ocean. He saw a broken road, armored trucks, and a crater in front of them. There was Dillon. Looking straight ahead, then turning his head. Lester took a step back and gasped. Dillon's mouth opened, ready to speak . . .

"Sir?"

Lester snapped his head in the direction of the female voice.

"Sorry. What?" he asked.

"Welcome to The Java Box. What can I get started for you?"

Lester wiped his eyes with the back of his hand and sniffled. "Uh. Coffee, please. Black, no sugar."

"Yes, sir. Anything else for you today?"

He started to shake his head. He looked back and saw the vehicle. It was moving, but Dillon was not inside. The passenger seat was empty. Lester's mouth opened, and he was about to shout, when a man tapped him on the shoulder.

"Hey, buddy, you gonna order, or what?"

The desert and the broken road vanished, replaced by a tall, muscular man of oriental descent. "Huh? Oh. Sorry." He turned to the barista and asked if he could have a breakfast sandwich with eggs and bacon.

"Absolutely." She paused and tilted her head to the side. "Are you okay, Lester?"

Lester straightened up and sucked in a sharp breath. "You know my name?"

The barista smiled. "Of course." Her smile went away in an instant, replaced by a stern look, and her eyes turned black. Electricity danced in them. "And much more." Her voice had turned masculine, baritone.

Lester backed up a step and bumped into the man who had tapped him on the shoulder. He turned and begged his apology, but the man just snorted and told him to watch it. Lester looked back to the window. A male barista was now standing in the window, holding a cup of coffee and a breakfast sandwich.

Lester blinked. It was all he could do. His body would not move, but it was shaking. He took heavy breaths, feeling his chest rise and fall. The world was silent. The barista was saying something, but Lester couldn't hear him. He felt a tap on his shoulder and nearly fell to the ground. He threw his hands up and jerked around, afraid of what he would see.

"Man, what is your problem?" The man he had bumped into was glaring down at him.

Lester stared. "I . . . I don't—"

The man held up a hand. "I don't care. Can you please just get your stuff and get out my way? I've got a job to get to, you jerk."

Lester's fear was replaced by an angry heat rising up in his chest and neck. He bit back a reply and the urge to hit the man. He turned back to the counter, took a step forward, reached out with trembling hands, and took the items from the man. He set them on the ledge and pulled out his wallet as if he was showing it to a police officer.

"Where'd the girl go?" He tried to sound nonchalant, but his voice cracked.

The man in the window scrunched up his face. "What girl, dude?" He shook his head. "Seven sixty-five, please."

Lester snatched a ten dollar bill out of his wallet, shoved it into the man's hand, and then grabbed his items without bothering to put his wallet away. He walked away from the counter, trying his best to quicken his pace and ignore the scowls and gawking coming from the people still in line.

He thought about sitting at one of the outside table and chair sets; but when he got past the line, he looked up and saw trees and freshly cut, dark green grass paralleling a trail. He paused, holding his items tightly to his chest, and scanned from left to right. There were benches and a playground to one side of the trail and a short bridge over a narrow stream to the other. He looked over his shoulder at the coffee shop and realized that it was the same one he and Draven had gotten chai from the night before. As he slowly turned his head back toward the park, he saw a homeless man sitting on one of the benches—the same bench the man had been sleeping on before. Lester shook his head and laughed, then fumbled through putting his wallet away without spilling his coffee before crossing the street to the park.

Khufia

Yusef Asad lifted his boot from the back of the pitiful man's neck. With a whimper, he looked up at the Al-Shabaab leader. Yusef turned his head, thankful his face was covered by a shawl so that the stench from the man's soiled pants did not fully reach his sensitive nose.

He shooed the man away with the flick of his wrist and smiled when he heard the grunts and then the shifting of sand beneath the man's feet. He eyed the other three men under his command, delighting in them averting their eyes and shifting their feet from side to side whenever he made eye contact.

"The rest of the interrogations have been like that one?" He walked up and down their ranks, pacing with his head toward the ground.

"The same."

Yusef hated the squeaky sound of his brother Diric's voice, but he was more annoyed by the answer. He paused and looked at Diric, similar height at five feet and ten inches. Diric's face was uncovered, revealing the trademark, hawkish nose of their tribe. He stepped close to Diric and cleared his throat.

"I want to know who the sorcerer is, and I want to know now."

Without warning, he slapped Diric on the cheek with enough force to send him stumbling into Yasir, a tall, dark-skinned man to his left. Yasir shoved him away and down, and Diric fell to his backside. He looked up with his mouth open. Yusef noticed Yasir shoot him a warning glance before turning back to face the front. He laughed at Diric and moved to stand in front of Yasir.

"You know what the sorcerer will bring."

Yasir nodded. "Hope."

Beneath his shawl, Yusef smiled. He patted Yasir on the shoulder. "Yes, hope. And we cannot allow them to hope in anything but Allah and the law."

"But are you sure the sorcerer came from among them?"

Yusef turned to his left slowly and cocked his head to the side. Tahiil, the shortest of the four men, had stepped forward and held his hands to his sides.

"We destroyed their church. The Christians are gone."

Yusef nodded. "You are right, Tahiil, which is why I don't strike you for speaking to me out of line, but we cannot be negligent. We must weed out any dissenters and deal with them swiftly." Tahiil lowered his head and stepped back.

Yusef looked back at Yasir. "Find them. Beat the truth out of them if you have to."

"With pleasure."

As Yasir walked away, Tahiil reached down and helped Diric to his feet. Yusef chuckled to himself as they followed Yasir, Diric looking over his shoulder.

CHAPTER FIVE

Olympia

MORANE WALKED BEHIND LESTER, LESS than ten feet away, until he stopped at a park bench and exchanged greetings with a filthy, ungroomed man. Morane wrinkled his nose at the mere thought of smelling the creature, thankful his nose could not actually be poisoned by the stench in the relative safety of the spirit realm. As he watched Lester sit down next to the man, Morane began to inhale and exhale with a hissing sound, and his eyes narrowed.

Lester handed food to the homeless man, and Morane growled.

"Your kindness is weakness, fool." He wanted to emerge onto the material plane and rip them both apart, but he was restrained. The demon despised the limitations, yet he had no choice but to remain within his boundaries.

He inhaled the stagnant air of his hidden realm and smiled. There were other ways to destroy a man, after all. He chuckled to himself, a sound not unlike the scraping of a tool over gravel and the growl of a bear joined in a sinister symphony. The smile vanished when he overheard Lester asking the man about his family.

He had none.

Lester asked about his previcus work.

He had been out of work for years.

Could he sweep?

Yes.

Mind making minimum wage?

No. He'd take anything.

Could he make it to the shop in two hours?

Morane clenched his fists and roared. Though he was well-hidden in the realm of spirits, Lester lifted his head. The demon hissed and spat. He seethed as Lester shook the wretched man's hand and then stood. He tried to stare through Lester as he passed in front of Morane, oblivious, and walked back to the coffee shop.

He shifted his focus away from Lester, momentarily. What did it matter to him if the man was ordering more food? It was time to take Lester's thoughts away from the needs of others, and the only way to do that was to get him to look at something more powerful. Morane felt himself calming as he looked toward the impound lot and drifted on the air toward it.

He passed through the wall and came into the office where a short, Hispanic man around Lester's age was sitting behind a low desk. For a salvage yard and towing service, the office was immaculate and well-furnished. Though it was more comfortable than Hades, Morane paid it no attention. He crept around the desk and hovered over the man. He could feel his weakness. A few sentences uttered from the mouth of this mortal and Morane would have all the information he needed.

A few minutes later, a bell above the door chimed, and Lester walked in. He held a new cup of coffee in one hand and a half-eaten sandwich in the other. Morane smiled and relaxed, standing to his full height behind the clerk. His skin tingled as he began to listen.

The man lifted his head and gave Lester a wave. "What can I do for you, sir?"

"Tito?"

The clerk leaned back and tilted his head. "Lester?" There was an awkward silence, an exchange of bewildered looks, then they both laughed, and the man stood up to shake Lester's hand. "That you, man? How you been, bro?"

Lester released Tito's hand after giving it a hearty shake. "Yeah, man. I'm good. What about you?"

"Same old, same old, bro. Just work. That's about it." Tito motioned around the office and to his desk. "Sit here and pretend to be working, that is."

Lester laughed and leaned over the counter, folding his arms on the top of it. "I hear ya. Married yet?"

Tito nodded. "Dude, three times. Never again, bro."

Lester stuck his chin out. "So, you're not married anymore?"

"Nah, that's what I mean. I'm married to my third wife, but I'm never going through that again. I had to grow up, y'know?" He smiled. "This one's for life."

Lester nodded once, moving his head up and down deliberately with a "hmm."

Tito sat back down, and Morane chuckled. The two of them had not even been talking for a full minute, and they had already given him what he needed. He leaned down and whispered into Tito's ear.

"What about you, bro?"

Lester pulled his hand away from the desk and shook his head.

"Never married? Not even dating?" Tito folded his arms. "Whatever happened to you and Quinn?"

Morane nearly roared with elation but held himself together when he saw the smile being erased from Lester's face.

Lester shrugged. "Haven't seen her in a while. Why?"

"No? I heard you two broke up. I was gonna come to the wedding, too."

Lester scratched at his cheek. "What can you do, you know?"

Tito sat forward. "Unfortunately, I do. You should look her up."

Lester shook his head and sighed. "Not happening, Tito. Man, I stay so busy with the shop, I just don't have time. Honestly, until you mentioned her just now, I hadn't thought of her in over a year."

Tito nodded. "That's cold, bro. But hey, I heard your place is doing pretty good. I also heard that's why you two weren't together anymore." He held his hands up and shrugged. "It's not really my business, but you messed that one up."

Lester opened his mouth, but then quickly closed it. He shook his head and looked down. "Don't I know it." He scratched his cheek again and then ran his fingers over the side of his head. "Anyway, it doesn't matter. Like I said, I don't really think about it."

"Hey, man," Tito said with his palms facing Lester. "I didn't mean to get you all upset. Just something to think about." He pointed at Lester. "What's with the shirt? You back in church?"

Lester looked down at his shirt and then at the floor. Morane shook with pleasure.

"Just a shirt, man. Listen, Tito, I don't mean to cut you off, but I really need to get going."

"Sure," Tito said. "What brought you by, though? You just swing in to say hello?"

Lester was shaking his head. "No. My car got impounded. They told me at the police station they would call ahead."

Tito smacked himself in the forehead with the palm of his hand. "Lester Sharp! How did I not make that connection? I guess it's been that long, huh? Anyways, they called from the police station a while ago." He looked around on the desk until he found a piece of paper. "You got your key?"

"Yeah." Lester pulled his keys from his pocket. "You need I.D. or anything?"

Tito slid the paper toward Lester and looked up. "You serious?"

"Just asking."

"Bro, we wrecked my dad's Toyota on graduation night. I think I know you."

Lester laughed. "Man, was that crazy, or what? I thought your dad was gonna rip your head off."

Tito was nodding. "I thought Quinn was gonna rip yours off."

They laughed again, but the laughter faded into awkward "huhs" as they both looked away and nodded. Morane watched the rest in a state of pure bliss. Lester signed the paper; they shook hands again; and they promised to stay in touch.

As Lester exited the shop, Morane smiled. He wished he could capture the look on the pitiful man's face at the mention of the woman. The turmoil was clear on the man's face, and the question about his shirt and going back to church had been the icing on the cake. While Morane wanted to keep Lester as far away from that place as he could, running into a certain someone at a time like this was a risk he was willing to take. He laughed and slipped through the wall of the building. Lester's turmoil would unfold on its own, for now.

Khufia

Ibrahim pushed back the thick blanket that served as the door to his hut and entered. The air inside was cool and smelled like damp earth. It was too dark to see, so he looped the blanket onto a hook he had fastened inside the doorway to allow moonlight to shine a path inside. He fumbled his way through until he found an oil lamp and lit it. The sharp striking of the match in his hand broke the silence, and the flame sent the darkness away.

He held the match to the wick and smiled as the bright orange flame turned into a soft, growing glow. He did not use the oil very often. It was a scarce commodity for a poor man in a rural village, but he did not want to be in the dark at the moment. It was late, and his body screamed for him to put the light out and go to sleep; but he could only think of the man being held prisoner by Yusef and his men.

Yusef.

He spat on the floor as he thought of the militant tyrant who had terrorized Khufia for nearly a year. The image of Nala swinging from the tree and Guleed's body bleeding onto the hot sand intruded his thoughts. He held a hand out and braced himself against the wall as his emotions bubbled over. His shoulders shook as he sobbed. The sobs turned to groans and nearly a wail before he remembered his situation.

"This is no time to cry like a child," he said to himself. He studied the lamp, trying not to think about his trembling hand, which made the light dance on the walls.

Mustering his resolve, he quickly gathered the bread he had left over, put out the light, and exited the hut. He nibbled on a piece of the bread as he walked through the quiet village. All of the workers would be fast asleep for a few more hours until just before dawn, when they would start preparing for another day in the fields. He laughed at the thought. They spent their lives working fields that rendered virtually no harvest. The soil was nearly as unforgiving as Yusef.

As he passed by the round, pointed roof huts made of various combinations of mud, brick, and scrap metal, Ibrahim thought of the families asleep inside of them. Not all, but many fathers and mothers were huddled closely with their children and grandchildren. They slept soundly, not mourning as Ibrahim They were not hiding their granddaughters, and he envied them.

He had little time to contemplate such thoughts. The village was small, and he reached the edge in less than five minutes. He stayed close to the last of the huts and focused on the rusted cargo container that had been converted into a home. It was twenty feet away and unguarded. That seemed suspicious at first, considering Yusef's men had never taken a prisoner before. They either beat them or killed them after their false interrogations.

The container was twenty feet long and just tall enough for a person to walk inside without ducking. Windows and a door had been cut out and crudely fashioned on the sides and front. Ibrahim walked on the balls of his feet but soon relaxed when he reached the door. No one came. No lock on the door.

He checked over his shoulders and then peered around the side of the container that faced away from the moon. He held the side of the container and strained to see, but it was as black as a grave. He took a slow, deep breath, then walked over to the door. He opened it, pushing down on the simple latch that had been rigged to it, still amazed that it was not locked, and stepped inside.

A gasp preceded the sound of chains shifting and scraping along the plywood floor as soon as he was inside. Ibrahim nearly jumped, but he managed to keep himself under control and rushed to pull the door shut. Two rectangles of silver light shone through the cut-out windows and projected onto the wall to his right. They cast a shadowed glow, very dim but bright enough for him to see a slim man with long, thick dreadlocks.

The man tried to scurry to the back of the container, causing his chains to rattle. Ibrahim crouched and held a finger to his lips. He made a soft shushing sound and inched forward. The man jerked on his chains. Ibrahim paused. Again, he made the sound, but this time he held out the bread. The man made a whimpering sound, and Ibrahim saw a shiny, dark liquid trailing from the top of his head to the corner of his jaw.

Ibrahim lowered himself as far as he could without falling and placed one hand on the floor. He stretched himself forward and reached the bread to the prisoner. The man tried to get away, tugged at the short chains, and clenched his teeth. The heat inside the container was oppressive, and Ibrahim felt warm sweat trickling along his cheek. It itched and made his skin crawl. The dragging and scraping of the chain made Ibrahim cringe. He sneaked a quick glance over his shoulder and saw nothing but the door.

He turned back to the prisoner, placed the small piece of bread on the ground, and backed away, using his hands to walk backward and stand up. He focused on the chains as he moved, taking note of how short they were. Fastened to the wall and stretched to their limit, he could tell that the prisoner would not even be able to lay down properly when he moved forward and put slack on them. There was not enough light to make out all of his features, but Ibrahim could easily see cuts and bruises. The man looked exhausted, frightened, and in excruciating pain. With one last sympathetic look, Ibrahim turned and left.

To his surprise, the prisoner did not protest. There were no pleas for him to stay. No rattling of chains. Only silence, which he hoped meant the man had taken the bread. Outside, he silently scolded himself for not trying to unchain the prisoner, but male voices heading in his direction stopped him.

Ibrahim was far too old to run, but he made his best attempt in that moment, doing his best to put as much distance between himself and that container as possible. He had not gone far when he slammed into something solid that nearly knocked him backward and onto the ground. He heard a man grunt and looked up. Though the man's face was wrapped in a black shawl, and his dark clothes were indistinguishable from the three other men with him, Ibrahim knew he was looking at Yusef.

A raspy voice spoke through the face covering. "Out a little late, aren't you, Ibrahim?"

Ibrahim stood up straight and gulped. He could not pull his eyes away from the rifles they carried.

"Yusef?"

"You thought it was someone else, old man?"

Ibrahim looked down and rubbed his forehead. "I don't know how. What am I doing out here?"

The three men with Yusef started to laugh, but the leader held up a hand to silence them, never diverting his attention away from Ibrahim.

"I'm asking you what you're doing out here, and now you want me to tell you?"

He stuttered. "I . . . I . . . I am sorry." He shook his head and blinked several times. "Forgive me. I was in the sun too long today, and I am disoriented."

"The sun went down a long time ago, Uncle."

He despised hearing his son's killer use the common term of respect for an elder but checked his emotions and nodded. "Yes, of course. But I became delirious after fetching water, and I wandered off. I woke up in the fields not long ago, and I cannot get my thoughts straight. Would you and your men be willing to help me to my home?"

"You really must have lost your mind, old man."

This came from one of the other men. He thought it sounded like the youngest of them, Tahiil. He wanted to scold the young upstart and assure him that he was in full control of his mind, but going back on his ruse now would be certain death. He tried not to narrow his eyes as he glared at the masked face. He wanted to tell them to remove their face coverings. Everyone knew who they were.

He regained his composure and gave Yusef a pleading look. "Please. I might wander off again."

Yusef snorted. "That is your business. Ours is the direction you are coming from." He stepped closer and bent down so that his face was inches away from Ibrahim's. "You haven't been to see the sorcerer, have you?"

Ibrahim gasped, genuinely shocked. He hoped they took it as him being aghast at the thought and not the fear of his activities being discovered. "Me? Visit a sorcerer? Why would I do such a thing?"

"Your son was the father of the girl he tried to protect."

Ibrahim looked down and shook his head furiously. "No." Genuine anger boiled in him then, but it was quickly replaced by fear. He croaked out the lie he knew he had to say. "I have no son." He wanted to run as soon as the words escaped his mouth. To hide. To cry out to

God for what he was doing and what he was about to do, but he was frozen with fear.

"No?"

He suppressed his emotions and looked directly into Yusef's eyes, though he could barely see them in the dark. "No. My son died when he forsook Allah."

Yusef leaned back and nodded. "So you said earlier. Are you sure you weren't thanking the prisoner for sending your granddaughter, child of the infidel, to a safe place with his magic?"

Ibrahim turned his head and spat on the ground. "I have no granddaughter. I have no pity for the ones who died today." He felt like a sword was over his head, ready to strike him down. He was faint and wanted nothing more than for Yusef and his thugs to leave him alone so that he could go into the wilderness and wait for God's judgment upon his cowardice. *How quickly your resolve has failed you, Ibrahim*, he thought.

Yusef took a long breath through his nostrils and let his shoulders slump. "Go home, Uncle, before you get hurt."

Ibrahim nodded his thanks and moved to walk past the leader, but Yusef put his hand on his chest. Ibrahim looked up and to his left. Yusef was looking sidelong at him.

"If I find out you are lying to me, I will drag you in front of the entire village and make you an example of what happens to those who turn their backs on Allah and his law."

Ibrahim hesitated, nodded, and then hurried away. Toward home. To condemnation.

CHAPTER SIX

Olympia

ON THE HIGHWAY, SIPPING HIS coffee, Lester's mind was a chaotic whirlpool of conflicting thoughts. The glass towers of Hudson pulled absent glances from his peripherals, but the bumper-to-bumper traffic before him kept his sight mostly captive. Not that he was paying attention to it. He kept one hand draped over the steering wheel while he crammed the last bite of rubbery egg and razor sharp, dry bruschetta bread into his already half-full mouth.

Why hasn't someone called with the funeral arrangements yet? he thought. He sneaked a quick jerk of his head to the right and down so that he could see his phone, which was sitting in the center console cup holder. *Nothing from the old man, but there's another text from Dave.* He chomped the sandwich until it was beaten down enough to swallow. Washing it down with a lukewarm sip of bitter coffee, he focused his attention back on the road. He had to keep his foot on the brake pedal to avoid hitting a minivan as it cut into his lane.

"Where is all this traffic coming from?" He set the coffee cup in the second cup holder and leaned his head back into the headrest. "Must be a wreck or something." With both hands on the steering wheel, he tapped a quick rhythm. *Did anyone else survive the attack?* He sat up straight and shook his head. An image of a soldier in the gunner's hatch of an armored vehicle flashed in his mind. Then one of Dillon. In the seat behind the locked door of the vehicle. Then the seat was empty.

Lester shoved his foot nearly to the floor, pressing the pedal in as fast as he could at the sound of a blaring horn. The rear end of the car lifted, and his head snapped forward. He looked up and saw that the front of the car was so close to the minivan that he couldn't see the taillights. He turned to his left and saw a man about his age in a Jeep Wrangler waving at him. Lester waved back, thanking the man, and then looked back to the front. The minivan was moving. Relieved but embarrassed, Lester eased his car back into the flow of traffic.

Who was that guy at the police station? He tried another sip of coffee to distract him from thoughts of the giant of a man. *Why did he help me, and what happened at the coffee shop?*

He needed to get in the left lane to go in the direction of the shop, but he stayed in the lane he was already in. "You need help, Lester." He didn't care that he was talking to himself. Another image was creeping into his mind, one he simply could not resist allowing in. One that had not entered his thoughts in over a year. She was slim, with smooth, chestnut-brown skin and bright, hazel eyes. She was smiling. He was powerless against her smile.

He flipped his turn signal on as he approached a traffic light and then sped through it, turning right with a squeal of tires. Ignoring the angry looks and yet another series of horns, he weaved through cars until he was cutting a path down East Avenue.

In the direction of the church.

Lester saw three vehicles in the large but mostly empty parking lot as he pulled in. Two of the vehicles were fairly new and parked in designated spaces in front of a large, rectangular building with a covered drop-off area. Just outside the shade from the two-story building, the sun glinted off the rear windows of the cars. The front of the building was glass, and Lester could see inside to the two-sided stairwell accentuated by hanging artwork and brilliantly tiled floors. A row of well-manicured bushes and flowers extended to either side of the main entrance, providing an inviting ambiance.

Lester parked toward the middle of the lot and let his gaze follow one of the rows of flowers to the grassy field beside the building. The third vehicle was parked against the rounded curb next to the field. It was a white diesel with a trailer attached that had lawn maintenance equipment stacked on it. Lester glanced back to the glass entrance as he shut the car off. The immediate silence that followed disturbed him. In his driveway at home, that engine-shut-off silence was a peaceful, end-of-the-day moment he welcomed. But there, in front of the church he had not been to in so long, it was as ominous as the last moment of peace before a long day at work.

He took a deep breath and opened the driver's side door with a hesitant push, then got out. There was a rush of heat and wind that swept across his face and neck before swirling past him to go disturb some other stranger in another empty parking lot somewhere. Lester wondered who else would be touched by that rush of air and what they were going through. He imagined how far it would go before merging with another breeze, or maybe a storm. He wondered if it would make it all the way across an ocean. If it would caress the belly of a plane carrying a body to its final resting place. If Dillon was on that plane.

He shook his head and shut the car door more violently than he had intended and started across the parking lot. It was spacious enough to hold a few hundred people, but Lester was convinced that he would never reach the door of the church. Every step that took him closer to the door seemed to push him farther away. In reality, he walked only the length of about twenty yards before he was under the awning, then a few more steps before grabbing the door handle with trembling fingers.

"Lester?" A man's voice came from the inside as soon as he opened the door. "Lester Sharp?"

Lester stepped inside and let the door close on its own with the sound of air compressing into a tube. A tall man in boots and faded jeans was striding toward him. He wore a thin flannel with long sleeves, and his even thinner, black hair was slicked back. The man held one hand out when he was about three feet away. His other hand was gloved and holding a glove. Lester took the offered hand. The man's grip was firm and sudden, taking Lester by surprise.

"How you been, brother?" The title was unexpected, and Lester guessed that his own, wide-eyed response was the reason the man was suddenly furrowing his brow.

"Alright, I guess." Lester pulled his hand away when the man's grip finally relaxed. "Sorry, I don't—"

"Dale," the man said. He paused and raised his eyebrows. Seeing that Lester was not recognizing him, the man shook his head but continued. "Dale Parkman?" Disappointment. "I'm the groundskeeper. Your dad and I know each other from before he and your mom moved a while back. I know I'm not in a suit, but come on, boy. You've known me all your life."

Lester did his best to hide a flinch at the mention of his parents. And then it was there. A memory of waving at this man as he entered the church building. He was always outside, always tending to the grass or the flowers, or scraping up gum in the parking lot, even in a suit and tie. He remembered crowds of kids surrounding a laughing Dale, who always had a fist full of money.

"Dollar Dale," Lester blurted out without thinking.

Dale laughed and nodded. "Fifty-cent Dale these days, the way this place keeps growing. Seems like there's more kids here every Sunday. I'll be Nickel Dale or penniless if I'm not careful." He slapped Lester on the shoulder and let out a hearty laugh. "Here to see Pastor?"

Lester nodded.

"Well, he's here," Dale said and then laughed. "You sure you don't want to come back later, though?"

Lester shook his head and furrowed his brow. "No. Why?"

Dale shook his head and grinned. "Nothing. How you been, son?"

Lester shrugged and looked at the polished tile at his feet. "Busy."

"Too busy, from what I hear."

Lester looked up, wanting to be offended but finding himself agreeing. "Yeah, keeping the shop up and running takes a lot out of me. You know?"

Dale nodded. "I bet." He reached out his hand again, and Lester shook it. "I sure hate to run off on you like this, but they're not paying me to stand here and run my mouth."

"Oh. Okay. No problem." Dale pulled his hand away and put his other glove on.

"Good to see you, Lester. I'll be praying for you." Dale smiled and chuckled.

"Why?"

Dale shook his head and slapped Lester on the shoulder. "You'll see." He walked outside.

Lester turned his attention to the high ceiling of the lobby as he listened to the air push out of the hydraulic door closer. He thought it would be a good idea to get the door to the main entrance of the shop upgraded to something quieter, like that one. It reminded him of Dave and the multiple calls and texts he had not answered. He was about to pull his phone out of his pocket when he heard the unmistakable clicking of a woman's heels on the tile. He searched left and right but didn't see anyone. The spiral staircases were exactly in the middle and on either side of the lobby. They led to a balcony that extended out over the first floor. On the first floor, on the other side of the stairs, were hallways to the left and right.

A slim woman in her late twenties emerged from the hallway on the right. She was wearing black slacks and a loose-fitting, blue blouse that accented her chestnut-colored skin as if they had been made together. She stopped abruptly and got half of "May I help you?" out before she froze. Lester's heart skipped as he looked at Quinn. She was motionless, her mouth agape. Finally, she ended the awkward silence.

"Lester?"

He put his hands in his pockets and let out a slow breath. "Hey, Quinn."

She took a step forward, looked as if she were about to rush toward him, then stopped. "What are you doing here?"

He pulled one hand from his pocket long enough to run his fingers through his hair and then quickly replaced it. "I . . . " He was finding it difficult to breathe. He looked down. "I came to see Pastor Greene."

His sentence had ended in a whisper that echoed through the lobby. He lifted his head and puffed out his cheeks.

Quinn did walk toward him then. "You look . . ." She touched her finger to her lips, then yanked her hand away. "I mean, how are you?"

He nodded. "Good." He paused to consider whether he was lying. "Yeah. I'm alright. You? How've you been?"

"Good," she said without hesitation. "Really good."

They both nodded and resumed silence. Lester tried to get his hands deeper into his shallow pockets, while Quinn hugged herself and bit her bottom lip.

"So, what are *you* doing here?" he asked.

She opened her mouth and looked around as if she had forgotten where they were. "Oh. Well, I work here now."

"Really?" He pressed his lips together and wondered how many more times he could nod without his head falling off. "Wow."

"Yeah." She laughed. "Crazy, right? I had some decisions to make after . . . " She paused and met his gaze. "After . . . " She laughed again and shrugged. "The church hired me to be the pastor's assistant and handle the daytime logistics around here."

Lester thought about running but knew that he had to face this. "I'm glad things worked out."

She cocked her head to one side then and narrowed her eyes. "Worked out?"

Lester felt his heart pounding in his chest, and the thought of running was becoming even more enticing.

He swallowed before speaking. "I just mean with the job. I think it's great."

She touched her upper lip with the tip of her tongue and shook her head in tight, little jerks, letting out a puff of air. After a few moments, she took in a deep breath and forced a smile. "The pastor is in his office. He doesn't have any appointments until later today, so he should be able to see you." She turned and practically stomped her way back toward the hallway.

"Quinn." Lester called after her and held his hands out to his sides.

She stopped and spun around to face him. "Why are you here?" Her hands were balled up at her sides. "I'm doing just fine without you around. There's thirty other churches you could have come to, Les, and you had to come here?"

"I didn't know you would be here." He walked toward her, but she held up her hand.

"Don't." She smiled and looked down. He could hear her voice shaking. She looked up, and the forced smile was gone. "Do you know how many times I called you?"

"Dillon's dead."

He closed his eyes and mentally berated himself for blurting that out. The silence between them was instant. He opened his eyes and exhaled, shoving his hands back in his pockets. She stood up straight and lowered her hand. Lester's lip began to quiver, and his eyes felt hot. He tried to say he was sorry. Tried to take it back, but she had already turned and was heel-clicking her way down the hall, hugging herself with her head down.

Lester lowered his head and put his hands on his hips as the heat in his eyes turned to moisture.

CHAPTER SEVEN

Khufia

AS THE PRISONER'S EYELIDS SPREAD, light pushed through the foggy haze of his vision and yanked him from sleep. With his head lying awkwardly to one side on the ground, blood pumped through it and amplified the throbbing in his temples. He blinked rapidly, took in vacuum bursts of air through his bloody nostrils, and tried to sit up.

Pain like fire enveloped his right wrist, and his shoulder popped in protest. Remembering the chains binding him to the walls, he finished the laborious task of opening his eyes before contorting through another attempt. Several groans, coughs, and joint pops later, he was on his knees with his arms and hands as close to his sides as he could get them. After scanning the tiny prison, he guessed it was sometime in the evening. An orange light flickered outside the window, but he could not stand up to investigate.

The creaking of the door to his front interrupted his shock from the sight of a torch and he turned his head toward the sound. Hoping to see the nameless old man with another piece of bread, he was disappointed to see four men entering. They all wore black fatigue pants and t-shirts. Their heads and faces were wrapped in some kind of black cloth. His mind searched for a word and found *scarf,* but he knew that was not the right word. Each of the men held a rifle. They did not speak as they stomped their way across the creaky plywood floor.

The first one to him kicked him in the chest, not particularly hard but enough to knock him back and cause his shoulders to pop and wrists to burn when the chains jerked tight. Because he was sitting on his calves, he did not fall all the way back but bounced up and was met with another kick, this one from the second attacker to the face. White light exploded, blinding him, and he felt the ground rush up to hammer into his forehead. Strong hands gripped his neck and pulled him back up.

He stared into the dark, green eyes of a killer. The flames blazed on both wrists, and he saw the motion of hands removing the wrist braces out of the corners of his eyes. The man directly in front of him, holding him by the throat, was yelling at him, but the language was foreign. The prisoner shook his head and hoped the pleading in his eyes explained that he could not understand. He was lifted from the sides and then dragged out of the cell, held on either side by one of the men.

Outside, he saw a secluded village. There were many small buildings constructed from scrap wood and metal. Gray and black smoke spiraled out of the huts and disappeared into the black sky. The buildings were laid out randomly but connected by a wide patch of sandy dirt that trailed off between the houses. The men tossed him onto the dirt in the widest part of that road. He landed face-first and involuntarily ate a mouthful of bitter sand.

As he was pushing himself up and spitting out the grains, the men fired their rifles into the air and began to make hooting noises. Some of them shouted; and after several rounds had been fired and the men had settled their shouting, one of them began to yell. The prisoner was sitting now, bracing himself with his hands on the ground to his sides and slightly behind him. He was unable to understand what the man was yelling, but the meaning became obvious when, one by one, villagers emerged from their homes.

They wore nightclothes and rubbed at their faces. Several of them escorted children with hands on small shoulders. Others ushered their young back into their homes with waves of their hands and harsh whispers. He looked into the frightened faces of the children and willed them back inside the pitiful shacks. The faces of the adults held fear as well, but also disgust. He could not tell from the curled lips and flared nostrils if the disdain was for him or his attackers. When the houses had been mostly emptied of their inhabitants, one of the scarfed men began to yell.

"Anzur 'iilaa alsaahira!" he shouted while pointing his rifle into the air. The man lowered his rifle and used it to point at the prisoner. "Anzur 'iilaa alkafir!" The man leaned forward and made a half-circle, scraping the dirt as he turned. He then walked over and punched the prisoner in the jaw, knocking him to the ground where he clutched at his face.

"Anzur madha yahduth lah," the man said. He repeated himself.

The prisoner sat up and cocked his head to the left. *Had he understood one of those words?* He thought he had. The word was *witch*. The man was pointing at him again and repeating the phrase, "Anzur 'iilaa alsaahira!"

Look at the witch? His mind seemed to be racing through a thousand languages, which further frightened him.

The man again spoke to the crowd with words the prisoner could not understand. The villagers furrowed their brows and leaned their heads back with their chins tucked toward their necks. His attacker kept the muzzle of his rifle pointed at the ground but shook it and repeated his words louder. The prisoner was distracted by the throbbing on the left side of his jaw. He tenderly touched the spot and watched the man stomp over to a man and woman in the crowd.

The prisoner searched the crowd but did not see the old man who had brought him food. His search was interrupted by a scream, and he jerked his head to the front. His attacker held a man by the shirt and was pulling him toward the prisoner. The scarfed man stopped and pointed at the prisoner, then repeated himself.

"'Azhar walayik lilah."

The prisoner heard the words this time, and he thought he understood their meaning, but he did not know how. Could not. He did not speak this language. *What language did he speak?* he thought. He did not have to wait for a translation. When the accosted man bit his lip and shook his head, the scarfed man shoved the butt of his rifle into his gut. The man doubled over and groaned, and the woman screamed.

"'Azhar walayik lilah." The scarfed man leaned over so that his mouth was almost touching the man's ear. "'Aw aindama 'iilaa hdha alkafir."

The prisoner worked out the meaning. He wanted the man to beat the prisoner.

He wanted to get up and run. He felt an untapped amount of strength lurking beneath the surface of his beaten body, but it was out of his hopeless reach. He wanted to grab the scarfed man by the throat. To beat him and the rest of his attackers the way he had been beaten. But as quickly as the strength had attempted to rise, it fled when he watched the man stand.

He held his stomach with one hand and scowled at the man with the rifle. He took two gaping strides and then drove his fist into the prisoner's face between the eyes. The prisoner saw light and stars explode. He was on his back then with his legs tucked under his body. He rolled to his side, blind, and kicked his feet out. Enough of the haze that followed the stars cleared for him to see the man standing over him, shaking his hand.

The prisoner was snatched from the ground by intrusive hands. There were indiscernible shouts from his attackers. The villagers began to shout "Allah 'akbar" and pump their fists in the air. One by one, the men in the crowd walked over—some with disdain etched in their faces, some with tears—and beat him. He was struck repeatedly in the face, the stomach, and then all over when he slumped and was let go by the ones holding him.

His mind did not stay there; it drifted to another village, another city. Another time. He had never experienced this, but he did then. He had seen it in many places and in many times. He did not know how he knew this. He could not force his mind to give him the answers he knew he had. It had begun to accept the state he was in and told him he was no one. He was the prisoner. He was the infidel.

A rifle to the side of his head silenced those thoughts.

When Ibrahim woke up, he found himself in a dark room. He could hear his own breaths huffing out in loud bursts of panicked air. Cold, slick sweat smeared his face and neck. He swiped at it with a trembling hand, then forced himself onto his side and propped his upper torso on one elbow. He nearly screamed when he saw Yara's glassy eyes staring back at him. She was on her knees, silhouetted by the pale light of the moon, which had forced its way through a lone window.

Panting, he asked her what was wrong. She held his stare with her own, remaining speechless. Ibrahim said her name. Nothing. He said it again, then said everything was alright. She moved then, a slight move of her head from left to right. He wondered how long she had been watching him, wondered if he had been talking in his sleep. If sleep was the right word.

The memory of the nightmare lingered like a phantom in the air, kept at bay only by the fear for his granddaughter. He quickly scanned the room, then back to Yara. Her hands were folded in her lap, and she kept her unblinking eyes fixed on him.

Without warning, she reached out and put her hand on his forehead. Immediately, it was as if her tiny palm was attached to his clammy skin and could not be removed. Ibrahim saw a burst of light and felt himself being forced down. His shoulder, then his back, was pressed against the bed roll. Yara was above him then, her face indiscernible in the dark. She leaned down, eyes bulging, and there was another burst of light.

He stood on a dirt road. It was dark. There was a warm breeze at his back. He could hear insects—cicadas and grasshoppers—playing the rattling, screeching tunes that reminded him of being a boy. Something touched his hand. He looked down and to his left. Yara was standing there, wrapping her small hand around three of his fingers. She was trembling.

Voices in front of him stole his attention away, and he snatched his head up to see what it was. Four shadowy figures emerged from somewhere down a path, a path he now recognized. A moment later, from the opposite direction, came his own likeness in hobbling yet hurried steps. He watched with jaw agape as the image of himself bumped into the image of the tallest of the four other figures.

Yusef.

Ibrahim felt pressure around his fingers and glanced sideways at Yara. She inched closer to him and grabbed his arm with her other hand. He wanted to comfort her, but he was unsure. He tentatively turned his head back to the men on the path and watched as Yusef got close to his face. Awestruck that he was looking at himself, witnessing the event from a few hours before, Ibrahim could not move. Moreover, he and Yara were apparently invisible and unheard because none of the men, including the similitude of himself, had acknowledged his presence.

He watched in shame and listened to himself denouncing his son and denying Christ. He hung his head, unable to bear the sight of his own cowardice playing out before him. A few moments later, he heard laughter and the sound of shuffling feet scraping through the sand. He looked up to see himself running down the path. The image froze, and Yara's grip on his hand loosened. He swallowed a lump in his throat and shook his head.

"How are you doing this, Yara?" He faced her and knelt. On one knee, he was just taller than her, and he looked into her eyes. "Yara? What has happened to you?"

She did not speak, but the girl turned, head-first, and pointed at the large shipping crate the prisoner was being held in. She held her finger in the air for a few seconds before lowering her arm and turning back to face him.

His mind was a hive of questions, but he asked only one. "Do you know who is in there?" She hesitated, then nodded once. "The man from the field? You remember him?" Terror beyond anything he had ever known rippled through him. He grabbed her by the shoulders and forced her to look directly at him.

"What is he, Yara?" She was silent. He gave her a gentle shake. "Please, Yara. Do you know what the man is?"

Instead of answering his question, Yara turned her head and looked at the frozen image of the four Al-Shabaab men. He followed her gaze, and suddenly, he wanted to rush over and kill them where they stood; but he knew that was not possible. When he turned his head away, Yara slapped her palm against his forehead, and another burst of light brought him back to Nasteexo's home.

He gasped and pushed Yara's hand away as he sat up. He struggled to breathe, pulling in as much air as his lungs would accept. Yara had stepped back, lowering her head. Her lip trembled, and she turned away. He called after her, but she only went across the room to her sleeping mat. She laid down and pulled the thin blanket Nasteexo had given her over her head.

Ibrahim could hear gentle sobs. His instinct to get up and go to her was crushed by the weight of his sadness and shame. The memory of hearing himself deny his son played like a broken record in his mind, and the image of himself running away felt like a knife in his chest.

He laid down on his side. All of his questions over what had happened to his precious granddaughter had disappeared, replaced by that memory. He doubted he would sleep.

CHAPTER EIGHT

Olympia

LESTER STOOD IN FRONT OF the pastor's door with his head in his hands and his elbows pulled into his stomach. He breathed in and held it. Pushed the air out with a shudder. He rubbed his eyes, though they were fine. He dropped his hands to his sides with a slap and groaned. He shook his head and took one more deep breath before reaching up and lightly rapping his knuckles against the dark brown wood grain of the door.

He heard a baritone voice say, "Come in," and reached for the brass knob with his shaky hand. He paused to chew on his bottom lip, his fingertips poised above the door knob as if there was an electrical arc between them, and then he rolled his eyes and opened the door. He eased it open and leaned his head through. The room was like something out of a movie, and Lester took note of changes that had been made since the last time he had seen it.

A wide, navy blue carpet filled the room and was like a glistening sea of comfort beneath fully stocked bookshelves, snake plants, and a rock fountain on a stand in the corner. Lester had no time to admire the decor because the tall, barrel-chested man behind the immaculate cherry wood desk was standing. The high back, leather chair he had been sitting in rolled back as his legs pushed against it; and when the man stood to his full height, Lester remembered how imposing a figure

Pastor Nathaniel Greene had been when he was younger. Even now, with a head full of gray, curly hair and matching eyebrows that made his bronze skin seem darker around his eyes, Lester was intimidated.

"Lester?" Greene edged his way around the desk. "Lester Sharp?"

Lester nodded and stepped through the door. "Yes, sir."

Pastor Greene took measured steps, paused, shook his head, and half-chuckled. "Lester?"

Lester swallowed and pushed the door shut behind him. "It's me."

"Sorry." Greene took large strides, easily covering the distance between them, and extended his massive hand. "I'm just surprised to see you."

"Yeah, it's been a while." Lester took the offered hand, and his was engulfed by the pastor's. He had to look up to make eye contact. The handshake was uncomfortably long, so Lester tried to loosen his grip, but Greene didn't seem to notice.

"How long has it been?" Greene asked. He looked down at his hand and shook his head. "Sorry. Let me give you that back." He released his grip.

"I'm not really sure," Lester said. "At least a year."

Greene let his head tip forward and narrowed his eyes. "Or two or three?"

Lester could not resist laughing. "Yeah, probably."

Greene shook his head and chuckled. 'Come on in. Have a seat." He motioned toward two wide, leather chairs in front of his desk. Lester sat to the left, and Greene sat down opposite him. The leather felt cool and yielded to his body. Lester eased into the chair at first, but it seemed to swallow him; so, he sunk down and draped his forearms on the arm rests.

"So." Greene smiled and folded his hands in his lap. "How have you been? Shop doing okay?"

Lester did his best to hide his wince at the mention of the shop. "It's, um, it's alright, I guess." He paused, but Greene made no effort to respond, so he continued. "Busy. Really busy, but we're picking up a lot of repeat business, and we're slowly gaining a good reputation." He shrugged. "It just takes time."

Greene nodded. "Well, anything lasting takes time to get established." He waved one hand in the direction of the main part of the church and then set it back in his lap. "I'm still amazed at how much we've grown here. Not just the church, either."

Lester raised his eyebrows. "Oh? Did you and your wife have more kids?"

Greene chuckled. "Hard to believe at my age, but yes and no. We decided to become foster parents, and we're looking into adopting a refugee."

"Really?"

Greene nodded. "Several of our families are doing that. We had a missionary come through about a year ago to discuss his work in northern Africa, and it just broke our hearts. We took him and his work on for support, but we also decided to start trying to help as many of those kids as possible."

Lester had sat forward while Greene was talking, but he eased himself back into the chair and looked at his hands in his lap. "That's amazing." His mind drifted to the scene at the Horn of Africa he had witnessed during the glimpse. He remembered the headless body and the believers on their knees before the rifle-wielding men.

"Lester." Greene's tone was sharp and abrupt. Lester snapped his head up. "I could talk about this all day, but that's not why you came here. Any man with two eyes could see something's troubling you, so what is it, son?"

Lester opened his mouth, but nothing came out. He felt an urge to run but suppressed it. He found himself wishing he was back in his study, back to the day before, consumed by invoices and OSHA paperwork while consuming bitter coffee. His mind, however, did not want to go to that place. His mind only wanted to travel to a barren road near an ancient temple. To a bomb hastily buried in that road. To the vehicles headed for that bomb. The vehicles filled with soldiers only one second from their death. Filled, except for one seat.

"My brother is dead." He looked up at Greene through watery eyes and felt the sting as he fought to hold back tears.

Greene lowered his head and rubbed his face. "Oh, no." The giant of a man's shoulders slumped, and his breaths turned to loud sighs. "Oh, no. Not Dillon." This went on for more than a minute, but the pastor finally looked up with his elbows propped on his knees. "What happened?" he asked with red eyes.

"Roadside bomb." Lester felt his lip trembling and fought it by clenching his jaw. "I'm waiting for my dad to call back with the details."

"Lester, I'm so sorry." Greene sat up and shook his head. "I don't—"

"That's not why I came here today," Lester said, interrupting. He sat up straight and looked directly into the pastor's eyes. Greene closed his mouth and sat back.

"Okay. What's going on?"

Lester didn't know where to begin, and he didn't know how much to say, so he just let his frustration boil over until words came out.

"I want to know why everything has to be so hard. I want to know why I can't just live my life and be left alone. I want to know why this world's been messed up since forever, but all of a sudden, it's my problem. You have any answers for that?"

Greene did not respond right away. He narrowed his eyes, blinked, and then smiled. "Lester, the things you want to know are—"

"How long has Quinn been working for the church?"

Greene looked as if he'd just been slapped in the face. "About a year. Lester, what happened to you? It's not just your brother's death that has you asking these questions. What do you mean, 'it's all of a sudden your problem'?"

Lester shook his head. "I don't know. I shouldn't have said that." He pushed himself up. "I shouldn't have come here, either."

"Hold on," Greene said as he got out of his chair. "Just calm down." He touched Lester on the shoulder. They both eased back into their chairs.

Lester took a deep breath. "How come when you decide to do right, the world falls apart?"

Greene smiled. "Because you have a real enemy, Lester. An enemy that doesn't want you to do right. He is a lion, walking about, seeking whom he may devour." Greene pointed at Lester's shirt. "What's with the shirt?"

Lester glanced down at his chest and shrugged. "A long story."

"I've got time."

Lester looked up and frowned. "I don't. And I don't mean that to be rude; I just have to get to the shop before the place burns down or something. The guy I hired to manage the place has been blowing my phone up."

Greene laughed. "Fair enough, but what about your questions? Where is all of this coming from?"

Lester sucked his teeth, pondering how much to say. "I had a long night, I guess you could say, and, well . . . " He paused. "Well, I had my eyes opened to a lot of things. A lot of things that I should have been noticing all the while, but someone had to show me."

"Like what?"

Lester waved his hand. "A lot. And I'd rather not go into detail, but it was enough to shake me up. Anyway, I made up my mind last night to come back."

"To church?"

Lester shook his head. "To God."

Greene smiled. "I'm listening."

"Yeah," Lester said. "I've been selfish. I see that now, but I don't want to be that way. I mean, I know better I was raised in this church, way before it was this big, and I've heard you preach all my life about what God's done for me and how much He sacrificed."

"Gave up His own Son."

Lester hesitated, still uncomfortable with this conversation. "Well, yeah. That's what I'm saying. You know, He did all that for me, but I never do anything for Him." He cleared his throat. "Anyway, I made up my mind about that last night; and this morning, I wake up to a phone call telling me my brother's dead. Now I run into Quinn, whom I haven't even thought about in over a year."

Greene patted the air with his hands and sat forward. "Lester, slow down. Look, I get it, but you've got so much going through your mind right now that there's no way you'll ever make sense of it until you can see it from a rational frame of mind." He folded his hands in his lap and looked at the carpet at his feet. "What you're talking about is normal. I know, I know. That sounds crazy, and you don't want to hear it, but it's true. You make a decision for Christ, and the devil rears his ugly head. Happens to everybody."

"Why?" Lester held up his hands and then let them rest back on his thighs.

Greene let out a laugh. "We're in a war, Lester. A spiritual war. We don't fight with our hands; we fight with prayer and the Word. The last thing the devil wants is for God to be glorified. The devil wants the glory, and he thinks he gets it when the world keeps spinning on the course he set it on. All this anger and death out here? He thrives on that. People like us come along and try to stop some of that, and he's sure to give us some opposition. You think things have been easy since people in this church have started taking on refugees?"

"What's been going on?"

Greene waved his hand in front of his face. "Doesn't matter. The point is, when you set out to serve the Lord, you become a target; and the one taking aim is a good marksman. He's been doing this for a long time, and he knows what he's doing."

"So, what do I do?"

"Pray." Greene turned his hands over in his lap and shrugged. "Read your Bible. Come here every time the doors are open, if you can make it. Tell others about God's love through His Son. Share the Gospel. Have faith."

Lester scrunched up his face. "That's it?"

Greene leaned back. "What do you expect me to say?"

"I don't know. More."

"Sorry to disappoint. You have to start with the basics."

"I don't know if I can come back here," Lester said.

"You still care about her?"

Lester tried to fight back laughter, but it just came out in a burst. "Saw right through me, huh?"

"Boy, I've known you all your life. You're about as transparent as a window missing the glass."

Lester leaned his head back. "This is too much. I really hadn't thought about her, you know? I mean, I was just fine. Now, Dillon's gone, and I have to go to my parents' place out in Huron."

"One thing at a time," Greene said. "When's the funeral?"

Lester took a long, deep breath, and let it out with a puff of his cheeks. "Don't know. I'm waiting on that call."

"I know things are tense, but you have to keep the peace and try to get through this without going to war with your parents, Lester. Dillon made his own choices. They'll see that someday."

Lester nodded. "I hope so. My heart sinks every time one of them calls me."

"Let's just focus on what we can," Greene said. "How about you call me when your dad calls you? Good? Alright. Meantime, I want to see you here in the morning. The situation with Quinn will work itself out. You just come on. You can't fight spiritual warfare on your own, Lester."

"Yes, sir."

They stood and shook hands. Greene walked Lester out. Lester thought it was an abrupt ending to the meeting, and he still had a lot of questions; but he was somewhat relieved to be done with the conversation.

"I'm bringing a neighbor, if that's alright," he said as Greene opened the door for him.

"Glad to have him."

"He's a bit rough around the edges."

"So's my preaching," Greene said. "We don't turn people away here, Lester. You get him, and y'all come on. Be glad to have both of you, and you just take all of this one step at a time. We'll talk more after tomorrow."

Lester nodded.

"You good the rest of the way out?" Greene asked.

Lester assured him he was and gave one last goodbye before hurrying out of the building.

CHAPTER NINE

LESTER SAT AT A RED light in downtown Olympia, tapping his fingers on the steering wheel. This was the fourth light he had been stopped at, and each one seemed to take longer to change than the last. He did his best to avoid looking left or right. There were the faces, and his mind would wonder about the story behind those masks of smiles and frowns. Needs and wants. Worries and burdens. Things he had not seen only a day before. At each light, he inevitably scanned the road ahead; and the sidewalks and parks filled with poverty, hunger, and fear etched into the wrinkles of foreheads. The people had billboards advocating for change. Billboards everyone ignored.

The latest red light finally turned green, and Lester accelerated through the wide intersection without bothering to check for cross-traffic. He left the billboards behind, relieved, but only for a moment. The motion of the car caused flashes of the subway ride, and then his mind was carrying him across an ocean again. He was in the mountains watching a scene of starvation unfold. He was in a city watching a murder scene unravel, then an African plain watching an execution. A roadside bombing in—

Lester saw the couple holding up their hands in the crosswalk just before he locked up the brakes. The front bumper was only inches from them. A quick, wincing glance in the rearview showed a car so close to his that he could see details in the driver's face. He was holding his hands in the air and obviously shouting at Lester. In front of the car, the couple was doing the same thing. Lester gripped the steering wheel, closed his eyes, and breathed.

He felt a burning in his skin, and his heart was pounding like drums at a heavy metal concert. He snapped his head up and opened his eyes with such rage that the man and woman took a step back. Lester clenched his teeth and curled his upper lip. The man held up a hand and led his wife away, rushing her to the other side of the crosswalk. His eyes followed them, daring further retaliation to his negligence. As quickly as his anger had arisen, it melted into another emotion. The man was about Lester's height and build and probably the same age. The woman looked a little bit like Quinn, although pale with red hair.

The smell of smoke and the blaring of horns pulled his attention away. He looked up, saw a green light, and eased through the intersection, his thoughts now fully fixed on the scene unfolding before him. He didn't just smell smoke; he saw it. Two blocks ahead, in front of a circle of emergency vehicles parked in a perimeter outside his shop.

Lester parked next to the curb in front of a sandwich shop and shut the car off. He got out and ran over, past two police cruisers and a fire truck, and made it halfway to the smoldering remnants of the front door before a police officer got in front of him and physically accosted him. Lester tried to push past the officer, but another joined to help restrain him. He barely noticed their shouts of protest. He pushed against them for several moments, pleading, shouting that he was the owner. Ultimately, it was not their strength or authority that stopped him, but what he saw with his own eyes.

He relaxed and took a step back, looking around. The brick tire shop next to his had scorch marks along its walls. He tried to focus on the first police officer explaining to him what had happened and asking him who he was, but the site of his heavy-set general manager stomping toward him stole his focus. The officer must have noticed the alarm on Lester's face because he turned and held his hands up, planting them both squarely on the man's barrel chest when he got close enough.

"Where have you been, Les?" Dave shouted over the officer, pointing with a stubby finger. Spittle flew out of his mouth and flecked his lips. "Does your phone not work? Huh? You practically live in this place; and all of a sudden, on the day it burns to the ground, you're not here?" Dave looked at the officer and held up his hands, signaling that he would stay put. "Well?" he shouted at Lester again. "Hey, do you realize my whole livelihood just went up in smoke, and you don't have the decency to pick up the phone?"

Lester watched the smoldering of the collapsed roof, sickened by the smell of steam and ash from where the large hoses of the fire trucks had distinguished the flames. Dave's shouts faded into the background. The front of the building was gone, so he could see everything inside. The wall behind the counter was no longer there. The verse he'd written on the wall was gone, but the words scrolled through his memory:

I have set watchmen upon thy walls, O Jerusalem, which shall never hold their peace day nor night: ye that make mention of the LORD, keep not silence.

Standing silently in front of the broken walls of his shop, the irony did not escape Lester. Melted shards of glass were scattered along the ground. He thought of Draven then, sitting on the subway car with him, telling him about the difficult times so many of his employees faced while he mindlessly went about the day-to-day business of running the shop. The weight of their misfortune stacked itself atop a mountain of guilt, and Lester's last sense of hope was crushed beneath it.

He turned to Dave and took a step forward. "Don't you ever talk to me like that again!" He was on his toes and pointing before he realized it. His body was shaking. "What were you doing this time, Dave? Huh? Back there with the boys, whining and crying about life instead of taking care of the shop? Maybe if you actually did the job I hired you for, this wouldn't have happened." He paused and plopped his heels back on the asphalt, his tense muscles practically vibrating because they were shaking so violently.

Dave rushed forward with such speed and force that he knocked down the officer who stepped into his path. Lester hit the pavement next when Dave's fist crunched into his jaw. Lester managed to get his hands down before his face collided with the ground. He turned himself so that he was sitting and looking up at Dave, who was standing over him and pointing.

"You know what? That shop was made up of people, Les. Real people with real problems." An officer came and pushed him back. Dave did not resist but continued to lecture Lester. "If you weren't so stuck in invoices and marketing, you might know something about that."

Lester got up and brushed off his hands. "You think I don't know people have problems? That it? You think I don't care?" The anger was gone from his voice, replaced by sorrow.

Dave was being held by one police officer, and the one he had knocked over was on his feet. He rushed to Dave, pulled at his arms, and began to cuff them behind his back. Lester held up his hands. "Officer, wait. Please, the man is going through trauma, and he didn't intentionally knock you over." He touched his jaw and winced. "And I probably had it coming, so there's no reason to press charges." The two police officers looked back and forth from one another to Lester. They alternated shaking their heads, nodding, then finally shrugging. The assaulted officer removed the handcuffs and put them away.

Dave laughed. "So, now you know people?"

Lester shook his head and held up his hands. "What do you want from me? I just kept you from getting arrested. That doesn't prove I care about you?"

Dave scoffed. "No, it doesn't. You don't care about me, any of those guys, or anyone else." He pointed at the smoking shop as he spoke, then swept his arm out toward Olympia and Hudson.

Lester let out a heavy sigh and took a couple steps forward. He spoke softly. "You really think I don't care?"

Dave hesitated, looked down, and shook his head. "No. If you did, you wouldn't have kicked that guy out last night, and you'd know that the guys working for you just lost everything."

Lester didn't respond. He put his hands on his hips and looked at his feet. He felt his phone vibrating in his pocket and heard the ringer, but he ignored it. He thought about the first time he had seen Draven, the night before when he had come into the shop and asked for help. Lester had dismissed him without reservation. Kicked him out without a second thought. Remembering Draven's promise that he would be watching, Lester wondered what he was thinking then. The phone ringing and vibrating became annoying, so he yanked it from his pocket and looked at the screen.

Harold Sharp.

He fumbled the phone but answered, and he heard Dave yelling about him all of a sudden wanting to answer the phone. He ignored Dave and lifted the phone to his ear.

"You really have a problem picking up the phone today, don't you?"

Lester snapped his eyes shut and sucked air through clenched teeth. "What is it?"

"I just got off the phone with a man from the air force. Dillon's remains will be en route in the next few hours."

"Remains?" Lester wanted to vomit at the thought of his brother being talked about like some piece of rotten meat in a box.

There was a pause and then a heavy sigh. "The truth is, there's nothing to transport."

"What?"

"I made that up."

Lester almost threw the phone but maintained his composure. "What are you talking about?"

"They . . . um." He heard sniffling. "They didn't recover Dillon's body." He could hear his father sobbing, and the next words he spoke were difficult to interpret. "I called to find out about his body being transported, and they said they couldn't find anything."

Lester fought back the flood. He wanted to melt into the street and disappear, break down right there on the phone, but he would not and could not allow his father to hear his emotions. He put one hand on his hip and looked to the sky.

"What about the funeral?"

"Tuesday. We're not going to tell anyone the details. It will just be a closed casket, and he'll get full honors."

Lester nodded. "Alright. I'll be there."

There was a beep, and the phone went silent.

"You've gotta be kidding."

Lester slid the phone into his pocket and looked down. He wanted nothing more than to turn and let loose a flurry of punches on Dave's face; but his limbs, and his mind, were numb.

"You don't answer my calls or texts all morning; your shop burns to the ground; but all of a sudden, you can answer the phone?"

Lester turned and felt his eyes burning. He saw Dave through a wall of blurry, shimmering water. "It was my father. My brother died in Iraq yesterday." The flood broke loose, and he trembled with sobs.

Dave opened his mouth, closed it, then looked at the ground. When he looked up, there were tears in his eyes, and he walked over to his boss with his arms spread wide. Lester had no strength to fight the convulsions of tear-filled sobs. He fell against Dave's chest and let a thousand memories pour from his eyes as the big man wrapped his arms around his shoulders.

The prisoner was free. He stood on an abandoned, crater-riddled road. Rubble lay everywhere before and behind him. There was no sound. No wind. He inhaled and heard the echo of his breath. Scanning from left to right, he saw only fields of brown, knee-length grass. He spun in a half-circle, scraping the aged concrete as he turned. In the distance, in one of the fields to his right, was an ancient structure made of earth-colored brick and mud. It rose at least a hundred feet into the air. The base looked like a pyramid, but the walls had been eroded into the shape of an inverted tear-drop.

It was strange yet familiar. There was a flash at the top of the structure from the side facing away from him. He backpedaled and craned his neck. His foot nearly slipped, causing him to look down. He was standing in a tiny pool of dark, red blood. He scrambled away, feet scraping, and looked at his hands, which felt slick in the next moment. Blood dripped from them, but it was only on his hands.

Not his own.

His heart beat wildly. The prisoner sensed danger and looked up. A lone figure approached, silhouetted by the setting sun. The prisoner was about to shield his eyes with his hand but, seeing the blood, decided to squint into the brilliant, orange-red light. As the figure came closer, the prisoner realized it was a man. A man he knew but could not name. The man was pale, drained of all blood. He was the prisoner's height, pale, and wore a red t-shirt. He nodded and pointed at the prisoner's hands.

"The blood is mine," the man said. "The guilt is yours."

A black, clawed hand wrapped around the man's throat from behind. The man's eyes widened. "Why didn't you protect me, Dra—"

The hand tightened around the man's throat and silenced him with a single, powerful squeeze.

Khufia

Cold water cascaded over the prisoner. He gasped and inhaled several drops of water, blinking rapidly to clear his vision. He was surrounded by villagers and the masked men. One of them was holding a wooden bucket and taking a step back. The largest of the masked men stepped forward, and the prisoner saw the villagers behind him holding rocks.

A chant began to rise among the villagers, and they hoisted the rocks over their heads. "'Aqtul alsaahira!" They repeated it over and over, the volume and anger of the chant intensifying. As the prisoner shook the last of the annoying drops from his face, he began to pay attention to the chant. At first, it was gibberish, but then he heard it as if it was being said in his own language. "Kill the sorcerer." He looked at the rocks in their hands as he listened.

Before he knew what he was doing, he was shouting to them, saying, "Please. I'm not a sorcerer. You don't have to do this!" The crowd paused long enough to listen but then turned to one another, shaking their heads. He shouted at them again, begging.

He felt the sting of a slap, and his vision was flooded with stars. The man shouted and slapped him again. After shaking his head to clear the stars, the prisoner looked back and saw the man was pointing at the villagers and shouting. The prisoner understood none of it this time, but the meaning was clear.

The first of the rocks hit him in the shoulder and forced his body to twist. Another struck his other shoulder, reversing his momentum. His body screamed in agony. The prisoner was forced to hunch over into a ball, but it did nothing to stop the rocks or the pain. He heard bones cracking. Felt them cracking. His mind drifted into a dark swirl of empty, sickening blackness. Then he felt nothing.

A distant scraping sound pulled the prisoner from the abyss. Out of darkness.

No. Still dark.

He strained to open his eyes. Nothing. The scraping grew closer and was joined with grunts from somewhere above him. His arms burned. Something sharp passed under his back. He cried out as pain like fire seared his spine. The sound of his own cry brought him closer to the scraping. He begged his eyes to open. A blurred wall of red appeared in the slit between his eyelids.

There were voices above him, talking in between grunts. The prisoner did not know what they said. Did not care. He understood the pain in his arms came from him being dragged. The red cleared enough for him to see his bare feet leaving a trail in the dirt. A trail marked by his blood.

He managed to get one eye open wider, and he saw his legs. The rags that had once been pants were smeared in blood. Large holes had been ripped away from the tattered cloth; and he saw black, swollen bruises on his legs. He closed his eyes. His body spasmed and was wracked by a cough that shook from his broken ribs out of his nearly collapsed throat and sprayed phlegm onto his bleeding lips.

The arms that had been dragging him released his wrists, and his head and shoulders slammed into the ground. A sound so sickening and indiscernible escaped his mouth that he hardly believed it had come from him. There was a shuffling of feet. More scraping in the dirt.

Two men stood over him. One of them pulled the scarf from his face to reveal an open mouth with dry, cracked lips hiding in a thick, bushy, black beard. He muttered something the prisoner could not understand. The two men went back and forth with whispered, rushed words for a few moments, and then one of them pulled a phone from his pocket.

He pressed several buttons before pressing the phone to his ear. He spoke into it, then waited. After a pause, he spoke again. The prisoner did not understand, nor did he want to. His eyelids were heavy, and the pressure in his head pounded against his skull. He wanted them to leave him there on the ground, leave him to die; but as the phone was returned to the man's pocket, he knew that was not going to happen. They would not leave him, but sleep would come. He knew this when the man stood and raised his rifle

The rifle came down and connected with his face, and the prisoner returned to darkness.

PART TWO

PRIDE IS THE GREAT ENEMY of grace.

Where grace would step in to end wars, pride is the kindling of the fires fueling the battles. Pride stays out in the cold, unwilling to accept the hand of grace offering warmth and comfort. Pride goes hungry in the presence of a feast and suffers in solitude with eyes blind to the grace resting beside it.

But pride does not simply ignore grace; it despises it. When grace tries to love, pride amplifies hate. When grace seeks to forgive, pride digs its feet into the muck of never-ending grudges. When grace comes to the center of the battlefield with terms of peace, pride assassinates the ambassadors of goodwill and harmony, for pride desires the chaos and feeds on self-destruction.

To walk alone is to walk in pride, away from grace.

Many live in the land of pride, which is not really a land but an endless road. It does not bend or curve. The road of pride is straight and broad; and though it is a solitary road, it is filled by multitudes. Millions walk the path of pride, which ends in only one of two ways: continue forward until the inevitable fall off the cliff into undying death or turn around. The first way is wide and exhausting. The latter is narrow and leads to rest. There is no light on that road. There is only a voice. The voice lies to the travelers, convincing them their path is the righteous road, the way of truth.

I walked that road for years. Walked away from grace and listened to the voice of my own, misinformed righteousness. I found only heartache along that road but also found it strangely comforting. It was as if every step made the road and me inseparable. It became a part of me, and I could not turn around, though I knew the voice calling to me and telling me to go forward was leading me to destruction. Turning around meant admitting fault, admitting the need for help.

I had grown accustomed to the battles, the cold, the hunger, and solitude. I was familiar with hate and grudges, with chaos and self-destruction. And so, I walked, until I was given the choice to walk no more. Until someone showed grace stronger than my pride. Now that I have turned and experienced the truth of grace, I wish my back could stay forever turned to pride.

- Lester Sharp

CHAPTER TEN

Olympia

IN THE SHADOWS OF A narrow alley, Morane stood over the two homeless men. Convincing them to fight one another had been a simple task of whispering in the ears of one that the other had been stealing items from his cart while he slept. He smiled to himself, pleased that Lester's offer of employment to the filthy wretch would go nowhere.

The fact that the other man—a young, nearly cherubic-looking man—worked at Lester's shop and just happened to be disgruntled with his employer made the brawl between the two vagrants so much more delightful. The older man—the one whom Lester had given food to—had taken quite a beating. He watched the chest of Lester's employee rise and fall, much to his dismay. Then he had a thought and nearly jumped with excitement.

"You get another day in your pitiful life, and I get another day to have some fun," he purred and slipped into the spirit realm. "Don't worry. I have plenty of time before I have to check back in with dear Lester."

He heard a faint sound, like someone gasping, but far away and echoing, as if in a chamber. He wheeled around, letting his eyes adapt to the ethereal plane. Where there was a wall on Earth was vast darkness to the roaming spirits. He scanned as he crouched into a fighting stance, bearing his fangs for anyone foolish enough to approach him to see. Seeing nothing, he relaxed.

The demon half-expected an emissary to be there, or perhaps the Dark Lord himself. Morane ran through a mental checklist. He had been given a short timeframe to complete his task, but he had already set the pendulum swinging in only one day. He knew allowing Lester to attend the church service was a risk, but he waved his hand at that notion as he thought of the angry woman who would be there to keep Lester too distracted to focus on whatever the weak pastor had to say.

No, the sound Morane heard and the presence he felt was not a demon or Lucifer. It was something entirely different. An archangel, perhaps? He shook his head. That would have been obvious, and none of them would lurk in the shadows. This was entirely foreign. He flared his nostrils and sniffed the stagnant air around him. He smiled. The strange presence was gone, but the mixture of scents was unmistakable.

Human.

Fear.

Khufia

Yusef rubbed his swollen knuckles and stepped back, allowing Tahiil to stand. The little man glared at the leader as he rose to his feet, then stood in silence, averting his eyes and massaging his jaw. Yusef walked over and placed his hand on his shoulder. Tahiil moved to yank himself out of the way but stood his ground instead. Yusef bent down and looked into Tahiil's dull, brown eyes.

"Forgive me, brother. I should not have struck you. This is not your fault."

Tahiil shuttered. "I could not have known."

"Of course not." Yusef pulled his hand away and stood to his full height. "You have been a loyal warrior, brave and faithful. The sorcerer's magic is strong."

"Are you sure it is magic, brother?"

Yusef spun on his heels, kicking up a tiny flurry of sand. Diric was three feet away with his arms folded, shaking his head. Yusef closed the distance between them in one step and landed two consecutive punches to his brother's temple before he could react. Diric's hands flew up to try and deflect a third, but Yusef jabbed him in the stomach. As Diric hunched over, clutching his stomach and gasping for air, Yusef spat on the ground and turned to his right where Yasir stood.

"I am not sorry for that one."

Yasir grinned, but Yusef shot him a warning glare; and the tall man's face quickly returned to its normally perturbed complexion. Yusef took a long, deep breath and then spent a few moments scratching his beard before addressing his men.

"As I said, the sorcerer's magic is strong. It has made us look weak." He studied Yasir's face to see if he agreed, but the man was a statue. Turning his attention to Tahiil, Yusef continued, "We must find a way to kill him."

Tahiil nodded. "There is truth to what you say, Yusef. He has made us look weak, but we still do not know how to kill him."

"Or why we cannot," Yasir added.

Yusef looked back and forth, giving them both respectful nods. "Both of you are wise, unlike this stutterer." He waved a hand toward Diric, not bothering to look and see if his brother had recovered. "What do you suggest, brothers?"

Tahiil did not hesitate. "We have beaten and tried to kill the man. Why don't we try to talk to him?"

"And give him the chance to cast a spell on us?" Yusef shook his head, but Tahiil held up a hand.

"Do you not think it strange that a sorcerer with such power has not used his magic to set himself free?"

Yusef's eyes widened at that, and he cupped his mouth with his hand. After a moment, he smiled and wagged a finger at Tahiil. "Ah, ever the thinker is Tahiil. Very well, we must gain more information. We will interrogate him."

"He does not speak our language."

Yusef turned his head toward Yasir. "True, but we speak several languages between all of us. Perhaps my punching bag can finally be of some use." He turned and looked at Diric, who was standing with his fists balled up at his sides. "Then maybe my mother will not have to look away in shame every time she sees him."

They all laughed at Diric. Yusef walked over, still laughing, and grabbed him by the shoulders. "Relax, my brother. I have let you stay with me because I know you will make me proud. Now is your chance."

He pulled Diric into a hug while Tahiil and Yasir continued to laugh.

Olympia

Lester sat on the edge of his bed, hands gripping the mattress. He studied his bare toes, curled into the carpet. He breathed in through his nose and held the fresh air before exhaling through puffed out lips. He stretched, popping his back, then his neck from side to side. Still droopy-eyed, he reached over to his night stand and grabbed his phone. As soon as he lit up the screen, he saw the downloaded airline ticket to Huron. He swiped it away and looked at the time.

Eight-thirty.

He couldn't remember the last time he had slept that late, but late nights often caused late mornings. He glanced to his right, eyeing his warm pillow and groaned. Although he had managed to sleep, it had been a fitful night, waking constantly with thoughts of insurance claims, flight arrangements, and payroll. His dreams had been no better, jumbled into a nightmare collage of jail cells, martyrs, homeless people, bodies, and employees like zombies trying to attack his home.

He had no idea how he had ended up in his photo gallery or how his thumb was swiping through old photos of Quinn. In fact, until the day before, he had forgotten there were pictures of Quinn in his photo gallery or that his phone took photos. He felt a twinge of guilt over forgetting so much, not thinking about anything or anyone but his shop and himself.

And Dillon. There was always Dillon.

He paused at a picture of him and Quinn holding one another by the waist in front of the platform at the church. She was slightly shorter than him, but he laughed, remembering the way she had been wearing heels that day and had made a big deal about being "almost as tall as him." He swiped to another picture with them in the same pose but in front of the church building. The next picture was of them with Dillon and Lester's parents. He frowned and backed out of his photo gallery, tossed the phone on the bed next to him, and stood. He had plenty of time before the eleven o'clock service, and he intended to take all of it.

He went through his normal routine, minus coffee because the sight of the coffee maker still sent his mind to the glimpse. The clock trapped at midnight. The steaming vapor from his burned coffee captured like a chilling still-life image. Poverty, desperation, and death were still vivid in his mind; and no amount of busying himself kept them away. It crossed his mind to talk to someone, to seek help, but he laughed at himself. Who could he possibly tell without them thinking he was insane? He cried several times while getting dressed. Uncontrollable outbursts he could not explain. He finally decided being in the house was too much, so he finished getting dressed and then ate a breakfast of dry toast on his front steps.

His mind superimposed a similitude of himself banging on the siding of his house, like a hologram playing out the last scene with Draven from two nights before. He saw Draven as well, hands in his pockets, relaxed, saying something that he could not understand. Lester tossed the toast onto the lawn and buried his head in his hands. The images were hidden there, as well. They waited for him in every direction. Eyes open, eyes closed; they were there.

When he could no longer stand it, he got up, walked to his car, got in, and shut the door. The silence and stillness of the air inside the vehicle reminded him of time standing still. He hit the steering wheel and yelled. It hurt his palm but drove the hologram away. He hit it again. Yelled again. Draven's hologram vanished, but a whispered, "I'll be watching, Lester" followed it into a cloudless sky. As he pushed the start button and felt the car crank to life, Lester clenched his teeth and growled another onslaught of unwarranted tears away.

He tapped his fingers on the steering wheel on the short drive down the street, and then he found himself gripping the gear shift tightly enough to make his knuckles pop once he put the car in park in front of Wayne's house. He was just about to slump down in the driver's seat and prepare for a wait when the front door opened and Wayne emerged.

Lester laughed when he took in Wayne's attire. The man appeared to be walking on stilts in the tightest pair of jeans Lester had ever seen. The starched pants legs were pulled down stiffly over a light brown pair of cowboy boots. The worn leather of the boots was a sharp contrast to the dark blue of the jeans; and the white, Western-style shirt tucked into the jeans must have had an entire can of starch sprayed into its razor-sharp creases. Wayne took long, stiff-legged steps toward the car. He paused to run his hand over his slick black hair before opening the door.

"Morning," he said as he slid into the seat and eased the passenger door shut.

Lester nodded. "Morning."

Wayne nodded in return, then looked out the windshield. "Didn't really have nothing to wear."

Lester laid his hand on Wayne's shoulder and waited for his neighbor to look at him before saying anything. "You look fine, Wayne."

Wayne's Adam's apple rose and fell with a gulp; and then the man smiled before Lester pulled his hand away, put the car in gear, and drove away.

Khufia

The prisoner tried to blink open his swollen eyes, but his eyelids were heavy and ached. He managed to open them enough to see into the darkness of the room. The air was moist, and he had to fight the retching brought on by the smell of ammonia. Though it put great strain on his throbbing neck, he turned to look around. There was no window. No stream of light on the walls. There was nothing but darkness. The floor was still the flexible, wooden boards, which he felt as he adjusted himself to his knees.

Had they moved him?

He looked down at his wrists and saw streaks of dried blood smeared along his hands and arms. His wrists were still bound by the chains, which were still fastened to the walls. He blinked, managing to get one eye all the way open, and did a double-take from his wrists to the stakes near the walls. There was no light source, yet he could see them both with clarity. He began to scan the room, and it was suddenly filled with colors and light that had not been there a moment ago. He searched the room, confirming there was no light, as he realized that he was seeing everything through the darkness. He looked up to the windows and saw that they had been covered, but how he could see that was more of a mystery than why.

The prisoner snapped his head up at the sound of the door opening. The old man from before entered, carrying a bucket and a covered dish. The old man eased the door shut with his foot, careful not to spill the items he carried, and then hobbled over to the prisoner. He set the bucket down and then stood in front of him with a solemn expression. He pulled something from his pocket and held it in both hands. There was a clicking sound, and the little black object began to glow from one side. The old man set the object at his side after grunting his way to the ground.

Sitting on his knees, the old man slid a dish of food toward the prisoner. He then reached into the bucket with his bony arm and removed a cloth. The cloth dripped water, and the old man squeezed it in one hand to force the excess water out. He reached out and took hold of the prisoner's wrist with gentle hands and began to wipe the blood away. The prisoner stared in disbelief.

"What is your name?" he whispered. At this point, he was not sure what language he was speaking, and he had no idea what language the old man spoke, but he hoped they could understand one another.

The old man held a finger to his lips, then patted the air in front of him. The prisoner simply stared back.

"Do you know my name?"

The old man's forehead wrinkled up. He shook his head and held his finger to his lips again. When the prisoner shrugged, it made his chains rattle. The old man looked around frantically, then waved his hand in front of the prisoner's face. He pointed toward the door, then made motions with his arms as if he was carrying a weapon.

The prisoner nodded but could not help himself. The need to know what was happening to him was too much. He asked another question, but in a whisper this time. "Where am I?"

The old man ignored this question. He dipped the cloth in the bucket, plunging it several times before squeezing the water out again. He began to clean the prisoner's neck and face, and the prisoner fell silent once more. If not for the hopelessness of it all, he would have yelled in rage. After another minute, the old man dropped the cloth in the bucket with an unceremonious plop and then pointed toward the dish. He picked up the glowing object, manipulated it in his hand, and the light went out.

Darkness enveloped the room once more; but after a moment, the prisoner was able to see through it, though faintly. He watched in silence as the old man grunted through the motions of standing and retrieving the bucket. The old man stumbled his way to the door, obviously unable to see, which only brought more questions to the prisoner's mind. He reached down, removed the cloth covering the dish, and found a piece of bread. Strangely, there was no growling of his stomach, though he knew he should be famished. The prisoner wondered at that revelation.

Outside the shipping container prison, Ibrahim let his hand slowly slip away from the latch. He remembered the dish, a small plate made of clay, and closed his eyes. Momentarily paralyzed with indecision, he scolded himself. Sneaking past the sleeping guard had not been difficult. The arrogance of Yusef's men knew no bounds, but to leave something behind was evidence.

He opened his eyes and slipped into the shadow of the building. The moon was behind him, casting the familiar, silver glow he had navigated by in recent days. Tahiil slept with his back to a boulder less than ten feet away, the small man's head hanging so far down that it almost looked as if his neck had been broken. Ibrahim knew he had to go. The longer he waited, the greater the risk of Tahiil waking up and finding him there; but the dish would bring trouble.

He took a step out of the shadow and reached for the latch of the door, keeping his eyes fixed on Tahiil. Confident the man was still slumbering, Ibrahim grasped the latch and was about to pull the door open when Tahill stirred and sucked in a deep, snorting breath. The man's head popped up, and he searched all around as Ibrahim snatched his hand away from the latch and shuffled back, deep into the shadow and around the side of the building where he sent up a rushed, silent prayer.

He managed to hide himself well enough and still be able to see around the corner as Tahiil got to his feet and started spinning back and forth on his heels. Ibrahim wanted to laugh at the disoriented man, delighting in seeing one of the members of Al-Shabaab in such a weak state, but he was gripped with panic. He pressed himself into the side of the building and tried to keep his body from trembling against the metal. Tahiil finally settled down and walked over to the building. He glanced left and right as he approached, and Ibrahim ducked his head back around the corner. He heard scraping and bumping noises, then Tahiil mumbling to himself.

"Yusef will kill me if he finds out I left this door unlocked." There was another grunt and another scrape, and then Ibrahim heard a distinct clicking noise. "But he will not know, will he, Tahiil?" the man said to himself. There was a chuckle. "Nor will he find out that I was asleep on guard. Not like it matters. Who would be stupid enough to try and get in here?"

The sound of Tahiil's voice was quieter and projecting away from the building, so Ibrahim sneaked his head around to look. Tahiil was still mumbling to himself as he sat against the boulder again. It was only a few moments before the mumbling became indiscernible, and then the man's head drooped to his chest again. There were a couple of head bobs up and down, more mumbling, and then the man was breathing heavily and not moving.

Ibrahim waited a few more minutes before moving from his hiding spot. He took a wide path around Tahiil, slipping in between huts and sneaking through on the balls of his feet. This took a while and was exhausting for Ibrahim's aching muscles and fragile bones, but he got out of the village without incident. As he hastened his way down the path to Khufiana, his sister's words echoed in his mind. She had warned him to stay away from the prisoner, telling him he was falling into a trap. The prisoner's questions also ran through his mind, and he was soon deep in thought.

Why would the prisoner be asking what his name was?

Less than an hour later, Ibrahim had an answer to that question when he knocked on Nasteexo's door. It swung inward, revealing Nasteexo's puffy face and swollen eyes. Her chest heaved with her breaths. She started to motion him in when Ibrahim interrupted her.

"He has amnesia!"

Nasteexo had continued motioning him in, ignoring him, but then she froze. She raised an eyebrow. "What did you say?"

Ibrahim pushed his way past her, into the small house. "The prisoner has amnesia." He heard Nasteexo's reply but did not stop or look back.

"The demon?"

Ibrahim walked up to Yara's sleeping mat and stood over the girl. "He's not a demon, Nasteexo." He looked at her over his shoulder. She was standing in the middle of the room with her arms folded. "He's an angel."

Nasteexo shook her head. "Do you hear yourself, brother?" She unfolded her arms and held them at her sides. "An angel with amnesia."

He turned back to face Yara and nodded. "Yes, and I know how to cure him." He smiled as his granddaughter stirred and opened her eyes, looking up at him as if she was wide awake.

CHAPTER ELEVEN

Olympia

A MAN WEARING AN ORANGE protective vest waved to Lester as he pulled into the parking lot of the church and directed him to the far right. He waved with the tips of his fingers, keeping his palm on the steering wheel, and proceeded to the end where another man was pointing to a parking space. He parked, turned the car off, took a deep breath, and leaned back against the headrest.

"Place seems bigger'n when I drive past it," Wayne said.

Lester turned his head just enough to see his passenger out of the corner of his eye. Wayne was rubbing the tops of both of his thighs. Lester chuckled and turned back to look out the windshield. "Yeah, it's a pretty big place, but trust me; the people in there will treat you like it's a tiny, little church."

"That's good," Wayne said. There was a pause. "Everyone sure looks nice. Nice place, too. Flowers and all."

Lester lifted his head from the headrest and shifted in his seat to look at Wayne. "You're going to be just fine, Wayne. You'll see."

Wayne was wide-eyed but nodded and swallowed a lump of anxiety. "Okay."

They got out of the car, and Lester led Wayne across the parking lot. He was trying his best to hide the fact that he was just as nervous as his neighbor, but that, inevitably, fell apart when the first round of "Oh my goodness; is that Lester?" made its way across the park-ing lot, accompanied by vigorous waves. He waved back and assured them that "it sure was" as he picked up his pace and avoided Wayne's confused look.

He was accosted by handshakes and hugs on the inside. Warm greetings filled with "I've missed you" and "Just where have you been?" were drowned in back slaps that could have formed instant scar tissue. He smiled and nodded. He returned hugs, waited patiently for his hand to be returned at least a half a dozen times. Somehow, he pushed his way through the crowd like a hero returned from war and even man-aged to introduce Wayne to a few people. Try as he may, that did not distract anyone from asking of his whereabouts.

There were plenty of people he had seen frequently since he had last been in a church service because they had done business in his shop or saw him in a casual run-in at grocery stores and gas stations, but most of the faces were unfamiliar. He exchanged awkward grins with Wayne. It was proof that Draven was right: Lester had been blind to everyone in the world except himself and Dillon. He shook the hands of a particularly large man with a military-style haircut and pushed the thought of his fallen brother away.

Wayne turned and slid sideways between two crowds of people conversing and stood in front of Lester. "You ain't been here in a while, have you, bud?"

Lester laughed and looked at his feet. He put his hands on his hips and looked up to see Quinn standing beside Wayne with her arms folded. He had been forming the words, "No, not since—" but Quinn cut him off.

"Not since he called off our engagement."

As if on cue from a hidden stage director, several of the people around them turned, looked, and then quickly stepped away. Wayne looked back and forth between the two of them, but Lester barely noticed. He was fixed on Quinn's cold stare. She was leaning to one side with her foot forward. Lester thought he would be thrown out for playing the drums so loudly in the hallway from the way his heart was pounding.

"Should I leave you two alone?" Wayne asked. He paused in between every word.

Quinn was silent, but then she smiled. "No." She turned and extended her hand. "Sorry for being so blunt and for interrupting. Lester and I have some history, and I thought I'd give him a hard time. I'm Quinn, and you are?"

"Wayne," he said and shook her hand. "Wayne Burmeister. Real good to meet ya, ma'am."

"A pleasure, Wayne." She let go of his hand and turned to Lester. Her smile faded. "Come here," she said and opened her arms. Lester hesitated for just a second, but then he hugged her. It was real, but he hardly believed it. She smelled like lavender and felt warm. He felt her head turning so that her mouth was near his ear. "I'm sorry for the way I acted, Les." She pushed herself back and let her fingertips linger on his shoulders. "I'm so sorry about Dillon." She paused and tucked in her bottom lip. "You know how much I care about you both."

Lester nodded. "Don't apologize, Quinn. I know."

She sniffed and straightened her blue blouse. "Well, I had better quit standing around like I don't have a job to do. I need to go check and see if the preacher needs anything, but I'll let you boys get back to your conversation. It was nice meeting you, Wayne."

He waved as she hurried through the throng into the sanctuary. He gave Lester a pressed lip smile, and they exchanged nods. "You alright?"

Lester nodded again. "Yeah." He put his hands on his hips again and laughed. "Well, I'm busted. What do you say you and I get some lunch after the service? Maybe just be real honest with one another and see if we can't figure some of this out?"

"You bet, bud."

Lester patted him on the shoulder and led him in to the sanctuary for the service.

The sanctuary was larger than Lester remembered, but it felt strangely small and comfortable. He kept his eye on Wayne throughout the continued exchange of pleasantries, handshakes, and awkward moments of not knowing someone's name. They found a seat near the back by the large, elevated sound booth and settled in for the service. They did not talk after that, and it was only a few minutes before the choir walked out on the enormous platform, dressed similarly in blue shirts and black slacks or skirts.

Lester wasn't sure if he had forgotten how powerful the song service was or if the singing had immensely improved since his last time there. The choir sang in perfect harmony under the direction of a small but animated director, and then the congregation rose to sing with them. The words to the song were displayed on the screen, which Lester thought was a clever way to avoid spending a lot of money on song books. He tried not to laugh as he thought about hiding gum between the pages of an old hymnal when he was five.

After the congregational singing, they all sat down and listened to the choir sing two more songs about praying through trials. Lester was moved to tears more than once and caught a glimpse of Wayne trying, discreetly, to wipe his eyes. He avoided eye contact with Wayne after that. It did not take long for him to become so immersed in the singing that he nearly forgot that anyone else was there.

After a brief intermission for announcements and a presentation of a gift packet to all visitors, the singing resumed. Wayne sat stoically through it all and did not raise his hand when the man on the platform asked for visitors to be recognized. The ushers clearly saw that he was not a regular, but they were respectful not to press the issue and continued past him with tightlipped smiles. There was one more special after that, sung by a tall woman and her husband, while the ushers again moved from the front to the back of the auditorium, politely extending offering plates to the people in the cushioned pews. When the special was finished, Pastor Greene walked out on the platform, and the auditorium lights were dimmed slightly so that the brightest area in the massive room was the stage.

Pastor Greene took his time placing his Bible on the glass podium, opening it with care, and then stepping back. He folded his hands at his waist in front of his dark suit jacket and surveyed the audience. His head moved from left to right, and his expression was calm but neutral. After nearly a minute, he spoke, his tone somber, yet filled with warmth and kindness. Though Lester knew the pastor was wearing a headset microphone, it was invisible from where he sat, so it appeared as if the man's voice naturally carried throughout the auditorium.

"Good morning," Greene said. There was a murmured response to the greeting from the audience, and then he continued. "Today, I'd like to speak to you on a slightly different subject than you might be used to for a Sunday morning." He began to pace across the platform.

"This week, I've had several visits from numerous and very diverse individuals, and there seems to be a common theme. Simply put, what do I do in the face of trials?

"Every time I counsel with these individuals, I'm reminded of Job. Job's story is one of the oldest, most timeless tales in the Bible. Chronologically taking place very early in the timetable of the Bible, it actually occurs very close to the middle of the Scriptures." He paused and smiled. "How fitting? In the middle of God's Word, between the beauty of His creation, the fall of man, and the final restoration, is a book about a man who must endure a trial.

"And not just any trial. No. This man endured suffering none of us could imagine." Greene unfolded his hands and began to move about the platform with more enthusiasm. He would approach the front of the stage, lean toward the people, and then stand up straight, pause, and then step back before walking back and forth again. "This was the richest and wisest man in the East, a pillar of the community, and greatly respected. He owned fields and flocks of animals. Many were employed by this man. All of it was gone in a single day. Ten children, his flocks, all of his crops, gone. All that was left for Job was his bitter wife and sorrow. As if that wasn't enough, just a little time passed before Satan riddled his body with sores.

"The man who had once been greatly regarded was now a nobody with nothing to show for his life but scars and a wife who came to him in the midst of all of that and told him to curse God and die. Who could endure such a trial? But, of course, that wasn't it. Next, Job had to suffer through the agony of his so-called friends coming to him and accusing him of his own sin being the root of the evil that had befallen him. Throughout this book, Job never forsakes the God he trusts and serves. That doesn't mean he didn't feel like calling it quits. It doesn't mean he didn't feel the pain of every bit of his trial. But Job did understand something. He knew he was being tried, and he understood something that I want you to understand when you're in the midst of a trial. Can I read you a verse?"

Greene didn't wait for an answer, though many people in the audience responded with *yes* and *amen*. He walked over to the podium, leaned over his Bible, and read, "Job twenty-three ten says, 'But he knoweth the way that I take: when he hath tried me, I shall come forth as gold.'" The words scrolled across and then froze on the screens behind him. He stepped back and looked up. "Job knew the trial was meant to make him better, not bitter. Can I share something with you? There was a battle going on that Job and his miserable excuses for friends couldn't see. There was somewhat of a contest between God and Satan, and God was showing the devil his true power. See, Job's trial wasn't about him; it was about the power of God. But there's another lesson we can learn. The trial was also to demonstrate that though the devil has great power, it's nothing compared to the power of our God.

"Know and understand this, brethren: when you make a decision to follow the Lord, when you become His child, opposition will come. Just like Job is in between the new creation and the redeeming of that creation, your trial will come before your final redemption. If you have been redeemed by God through His Son, Jesus Christ, you are 'a new creature: old things are passed away; behold, all things are become new.' But you still live in that body of sin in a world filled with sin. There's a reckoning coming to this world, and then all things will be forever changed. This world will be made new, and you and I will receive a new body to live for eternity with our Redeemer."

Greene paused to let the shouts of joy and amens settle down. "But in between those things, we'll face trials. Not one, not two or a dozen, but many. Stay strong, brethren. Follow the Lord, and stay the course. You will come forth shining like gold. You're on display for all the world to see, but you need to understand something." Greene was moving about the stage with passion then, and he stopped when he said no and raised his finger. "He puts His treasure on display; but before He does that, He shines them up. Brothers and sisters, if I can give you one piece of comfort in the midst of your trial, it's this: the tougher it seems, the greater the polishing! If the pressure is great, then great is the treasure.

"Your job is to continue steadfast in His Word and prayer. Don't think you're going to do this on your own. Go to Him in prayer. Go to your brothers and sisters in Christ, and ask them to pray for you and with you. Stay in the Scriptures. Stay in the service of the Lord. Don't listen to the voices that accuse you or try to lead you away from God. Those men wore Job down, but he didn't give in to their false accusations. Job stayed the course. Yes, he got depressed; and yes, he wanted to quit, but he endured. Trust me, I've read the rest of the story, and God showed up right on time. He was also listening all the while.

"He knows right where you are and what you're going through. If he heard Job, He can hear you. You cannot face your trial alone. Please be aware that the same spiritual warfare taking place in Job's day is still going on today. I'm not saying God and Satan are having a contest with you; but I am saying that there is spiritual wickedness in high places, and the weapons of our warfare are not carnal. This is not a flesh and blood fight, my friends.

"Don't forget Daniel. He prayed for three weeks, and then the angel appeared to him. When he did, he said he'd been hindered by one of the princes. Folks, he wasn't talking about some guy waiting for daddy to die so he could take the throne. Prince, in that context, meant a supernatural being, and there was a war being fought in the spiritual realm. Now, I don't understand how all of that works, but I know it's real. So, keep going, and keep praying. It may get worse before it gets better; but if you took all of the pain and hurt of this life and put it together, it's still just the blink of an eye compared to eternity."

Greene continued, but Lester could hardly focus on anything after hearing about the spiritual warfare. He began to think about Draven appearing to him and being in possession of supernatural powers. He thought of the man at the police station and the vanishing barista at the coffee shop. He wondered how it all tied together, or if it even did.

It wasn't until the pastor had finished his message and Wayne tapped Lester when everyone was standing up that Lester came out of his inner meditation on those thoughts. The rest of the service was a blur, and they left in silence.

Khufia

The prisoner opened his eyes but saw only thick, impenetrable darkness. He lifted his left cheek from the plywood and tried to exhale the scent of ammonia and rust. His shoulders popped as he rotated them, and the rattling of his chains reminded him that he had not simply fallen asleep. He blinked rapidly until his vision cleared. Faint at first, details of the room began to come into focus. There were cracks in the walls where they connected to the warped floor. It was not much light, but the prisoner's eyes adjusted to it as if he was a creature of the night.

He focused on his body, inspecting his wounds. He was relatively clean, considering his circumstances. The only blood on his arms and torso was dried. The old man had apparently washed away most of it, and the prisoner noticed that none of the wounds were open. This gave him pause, so he inspected further. Indeed, the wounds were closed, and many of them were gone. There were not even scars where, hours before, there had been gashes in his flesh.

He began to doubt this, along with his ability to see his flesh at all in the isolated room. Fearful it was another dream, he touched his arms and chest, rubbed his face, and then bit his finger. All of the sensations felt real, and he wondered how long he had been unconscious. No matter how long, he thought, there should still be scars.

In front of him, the door opened, and four men entered. Two of them were carrying torches. The intrusion of such powerful light made the room seem to be lit by the sun to the prisoner's mysteriously enhanced sight. These were the same men that had been attacking him all along, but they had lowered their scarves to reveal dark skin and long, scraggly beards. The prisoner wondered how closely related they were because they all looked similar. They spoke to one another in a language he had not heard them use before as they entered.

"Una uhakika hakuna mtu aliyekuwa hapa?" the tallest of the men said.

Swahili, the prisoner thought. *They are speaking Swahili.* He hid his surprise by keeping his head down, looking up at them with his eyes rolled up as high as he could get them. His mind quickly translated the words to, "Are you sure no one has been here?" It happened so quickly, and he understood it so precisely that the next words sounded like they were being spoken in his own language.

"No one," the shorter of the four said. "We threatened the villagers with death, and the door has been locked."

The tall man nodded and stroked his beard. "Locked the whole time?"

The shortest of the group looked away momentarily, then nodded.

The prisoner listened to the exchange in awe, fighting the urge to gasp and say something. His mind raced with possibilities as he continued to translate their words effortlessly.

"Someone is helping the sorcerer." The tall one pointed at the prisoner. "Look at his skin."

"Filthy, like his soul," another of the four said. This one was average height to the rest but had a powerful presence that was unmistakable.

"No, you idiot," the tall man said. "He has been cleaned. The wounds have been healed." He reached down, just in front of the prisoner, and picked up the dish left by the old man. "And someone has brought him food."

The shorter man stepped forward. "It does not matter, Yusef. If someone found him, we will find the traitor by monitoring this building more closely."

The tall man, apparently Yusef, growled. "Do not say my name, Tahiil. You fool."

The short man shook his head. "And now the prisoner knows both our names."

Yusef waved his hand and yelled. He turned to the prisoner and squatted down. In the language they had spoken the day before, he said, "Min aetak hdha ya sahira?"

Arabic, the prisoner thought. *Who gave this to you, sorcerer?* The prisoner did not answer the question. His mind was consumed with the question of how many languages he could understand and how he was able to suddenly translate them so naturally. A slap across his face interrupted that thought.

"Tell me. Now!" Yusef spoke in Arabic, but the prisoner heard it plainly with no need for a delay in translation. "Who cleaned your wounds, and how did they heal so quickly?"

The prisoner remained silent. He was wondering the same thing. He stared into Yusef's eyes and had a fleeting thought that, perhaps, he really was a sorcerer. That might explain the rapid healing and enhanced eyesight, but he did not recall casting any spells. That line of logic seemed irrelevant to him, considering he also did not know his name, where he was, or how he had gotten there.

Yusef stood and motioned to the other men. "If you will not answer, we will take the answers from your beaten flesh."

The other three were over the prisoner in the next moment, alternating punches to his head and body. He thought he would fall over, like he had all the other times; but the punches did not seem as powerful, and he remained in place. He felt their sting, heard and felt his skin breaking. There was a crack in his side that made him gasp and then clench his teeth in pain, but even that did not feel as severe as the previous assaults. Yusef talked the entire time the other three beat him.

"You will tell us who is helping you, sorcerer." The prisoner could see Yusef calmly picking at his nails. After each punch to the head or face knocked his head to the side, he would steal a look back and see the tall man scraping dirt from beneath them or scratching at them. "You will tell us how you got your power from the devil."

The beating continued, but the prisoner heard the grunting and heavy breathing of the men and was suddenly aware that they were tiring. He was not. He wanted the beating to stop, but he also knew that they would never get anything out of him. The prisoner was stronger than them. But how, he did not know. Yusef called to them, and the men ceased from their work and stepped back. Their shoulders rose and fell quickly. Their mouths were open, and the prisoner listened with a strange sense of amusement to their panting.

Yusef squatted down again and glared into the prisoner's eyes. "If you will not tell us, perhaps we will start taking the answers from the flesh of the villagers." He smiled without showing his teeth and stood. He stared down at the prisoner for many seconds and then motioned for the men to follow him out of the room.

The prisoner watched them go. When the door was shut and the light of the torches left him in darkness again, he rubbed his cheek. His eyes adjusted, and he saw blood on his fingertips when he pulled them away. The beating had not been without pain. The prisoner closed his eyes and hoped the old man was safe.

He also hoped Yara was hidden far away.

CHAPTER TWELVE

City of Hudson, near the town of Olympia

LESTER WAS WATCHING PEDESTRIANS PASS by on the sidewalk through the large window of the restaurant when the waiter's question pulled him from his thoughts. He turned his head, keeping his elbow propped on the back of the cushioned bench, and looked up at the teenager. He wore a white shirt and black tie, and he held a coffee carafe.

"Sorry. What?" Lester asked.

The waiter lifted the carafe and smiled. "Freshen that up for you, sir?"

Lester looked from the pot to his half-empty cup on the eggshell-colored table and exclaimed, "Oh!" He pulled his arm from the back of the bench and straightened up in his seat. "Yeah. Keep it coming." He cleared his throat. "Thanks."

The waiter topped off Lester's cup. "No problem, sir. Your food will be up in just a minute, guys."

Wayne's eyebrows were furrowed together, and he was looking at Lester intently. Lester nodded and looked down at the freshened cup as he grabbed it from the side. "Thank you."

Wayne laughed. Lester took a sip of coffee and regarded his neighbor from over the cup.

He set the mug down and shrugged. "What?"

Wayne shook his head. "Nothing. Anything interesting out there, bud? 'Cause you been lookin' out that winda like you's a waitin' on sumthin'."

Lester chuckled and shook his head. "Nah, I just love coming in to Hudson. This place is beautiful, man. Downtown market with plenty of police to keep crime down. Nice brick and cobblestone streets in the shopping area. The high-rise, spider-web bridges. I love it." He looked out the window as he spoke and saw a couple holding hands, carrying department store bags.

"Bit big and busy for me," Wayne said.

Lester turned back. "Yeah?" Wayne nodded. "You know, I've been meaning to ask you something, Wayne. You don't really have a Midwest accent. You from down South?"

Wayne shook his head. "Northwest, matter fact."

"No way."

Wayne laughed. "Yeah, I am, too. Most people think we talk proper and all, and most folks up 'ere do; but my kin come from the South, and I grew up in the mountains. Real high up. Ain't never been 'round cities 'til I moved out this way for work."

"Is that when you met your wife?" Lester eyed Wayne over the rim of his mug and took another sip of coffee.

Wayne nodded. "Yeah, they showed me how to drive one of them forklifts out at the tire plant. Suse was the clerk who handled all the certification stuff. Paperwork was her deal."

Lester scratched at his cheek. "You mentioned some paperwork when you were at my house."

Wayne sat up straight and let out a deep breath. "Yessir."

"How's all that going?"

Wayne gulped some coffee down and set his mug down with a soft thud. "Well, she done filed for divorce already. Can't say I blame her. I was clean and arrow straight 'til about three years ago.

Got to drinkin' too much when the bills was pilin' up. Then that wasn't enough. I couldn't sleep, so the doc put me on them real heavy pills. Messed me up. Guess I got one of them addictive-type personalities." He looked down and shook his head. "After Suse left, I was takin' whatever I could get. Lied to the doctor and everything. Lost my job not long after I run the forklift into a brand new pallet of winter tires."

Lester nodded and circled his finger around the lip of his mug. "That's rough, man. But I think you should keep trying. Get cleaned up, you know? Let Susan see that you've changed."

Wayne laughed. "Shoot, man. Ain't been but a day."

"One day *clean*," Lester said. He looked up and shrugged. "I don't know. Maybe just hold off on signing the papers. You never know."

Wayne shrugged as well. "Don't know it'd make much difference."

"You should call her."

Wayne looked out the window, and then his mouth spread into a wide smile. He looked back at Lester and pointed. "Maybe you should do some callin', too."

Lester sat back and touched his chest with his index finger. "Me?"

Wayne nodded. "Certain woman that seemed to give ya just a bit more'n a 'been a while' hug this mornin'."

Lester rolled his eyes.

"Here you go, guys."

They both looked up to see the waiter beside the table with two large plates of food. He set them down and then stood back. "Can I get you anything else?"

Lester looked at his plate of eggs, sausage, and hash browns, and shook his head. He glanced over at Wayne's burger and fries and tilted his chin toward the man. Wayne shook his head, as well. "Nope. Think we're good," Lester said.

"Alright, sounds good," the waiter said. "Just call me over if you think of anything."

"Thanks, bud," Wayne said as the waiter strolled away. Wayne reached for a French fry, and then paused with his hand hovering above his plate. "Say, do you . . . uh . . . " He stopped and looked around.

Lester looked at Wayne's perched hand for a while before he understood the man's unspoken question. "Oh!" he said. "Yeah, um. You mind?"

Wayne retracted his hand and lowered it to his lap. "Go 'head, bud."

Lester folded his hands on the table and cleared his throat. "Uh, Lord. We, uh, we thank You for letting us meet and get to know each other. Thank You for the food, and please let it nourish our bodies. Amen."

Wayne grunted something similar to an amen; and when Lester looked up, the man was shoving the fry in his mouth. He chewed for a few seconds and then started talking. "You sure you're a Christian?"

Lester was just about to grab his fork to get a bite of the steaming hash browns but let his hand rest back in his lap. He sat back and looked at Wayne for a few seconds, then shook his head and shrugged. Opened his mouth. Closed it. Finally, he reached for the fork and picked at the eggs, but he kept his back pressed into the bench.

"Yeah, I'm sure." He sighed. "Just been away for too long."

Wayne swallowed and nodded. "I figured as much, but how's that work?"

"What do you mean?"

Wayne shrugged. "You gotta, like, get baptized again, or something?"

Lester smiled. "No. It doesn't really work that way. See, I grew up in church. My parents were really dedicated, so I was there whenever they were, and that was just about every day. Worship services, choir practices, Bible studies, church outreach; you name it."

"What happened?" Wayne took a huge bite from his burger then, and Lester was secretly pleased to see the man's appetite strong.

"Well," Lester said, shaking his head. "Like I said, I grew up in church, but it was just a place we went until I was about fifteen. That's when I got saved. After that, I was all in. I was in the youth group, preached, choir. Everything. When I was old enough, I got involved with outreach. The church had this thing called The Midnight Cry that I would go to. Basically, a group of people would go to troubled areas in Olympia, and sometimes Hudson. We would just talk to people about the Lord.

"I did that for a long time, but I was also learning about retail. I made my money in sales, but it was just how I supported myself. All I cared about was church. I never knew anything about cars; but when a guy in our church offered me his business before he passed away, I took it."

Wayne held his drink and pointed at Lester with it. "You own a body shop, and you don't know anything about cars?"

"Nothing." Lester laughed. "That's why I eventually hired a general manager. His name is Dave. That guy knows everything about cars, and he's really good with people. Me? I'm just a business person. I spend my time looking at the numbers, and that's what got me in trouble.

"Quinn and I had been dating for a while; but when I started getting more involved with work, she started getting more involved with church events. I stopped going to The Midnight Cry, stopped singing in the choir, and just focused on business. It took a long time for that place to get up and running, especially with me in night school for my business degree. I just never had time for church. Quinn and I were supposed to get married somewhere in there, but I was too career-focused."

"So, she broke up with you?"

Lester took a small bite of eggs, found that they had turned cold, and shook his head. "No," he said after swallowing. "I left her. Broke off the engagement. I didn't even really tell her why. I know I hurt her pretty badly, but I was too caught up in my own world. Honestly, man, I stopped thinking about her. Stopped thinking about church and everything else a long time ago. Until the other night, the only person I thought about, except myself, was Dillon." He scooped up a bigger bite of eggs and looked at his plate while he ate.

"When time froze."

Lester stopped chewing and looked up. Wayne was staring at him with glassy eyes and clenched jaws.

"How did you—"

"Shut up, Lester." Wayne's voice was low, unnaturally low. His eyes were onyx black and flashed with electricity. "Enjoy your time while it lasts, human. It will not be long."

Lester sprang from the table, sending his fork clattering to the floor and scattering eggs. He stood, panting, with his eyes and mouth wide open. The next second vanished. Simply did not happen. Wayne was standing in front of him, holding and shaking him by the shoulders.

"Hey, you alright, bud?"

Lester slapped his hands away and backed up. "Get away from me!"

Wayne held his hands up with the palms facing Lester. "Hey, hey. Just calm down, Les."

Lester felt his body trembling and heard his breath coming out in tremors. "Wayne?"

Wayne nodded. "Yeah, bud. It's me. What just happened?"

"You don't know?"

Wayne shook his head. "Man, no. I just lost the last minute of my life. One minute I was listenin' to you talkin' 'bout leaving yer gal; next minute, I was standin' in front of you, and you was panickin'."

"Is everything okay, sir?"

Lester turned and saw the waiter. He was looking at Lester with his head cocked to the side, concerned.

Lester nodded. "Yeah. Sorry, I just had a bit of a scare. I got bad news about family recently, and it's just—"

The waiter held up a hand. "I get it. Been there."

Lester nodded and turned back to face Wayne. "I've got something to tell you."

Quinn flipped a slice of tomato over a bed of lettuce with her fork. The clinking of silverware against ceramic and a cacophony of some hushed, some loud conversations surrounded her. She pushed the tomato back to where it was and stabbed at it. The fork missed, so she settled for picking at the lettuce. She was vaguely aware that Pastor Greene and his wife, Laina, were watching her from the other side of the booth.

As she slid her fork across thinly sliced carrots, her mind wandered to a collage of memories. A game night in youth group, years ago. A movie. Dinner. Picking out a wedding dress, the same dress still hanging in her closet. She successfully skewered the tomato this time around, and felt a small twinge of pleasure at the metal stabbing through the flesh and down against the plate. She let her shoulders slump, remembering the way Lester had felt in her arms less than two hours before. The scent of his cologne.

"Wouldn't happen to be thinking about a certain young man, would you, Quinn?"

Quinn glanced up and across the table. Nathaniel and Laina both had their arms folded on the table and were leaning toward her, smiling. She raised the tomato to her mouth, paused, then set it down, let the fork fall on the plate, and leaned back against the cushion of the booth.

She sighed and looked to her right. A mother and father were teaming up to clean spaghetti off their daughter's face and shirt while the girl giggled. Quinn smiled and shook her head.

"It's just so strange," she said as she looked back to the pastor and his wife. They nodded. "I mean, I'm in a really good place in my life. You know? I love what I do at the church. I'm close to the Lord and feel spiritually stronger than I ever have."

"That may be a dangerous mindset to have when it comes to spirituality," Greene said. He sat up straight and unfolded his arms. An empty plate with crumbs and a paper napkin on it was in front of him.

"I don't mean it pridefully," Quinn said. "Just that I'm happy. I thought I was over this. That I was past it."

"And now you're second guessing that?" Laina asked.

Quinn frowned. "Yeah. Unfortunately."

"Sweetie, can I tell you a story?" Laina pushed her mostly finished salad away and brushed her hands together.

Quinn shrugged. "Of course."

Laina smiled. "You might have trouble believing this, but this old guy sitting next to me wasn't always the pastor of a church." Greene smiled and pushed his shoulder into hers. Quinn felt her eyebrows go up. "No, it's true. My husband, your pastor, walked away from the Lord for about five years."

"Really?"

Greene lowered his eyes, and frowned. "Sure did."

"Yes, he did," Laina said. "Did more than just walk away, too, but I don't want to bring up the past. I've forgiven him and, more importantly, so has the Lord. The point is that Nathaniel did some things Christians shouldn't do, and I wasn't sure our marriage was going to make it."

"That's hard to believe," Quinn said as she sat up straight.

Laina shrugged. "Maybe, but it's true."

"Five years?" Quinn asked. "What did you do?"

Laina turned just enough to look at Greene and kept her gaze on him while she replied. "Baby, I held on to my Jesus like I was being thrown from a moving vehicle; and the more I held on to Him, the more He held on to me. I cried so much and so often, I thought my insides were all dried out. I prayed every day, and I had people all over the country praying for this man." She paused and wiped tears from the corner of her eye.

"And it worked?"

Laina faced Quinn. "Prayer always works, honey. Sometimes we don't like the wait, and sometimes we don't like the answers; but God is always listening to our prayers. See, what I knew was there was a powerful force trying to pull Nathaniel into the world, a spiritual force that didn't want him serving God. Didn't want him preaching. So, I prayed for God to show Himself more powerful than that force. After trying it on my own and hiding it for years, I finally went to the ladies of my church and asked them to pray for us. Soon that prayer request got out to women everywhere, and we prayed this man back to Jesus."

Quinn smiled and shook her head. "That's incredible."

"That's God," Greene said.

Quinn picked up her fork and touched the tip of it to another slice of tomato. "I don't know if it will be that simple with Lester."

She saw Laina's hand on the table, just in front of her, and looked up. The pastor's wife was leaning toward her. "Have you forgiven him for what he did to you?"

Quinn nodded. "I have, but it still hurts."

Laina pulled her hand back. "Of course, it does, Quinn. And it will, but that wound will heal all the way up, eventually."

"Will it?"

"Sure, but don't think it won't leave a scar. There's a big difference between healed and never hurt."

"Quinn," Greene said, "we are not suggesting that you try and re-kindle a relationship with Lester just because he has come back to church. Neither of you should even be thinking about that right now. You just need to focus on truly forgiving him so that you can be his friend and pray for him. That is what he needs right now."

Quinn took a deep breath and then exhaled with a groan. "You're right. I just worry that him coming back won't last. I mean, he lost his brother, and they were really close; so, it's natural to run to the church when you're dealing with loss. But that loss, plus the loss of his business, might push him even farther away."

Greene and Laina nodded. "It's possible," Greene said.

"Which is why you really need to pray for him," Laina said.

Quinn looked away and fought back the swelling tears. "Tell that to my heart."

Khufia

Morane stood in the shadow of Draven's prison building, looking out over the village. His smile felt good as he thought about Lester's panic at the restaurant. How delightful it had been to slip in and out of the wretched man's life over the past few days to haunt him. To toy with him. Terrify him.

The demon breathed in, inhaling the victory. A part of him wanted to go inside and talk to Draven, but he knew that would only trigger the watcher's memory and ruin everything. It was foolish to think that Draven would not return to full strength soon, but Morane desperately wanted to enjoy the moment while it lasted. Allowing better judgment to prevail, he crept around the building and walked through the small village.

Of course, he thought, he could just grab Draven and chain him in Hades. Leave before the watcher recovered his faculties. But that would be only surface-level misery for his enemy. No, their battle had raged for centuries, and Draven had gained the upper hand far too often. It was Morane's turn. The time of the true champion to reign. He would torture Draven, and he knew just the way to do that.

He approached a hut made of mud and a thatched roof. He did not bother to step softly, for none could hear or see him in the spirit realm. He slipped through the wall and entered the single room hut where the boisterous array of voices he had heard outside became a somewhat comprehensible argument between the fool, Yusef, and his imbecilic crew. Convincing Yusef to avoid attempts at burning Draven—or something equally extreme—to be rid of him had been so simple. The man was influenced easily. Morane slipped into a corner and listened to the men.

"They are infidels and must be punished," the fool named Tahiil said. Morane especially despised this tiny creature. The runt of the litter of shiftless dogs, he was prone to speaking without thinking.

"Of course, they will be punished, Tahiil, but not until we give them a chance to renounce their Jesus." This was spoken by the second tallest of the band, Yasir. Morane was oddly fond of this one. He was rational yet cruel, a pragmatist with a streak of hatred that made him slightly unpredictable.

Tahiil waved his hands. "Never. They would rather die. They all would."

"Perhaps their beliefs are that sincere to them."

The others fell silent and turned to the newest participant in the conversation. Yusef's brother, Diric, was the least committed of them all. In fact, the others would have killed him months ago if not for Yusef's warnings.

Yusef, who had been leaning against the wall opposite of Morane behind his brother, stood up and unfolded his arms. "You doubt Allah, Diric?"

Diric turned quickly and looked at Yusef. "No, brother. I do not wish to follow these zealous fools. I say what I do to point out the obvious."

Yusef held his hand with the palm up. "Which is?"

"Which is that no one willingly dies for something they do not believe in." Diric turned back to the group and shrugged. "Perhaps fear is useless when dealing with such strong belief."

"You make a good point," Yasir said. "But the point is that this new group of Christians cannot be allowed to gather. They will proselytize the village."

"But how do we even know there are any of them left?" This came from Tahiil. Morane fixed his onyx eyes on the man. "We sent an entire congregation of them to their graves."

Yusef shook his head. "And yet someone is helping the sorcerer."

Morane shook his head. He had more important things to do than listen to these men squabble over the best way to terrorize the village. He had been paying close attention to Draven, and he knew the time of the watcher's amnesia was running out. He circled the room and stood next to Diric. He was the easiest. The weakest.

Morane leaned down and put his mouth next to the man's ear. "The real threat is the sorcerer."

Diric stiffened and looked straight ahead. "Wait!" He held up both hands, and the others stopped talking. They all faced him. "We can deal with the infidels easily enough, but the sorcerer makes us look weak."

They were all silent.

Yusef stepped away from the wall and walked into the circle of men. "I think Diric has been reading books, or perhaps Allah decided to give him a brain for temporary use because that is the first intelligible thing he has said today."

Diric opened his mouth but quickly shut it. Morane chuckled as the man balled his fists.

"The sorcerer is in chains," Tahiil said. "I say leave him and let him starve. He will die eventually." Morane moved closer to the smallest of the group and saw a bead of sweat forming on his forehead. The demon raised an eyebrow at this.

"You are a fool," Yusef said. "He has been beaten and stoned. We have given him no food or water, and yet he heals and grows stronger. He understands our language, even though he did not when we captured him. The man will not die because he is possessed by some demon."

Morane spun around and walked toward Yusef. The irony nearly made him fall over with laughter.

Yasir chimed in. "It is true. The man should not be alive after all we have done to him."

"Why don't we just shoot him and keep shooting until he is dead?" Diric asked.

Yusef shook his head. "Please, Allah, restore the brain to this man that you have taken away in the last ten seconds." He pinched his nose between his thumb and forefinger. "We have tried to kill the man, Diric. We cannot do it."

"Then what can we do?" Tahiil held up both hands.

Morane sneaked behind Diric and got next to his ear. "Where did he get the plate?" he whispered.

Diric stiffened again. "Wait a minute. Where did the sorcerer get the plate that we found?"

"From someone helping him, Diric," Yusef said, irritated. He turned and glared at his brother. "We questioned the prisoner. Were you paying attention while you were beating him? He told us nothing. I only hope the men I called in from Khufiana will do a better job of guarding the prisoner than all of you have."

Yasir snorted. "No one has been near the prisoner on my watch."

Tahiil took a step forward. "What are you implying, Yasir?"

Yasir grinned, revealing his white teeth. "I was not implying anything, Tahiil." His face became stern. "Perhaps you have something to say? We did find the plate on your watch."

Tahiil was about to rush forward, but Yusef held up a hand and shouted, "Enough!" He glared at both of them, looking back and forth, daring them to move. "The prisoner has been helped on more than one watch. All of us have failed. We are not here to lay blame, my friends." He smiled. "But I promise that if there is another failure, someone will pay."

The room fell silent for several moments. Morane was slightly upset that the argument had not escalated, but he was also impressed by Yusef. Perhaps the man had more intelligence than he thought. He leaned back toward Diric, hoping to regain the momentum he had established.

"Think," Morane whispered. "There must be some way to figure out who is helping him."

"We could question the people," Diric said.

Tahiil took a step forward, exclaiming, "That would be a waste of time."

Morane stepped back to the corner so that he could see all of the men at once, tiring of turning back and forth to keep track of whom was speaking.

Yusef shot Tahiil a curious glance before turning to Diric. "We have interrogated the people. They will protect one another with their lives."

"Fools," Yasir said.

"Yes, but loyal fools," Yusef said.

Morane walked over and whispered into Yusef's ear. "But what of Ibrahim?"

Yusef stiffened, just as his brother had. "Have any of the villagers been missing?"

They all paused for a moment and then one by one shook their heads.

"No," Tahiil said, "they all come when we demand."

Yusef shook his head. "Ibrahim was not there when the village stoned the sorcerer." He slowly turned and faced them all individually. "Was he?"

They exchanged curious looks, looking back and forth between each other. Almost simultaneously, they all said, "No."

"He has been acting strangely. Has anyone seen him?" Yusef looked directly at his brother.

Diric looked up and to his left for a moment and then back to Yusef. He started to shake his head, but then he opened his eyes widely. "Wait. I remember. He has requested to remain in his home while he mourns the loss of his granddaughter."

"Yara?" Yusef furrowed his brow. "She was with her parents when we burned the church?"

Diric nodded. "Yes, but she disappeared."

Yasir waved his hands. "She was with them. She died as the rest of those infidels died. If Ibrahim wants to mourn traitors to Allah, then he is a traitor to Allah!"

Diric shook his head. "No. Ibrahim is loyal to Allah, and to the prophet. His granddaughter was with her parents because she had no choice. How can we be upset with the man for mourning?"

"Because he is the one helping the sorcerer," Yusef said.

Diric held up his hands. "How can you know that, brother?"

"Maybe I do; maybe I do not know that." Yusef smiled. "Perhaps it is time to pay the dear, old man a visit." He turned to look each of them in the eye, and they all, eventually, returned his nod.

Morane smiled and backed away, vanishing through the wall behind him.

"That should keep you busy for a while. Now, it's time to pay your good friend, Lester, a visit."

Ibrahim rubbed his temple for what seemed like the hundredth time in the last hour. Nasteexo's voice from the other side of the room was like a knife cutting through a block of ice, and he buried his head in his hands. He felt soft but strong hands yanking on his wrists and looked up. Nasteexo pulled on his arms again, jerking them away from his face with enough force to surprise him.

"Be careful, Nasteexo." He held his wrists as she stepped back. "I am an old man with brittle bones."

Nasteexo stood over him and sighed. "I am sorry, brother, but you are acting like a madman."

He reached his hands up to her, and she helped him to his feet. "I want only to do what is right."

She snorted. "You want to prove you are not a coward."

He shook his head. "No. I am a coward. There is no point in trying to prove otherwise. This is about helping someone who needs our help."

"Yours." Nasteexo pointed at him. "Needs *your* help, not your granddaughter's."

Ibrahim turned his head and looked at Yara. She sat in the corner with her legs crossed, playing with a doll he had carved for her. He smiled, enjoying her brief moment of being a child again. She still had not spoken, and she had taken her meals only because she was told to do so. Watching her, he wondered if Nasteexo was right. He faced his sister again.

"I do not want her to be harmed."

"Then leave her here." Nasteexo folded her arms. "And you stay as well. Leave Khufia to Yusef."

He shook his head. "They will not stop until everyone is dead, sister. Helping the angel may be our chance to save the village."

She laughed. "An old man and a little girl are going to help an angel? Can you not hear yourself?"

"They have tried to kill him twice. He lives. He grows stronger, despite what they have done to him."

"Then let him heal, and maybe he will break free on his own."

Ibrahim tapped his forehead. "He does not remember who he is."

Nasteexo unfolded her arms. "Oh, yes. Your 'great angel with amnesia theory.'"

"Enough," Ibrahim said. "I will help him. Whoever he is, he does not deserve to be a prisoner, and he saved my granddaughter."

He walked over to Yara and called her name. She paused her private game and looked up at him. He looked into her big, dark brown eyes, and could not stop himself from smiling.

"Yara." He paused, choosing his words. "The man who saved you, the one from your dream? Do you want to help him?"

Yara looked down and touched her index finger to the head of her doll. Ibrahim looked closer and then nearly collapsed. He had carved the doll nearly a year before that day, and he had tried his best to make it look realistic; but his skill with carving was limited. It was made of dark wood, and he had chipped it several times. After trying but failing to make it look the way he wanted, he had simply handed it to her. In that moment, however, he saw the shape in a new light.

It had gashes across it. The wood was dark brown from Yara's dirty hands, and it looked like a man with thick dreadlocks. He knelt down and took the doll in his hands. As he held it, Yara kept one hand on it, and an image of a very strong man with hair flowing like water and skin that blended into his surroundings flashed through his mind. Ibrahim felt himself breathing hard, and he looked away from the doll to Yara's sad face.

"We will free him," he said. "But we must help him remember who he is. Do you want to help me do that?"

Yara took the doll back and held it in both hands. She placed it in her lap and stared at it. After a long silence, she lifted her head and nodded.

Ibrahim smiled. "My brave Yara. Come. We have much to do."

After he stood and helped Yara up, he turned toward Nasteexo. She had folded her arms again and looked away from him. He tried to speak, but she held her hand up. Reluctantly, he led Yara by the hand, and they left.

Olympia

Lester paced his living room floor, leafing through a heavy stack of papers that made up his insurance policy. The Google search he had completed a few minutes ago had assured him that the most important thing to do before getting too deep into a claim was to check his policy. He licked the tip of his forefinger with his semi-dry tongue and then separated yet another page from the stack.

No title. More text. He closed his eyes and let his head fall back so that he could stretch his neck. He let out a noise that was somewhere between a sigh and a groan before opening them again. He walked over to his coffee table and dropped the stack with an unceremonious thud. The top page caught the updraft and flew to the floor in a back and forth pattern. Lester shook his head and stomped to the bedroom with his shoulders hunched forward.

His bed was made, but it looked so inviting that he flopped down on it face-first with his toes still touching the floor. As soon as his face sank into the pillow-top mattress and he felt the simultaneous warmth and cool of the comforter, Lester saw onyx eyes pass through his mind. He pushed himself up with a gasp and stumbled backward.

His phone, which he had left on his nightstand, buzzed and chimed. Lester stood, glancing at the phone and panting, but he could not see who had texted. He closed his eyes and took a deep breath. He hoped to find only the darkness behind his eyelids, but he found those eyes waiting for him. He rubbed his face with both hands and leaned back against the wall.

He lowered his hands and shook his head. "Get it together, Les," he said to himself. "You're hallucinating. There's no demon. No one is out to get you." Saying the affirmation aloud made it seem rational enough for him to believe it, and he stood up. He looked over at his phone once more and saw Quinn's name with three words below it:

Can we talk?

Lester reached for the phone. Stopped. Pulled his hand back. Reached again but stopped. He flexed his fingers in the air above the phone as the screen went black. He finally growled and slapped his leg. "Come on!" he yelled with his face toward the ceiling. Before he realized what he was doing, and then regretting every step but unable to stop himself, he was walking into the bathroom. Then he was in his closet, reaching up to the highest shelf and pulling down a shoe box.

He slid to the floor with his back against the closet wall and set the shoe box in between his spread legs. When he removed the lid, he immediately saw a picture of him with Quinn and Dillon.

Lester reached in and removed the picture, letting the lid to the shoe box fall to the carpet. He knew the picture: the day Dillon had come home from his training to become an infantry soldier.

The picture trembled in his hand, but Dillon's face was clear. His smile was as bright as the marksmanship badge on the chest of his dress uniform. Lester's mom had made a special request for Dillon to wear his uniform for the pictures. Fake, just like the manufactured smiles they were all wearing in the photo. His mother had not spoken to Lester after the pictures.

Lester shook his head, remembering his mother walking away after taking the photo. There was another fleeting memory of standing in the driveway as his parents drove off in a moving truck. He thought of the day Dillon left from leave to report to his first duty station, and the day he had called—a few years later—to tell Lester he was going to Iraq.

He thought of Quinn and her asking him so many questions after that picture had been taken. How upset she had been when he'd refused to answer.

He wiped the corner of his eye with the side of his hand and took one more look at the picture. He tossed it back in the box and rested his head against the wall. He closed his eyes and found only darkness. No demon's eyes or memories to chase sleep away.

CHAPTER THIRTEEN

Khufia

IBRAHIM STOOD IN THE FLICKERING light cast by the lone candle on the floor next to a thin sleeping mat. Lying on a separate, smaller mat, Yara breathed softly, tiny bubbles forming on her cracked lips. Stray strands of her black hair were lying across her tiny face, and he was tempted to kneel next to her and move the hair away but restrained himself.

He sighed and turned away. Nasteexo's warnings still rang in his mind like incessant wind chimes *How can I risk getting her killed?* he thought. He had managed to sneak away for a few minutes and inspect where Yusef's men were keeping the prisoner. Two guards were posted. Yusef had apparently called in more people to help because neither of the men kept their faces covered, but Ibrahim did not recognize either of them. There would be no getting past those guards.

His granddaughter stirred, smacked her lips together, and stretched. He turned to face her again and was about to crawl to her when the door to the hut flew open and Yusef's men rushed in. They carried rifles in their hands and stalked toward him. Ibrahim looked quickly back to his granddaughter and saw that she was peeking through half-shut eyes. He made an exaggerated face of himself pretending to sleep, and she apparently understood because she shut her eyes all the way.

He kept his vision fixed on her as they grabbed him roughly by the shoulders and dragged him from the hut. He did not struggle, for he was too weak and terrified. Without explanation, without a word, they dragged him outside and into the night.

The prisoner awoke to the sound of the door opening. He snapped his eyes open and snatched his torso off the ground to sit back on his knees. Two of the masked men were in front of him before his eyes adjusted to the ring of flickering light cascading into the room. They pulled him to his feet, unlocked his shackles, and pulled him out of the building. He heard shouting and orders being yelled in every direction.

The masked men forced the prisoner through the village until they came to the edge of a crowd. Most of them were in night clothes, but a few were fully dressed. He was shoved into the center of the crowd and saw the old man who had visited him. He was on his knees, being held by the smallest of the gang. The old man's eyes were wide, and his body shook visibly.

Yusef was unmasked, and he stepped away from the crowd he had been yelling at to walk over to the old man. He towered over him for a moment, then leaned down and stared into his eyes. The old man leaned away from his face and tried not to turn his head to the side. Yusef clasped his hands behind his back and stood up, continuing to stare at the old man. He then unclasped his hands and slapped the old man. The sound silenced all murmurs in the crowd and forced a grunt from the old man. His face turned all the way to the side.

"Ibrahim, you know the rules better than anyone." Yusef's voice was strong and clearly held power over the onlookers. "You know that helping this infidel will cost you dearly, don't you?"

The old man, whose name was apparently Ibrahim, stared at Yusef as if nothing had happened.

Yusef's shoulders heaved up and down, and he growled. "And that goes for all of you!" He turned and shouted to the crowd with a sweep of his arms. "Anyone caught delivering food or supplies to this sorcerer will suffer the consequences."

"He is only an old man," someone yelled from the crowd. It was a man, but the prisoner could not see who it was. "Leave him alone," the man continued.

Yusef had apparently seen the man while he was speaking because he walked over to him and grabbed him by the back of the head. The man—young and tall with dark, black hair—winced and grabbed at Yusef's hand but followed his pull into the center of the circle. When they were close to Ibrahim, Yusef whispered something into the man's ear and then punched him in the stomach. The man groaned and fell to his knees, clutching himself. Yusef turned and faced the crowd.

"Anyone else?" He paused with his palms up. No one responded. The women did not make eye contact with him. After a few moments of silence, he turned back to Ibrahim. "As I was saying, we will not tolerate anyone aiding the infidel, even your beloved Ibrahim."

He nodded to the man holding Ibrahim. Tahiil, the prisoner remembered. Tahiil hesitated, exchanging looks with Yusef, and then began beating Ibrahim.

The prisoner wanted to turn away at first, but then he was intrigued by something. A feeling. The situation was oddly familiar to him, as if he had seen this same scenario played out many times before. Though he detested it and wanted to help the old man, it did not bother him as much as he thought it should. Worse, something told him he would see it again if he survived his captivity.

By now Ibrahim was on the ground, balled up. Two men attacked him, alternating kicks to his head and ribs. The people in the crowd murmured, some shouting but most too afraid to say anything. Yusef was to the side, watching and making comments about the punishments for helping "the sorcerer." He turned and looked at the prisoner. He tilted his head to the side and took a step back. Without looking away, he held up a hand, and the men beating Ibrahim stopped.

"That's enough for you, Uncle." Yusef nodded toward the prisoner. "Get the sorcerer."

The two men stalked toward the prisoner. It was then that he noticed how large the man helping Tahiil was. He was head and shoulders taller and extremely broad, and even Yusef stepped back when the man passed by. The prisoner heard Yusef shouting to the man, asking who he was and where he had come from. The giant of a man ignored him.

The prisoner was shoved to the ground. He heard the shuffling of feet on sand behind him. *They're trying to get away!* He pushed himself to his hands and knees but was grabbed by the throat and lifted into the air. He slapped at the corded forearm of the beast of a man as his windpipe was closed off by an impossible grip. The man stared into the prisoner's eyes with hatred. The giant's face was wrapped in a black cloth. Only his onyx eyes were clear, and electricity danced deep within them. The prisoner recognized them. Hated them for reasons his mind would not reveal.

The man hoisted the prisoner and thrust him into the air. The prisoner soared and landed with a sickening crack of his back and head against the ground. He tried to get his bearings and stand, but then the eyes were inches from his. The man's breath was hot and smelled of decay, like carrion. He grabbed the prisoner by the remnants of his tattered shirt and pulled him to his knees.

"Time for you to experience true pain, watcher," the man said in a snarling voice. He hit him with a right hook that sent the prisoner to the ground, where his face bounced. He looked up and saw his blood splattered in streaks. It glistened like crimson lava in the torchlight.

The force of the punch was nothing like he had felt at the hands of the others. This one had hurt him deep. The prisoner rolled to his side. Yusef was screaming at the man, screaming at his men. Screaming at the crowd and at nothing. It took the prisoner a few moments to understand the shouting well enough to gather that none of them knew who this latest attacker was. But his assailant knew who he was. The word "watcher" was both foreign and familiar at the same time.

The man grabbed him by the throat and hair. The prisoner's long dreadlocks fell across his face. He glanced at his arms as he was being pulled up and noticed that they were dark brown and slender. Solid. That seemed important, but he could not understand why.

He felt his heart pounding, felt power coursing through him, and he acted on instinct. He planted his feet firmly, grabbed the hand that was clutching his throat, and with force he did not know he possessed, snatched it away. Before he could think, he hit the man in the stomach. The giant stepped back with a gasp and hunched over. The prisoner rushed forward, grabbed the man's head, and slammed it down into his raised knee. The enormous head bounced off his knee. The man yelled in pain, but then he was no longer off-guard.

Lightning surged in his eyes, much to the amazement of the prisoner, and the man hit him with an uppercut to the jaw that sent the prisoner flying again. He landed on his back, and his head bounced against the ground. He looked up and saw three blurry versions of the giant man stomping toward him. As the three came into focus, merging into one, a memory flashed through the prisoner's mind.

The man was taller and much stronger. His skin was as black as midnight, and lightning surged all along his body. He was standing on a cliff, silhouetted by the light of a full moon, and his razor-sharp fangs were bared in a wicked smile. The prisoner was there, but he was not cowering or on the ground. He was facing the man—who was not a man but a demon—at the edge of the cliff. The prisoner glanced back, below him, and saw two armies clashing in battle with swords and axes. Fires blazed all around the field below.

The prisoner inspected himself. He was no longer slender, no longer dark brown. His arms changed colors as he moved them, blending in with the colors of his environment, and they were thick and corded. His legs were equally powerful, and he felt taller. He looked up and saw the demon in a fighting stance. The prisoner slid one foot back and bent both knees. He brought his hands up and felt the power of a force he did not understand gathering. He spoke: "Come on then . . . "

"Morane." The prisoner said the words just before the giant hit him with a punch that sent him into darkness.

CHAPTER FOURTEEN

Olympia

QUINN YANKED AND KICKED HER way out of her blankets. She sat up and let her legs swing over the edge of the bed. She looked at her trembling fingers, which appeared shadowed and almost silver in the beam of moonlight peeking through the crack in her thick blinds. She had been in bed for hours, exhausted, but sleep eluded her.

She tapped her temple and closed her eyes. "Why are you thinking about him?" She leaned her head back, stretching her neck, and let out a long breath.

Having her eyes closed made it easier to picture Lester, to imagine him showing up at the church in his red Watchmen shirt, then in his striped shirt and dark blue jeans on Sunday morning. She opened her eyes and stood. She stretched, then shuffled to the bathroom, dragging her feet across the thick carpet. She hugged herself, rubbing her shoulders vigorously.

She flipped the light switch up without looking and reached for the faucet on the sink to the left of the door when she entered the bathroom. She turned on the hot side and let the water cascade over her fingers with one eye open until she felt the comforting heat replace the bitter cold. She turned the cold side on just enough to prevent herself from being burned. She leaned down with an exhale, cupped her hands under the flow, and began splashing water on her face. The water was so soothing that she wanted to bury herself in its warmth. She stayed that way for nearly a minute, repeating the process of baptizing her eyes.

She finally turned the faucet off and slid her hands over her face several times to wipe away the dripping water. Her face cooled as the chill of the room touched the thin layer of water. When she was finished, she stood and leaned over the sink with her palms planted on the edge of the counter. She looked into the mirror, blinking water away. She saw a woman she wished was prettier. A girl she wished was older. A woman with lines on her forehead that made her wish she was younger. She traced her jawline with her fingertips, turned her head to the side, and let her fingers trail to her thin nightshirt.

A smile crept onto her face as she imagined the shirt was a long, flowing, white dress with a veil and train. The straps were thin but modest, showing off her smooth shoulders but not revealing too much. The secrets beneath the dress were saved for someone special, someone who would never betray the holder of those secrets.

"Girl, stop it." She shook her head and sighed. Looking away from the mirror and heading out of the bathroom, she reached up and grabbed the soft, cream-colored hand towel hanging near the light. She flipped the switch as she exited the bathroom and entered the dark, moonlit bedroom.

She patted her face dry and tossed the towel on the foot of the bed as she passed by. With a flop, she got back in the bed and pulled the blankets over her. Thoughts of Lester walking away from the woman trapped in the mirror—the woman in the secret dress—assaulted her, and she pounded her fists into the mattress.

You're staying up late thinking about a man who walked out on you, Quinn. Her thoughts began to stream, nearly audible. *Just like his family walked out on him.* She wanted to cry at the memories of Lester around his parents when Dillon had joined the army. The screaming, the accusations, and finally the silent treatment that had forced Lester to move out. Then there was the move. Lester's parents had left to pursue a career opportunity for Lester's father, and they had barely spoken after that.

And he's about to go see them again.

She tossed the blankets aside again and sat up in bed. She pushed herself against the headrest and then positioned a pillow in the small of her back. She reached to her nightstand and grabbed her phone from the nightstand, pulling it from the charger.

She hesitated, holding the phone in front of her with the screen lit up, but then she hit the call button, tapped on *Recents*, and swiped to the right over the word *Mom*. The phone was already ringing when she brought it to her ear, and her mother picked it up after only four rings.

The voice on the other end was dry and groggy. "Hello?"

"Hey, Mom."

"Quinn?" She heard her mother clearing her throat. "Baby, what're you doing?"

Quinn paused, thinking. "I can't sleep."

There was a chuckle. "Well, baby, I'm not coming over to sing you a lullaby and pet your cheek."

Quinn smiled at the memory, then winced at the irony. The last time her mother had done that was the day Lester had left her at the altar.

"No, I know. I just—"

"What's wrong, Quinn?" Her mother's voice was clearer.

Quinn sighed. "It's Lester."

There was a faint groan. "Are we doing this again?"

"Mom, no. It's . . . " She paused and squeezed her nose between her thumb and forefinger. "You know he was in church, right?"

"I saw him."

"Yeah, well, he's having a hard time."

"Ain't everybody that just shows up in church after two years?"

"Not like that."

Another sigh. "Girl, you letting this man pull the wool over your eyes?"

Quinn let her head rest against the headboard. "No, ma'am. You don't understand."

"Well, fill me in, baby, because it's late, and I still have a job to go to in the morning. Now, what's going on that's got you up this late?"

"His brother died, but he says that happened after he made a choice to turn back to the Lord."

There was a gasp. "Oh, no. Dillon? His mama must be sick."

"I'm sure she is, but that's the problem."

"He still ain't talking to his mama and daddy, is he?"

"Not that I'm aware of."

"Good gracious. What's wrong with folks these days?" She coughed. "Well, I guess he's on his way out there, and you're worried how that's gonna go. Am I right about it?"

Quinn nodded, then remembered she was on the phone. "Yes, ma'am."

"Baby, let me tell you something. That ain't none of your worry. And you ain't calling me because you're worried about Lester fighting with his parents at the funeral. I'll tell you right here and now: if them folks ain't got that right between them, and that boy went over the water and died, it's gonna be a fight at the funeral. Believe me."

"Then why shouldn't I be concerned?" Quinn asked.

"Because he's not your man anymore." Her mother sounded cold and flat. "Ain't but one reason you should be thinking about that."

Quinn rolled her eyes. "Which is?"

"You still love him."

Quinn sucked her teeth. "Mom, I'll just call you in the morning. I'm sorry I bothered you."

"Uh-uh. No, ma'am." Her mother coughed again. "Don't you call me in the middle of the night with all that attitude and then try and hurry up off the phone when I tell you the truth. I didn't raise you to disrespect me."

Quinn felt a tinge of regret. "You're right. I'm sorry."

"I don't need your sorry. I need your honesty, little girl. But let me break it down for you even better." There was a pause before she continued. "You need to be honest with yourself. You thought you were over that man because you've kept yourself busy for the past two years. Now he shows back up, and everything changes. Baby, that's the Lord trying to show you something, and you better have your eyes open."

"You sound like Mrs. Greene," Quinn said, smiling despite herself.

"I know."

Quinn furrowed her brow. "What does that mean?"

"She called me."

"What?"

"Mm-hm. Told me all about it. Girl, did you know that woman is my friend? Baby, she changed your diapers. You think her and I don't still talk?"

"So glad my life gives you two a reason to keep talking."

"Oh, we'll always have reason to talk, but that's beside the point. What *is* the point is that you need to deal with these feelings for Lester. You pray about it?"

"Of course."

"And what did you pray?"

"Mom!"

"Don't 'Mom!' me. What did you pray about?"

Quinn shook her head. "I asked the Lord to help me, to show me what to do."

"And what about when you prayed for Lester?"

Quinn nearly dropped the phone.

"I'm judging by the silence that I struck a nerve."

"I didn't pray for him," Quinn said in a breathy whisper.

"Well, there you have it. The problem with you kids is that you think there's some magic formula to praying and living for the Lord, but there's not. You have to just be honest with Him. Go ahead and be vulnerable and let Him work."

"Mom, that doesn't make any sense."

"Does if you're not trying to do everything in your own strength. But you always were headstrong. So was Lester, and that's your problem. Sometimes, the Lord has to break people before He can build them."

"I haven't been broken enough?" Quinn asked.

Her mother laughed. "Why don't you ask Jesus about being broken, then talk to me."

Quinn sighed and shook her head. She knew she wasn't going to get any further with this. "Thanks for the help, Mom. I feel so much better."

"Anytime, baby. Now go on to bed. I'm tired."

"Are you serious?"

Her mother made an uh-huh sound. "Got me up all late, talking about that man, and you know I don't like him."

"Um. Okay. Night, Mom."

"Night, baby. Love you."

The phone went silent before Quinn could say she loved her back. She tossed the phone on the bed beside her and closed her eyes. And there was Lester, his image waiting to keep her up and confuse her even more.

Lester felt his phone vibrate in his lap while he looked out the passenger window of Wayne's pickup. The city of Hudson streaked by. It was gray and silver, black and light, dark and green. All yesterday and tomorrow streaming past his window, and he felt nauseous from the passing. How many moments lost? he wondered. How many lives changed? Erased? Created?

He turned his head and picked his phone up. It was a text message from Dave, asking if they could talk when he got back. Lester cleared the notification and dropped the phone back to his lap. He had talked to Dave only a couple of times since the fire. There had been questions from the insurance agent, payroll to be distributed to everyone, and then informing his general manager that he would be out of town for a while to attend the funeral.

"Must not be good news."

Wayne's drawl pulled Lester from his thoughts, and he turned away from the window to look at his neighbor. The man looked like he belonged in a pickup. Or an eighteen-wheeler. His calloused hand was draped over the steering wheel with his free hand covering the gear knob.

"No news at all, really."

Wayne nodded. "You just ain't wantin' to answer it, I guess."

Lester smiled and faced the front. The Hudson International Airport was coming into view.

"I reckon so," he said with a pretend accent.

Wayne slapped his shoulder with the back of his hand. "Now you're talking like a real man, bud."

Lester shook his head and laughed. "Feel more like a boy right now."

"Oh?"

Lester ran his fingers through his hair. "Yeah. It's weird, y'know?" As he talked, he looked out the passenger's window again. This time, the Hudson skyline was in clear view, and everything seemed to be in slow motion as the pickup veered onto the access road leading to the terminal. "Dillon was a grown man, but all I can think about is him and me getting busted for stealing cookies when my mom used to lay them on towels on the counter." He laughed so hard that his shoulders shook, and he had to fight back tears. "Isn't that crazy?" When he looked at Wayne, his neighbor was turning the wheel with both hands and shaking his head.

"No, sir. Ain't crazy at all." He straightened the wheel and pointed at Lester. "No crazier'n me thinkin' about my my wife in her weddin' dress with her hair done up'n all."

"You talk to her?"

Wayne smiled.

Lester leaned back. "Wait. You did?"

Wayne nodded. "Meetin' with her tomorrow, just to talk. Took a bit to get her to hear me out, but I told her I got some things need sayin' 'fore we sign them papers."

It was Lester's turn to slap Wayne on the shoulder. "That's alright, man."

"Not too bad, huh?"

He pulled up to the curb at the terminal a minute later and put the pickup in park. They sat for a few moments, listening to the sound of the airport announcer telling people not to leave baggage unattended, and then they exchanged a nod and opened their doors at the same time.

Wayne told Lester not to worry about his bag and hurried around to the passenger side. He reached into the bed, grabbed Lester's suitcase, and pulled it out with a grunt. He set it down on the curb and pulled up the tote handle.

"Real sorry you gotta deal with all this, Les," he said, reaching his hand out. "Keep your head up out there, and I'll be here to pick ya up when ya get back."

Lester shook his hand. "I appreciate it. Thanks for helping me out."

"Shoot. After what you did for me?" Wayne shook his head. "I owe you, way I see it."

Lester had been apprehensive but relieved to tell Wayne about the glimpse, and more so about Wayne's part in that fateful night. Standing outside the terminal, he was glad to have a friend he could confide in. He patted Wayne on the side of the shoulder. "Rather just be your friend, Wayne." It felt strange to him. He had not said something like that to anyone in a long time.

Wayne smiled and winked. "For life, bud."

They shook hands once more, then Lester grabbed his bag and pulled it through the terminal doors, leaving Wayne behind. Ahead of him, people passed to the left and right in streaks of gray. Streaks of dark and light.

Two hours later, Lester power-walked down the accordion jet bridge to board the plane. At the end of the square tunnel, a flight attendant was waving for him to hurry; and Lester broke into a run, pulling his suitcase so quickly that the rollers sounded like a zipline on the metal floor. There was a significant amount of pressure on his bladder from the coffee he had finished right before boarding, but there was no time for a restroom break. He still didn't know how he had gotten so lost in thought watching the planes taking off and landing while sitting at his gate. He would just have to wait until the plane was in the air.

The flight attendant greeted him when he arrived at the entrance to the plane. "Thank you, sir." He motioned Lester aboard and stepped to the side. Lester nodded, impressed by the man's bright, heavily starched shirt and blue tie as the attendant wished him a good flight.

Lester said, "You too" before he could stop himself. He thought about trying to correct it with "thanks" but kept going instead. He returned the smile of the next flight attendant, a woman in her late forties who kept her hands folded in front of her waist. He exchanged nods with a couple of people who were sitting in their seats and staring up at him, but most of the people were looking straight ahead or already asleep. Almost every seat was filled. He glanced down at his boarding pass to double-check his seat number. Booking a flight so close to the departure date meant his seat was near the back, but he was thankful to see that it was an aisle seat.

When he got to his row, a tall, broad-shouldered man was in the seat next to Lester's. The man was the largest Asian-American man

Lester had ever seen. He gave Lester a cross between a wave and a salute, and Lester nodded with a thin-lipped smile. He pushed down the handle of his small carry-on suitcase, suppressing a groan, and then loaded it into the overhead compartment. He shoved his boarding pass back into his jeans, settled into his seat, and fastened his safety belt.

The flight crew was already going through the in-flight instructions by the time he sat down. Lester tried to pay attention, but he saw a hand stretched out in front of him. He turned his head and followed the hand to the arm and face of his seatmate. The man was smiling and gave a nod toward his hand. Lester blinked several times before turning back to the hand. He twisted his body back and to the side so that he could grasp the man's hand, and then his eyes opened wide at the instant pressure applied to his own.

"Simon Chester," the man said at full volume. "Looks like it's you and me."

Lester tucked in his bottom lip and offered somewhere between a frown and a smile, nodded, and pulled his hand away. "Guess so."

"What's your name, friend?" Simon apparently had no concern for the passengers staring at him because he continued to speak as if he was giving a speech to thousands, rather than having a conversation with someone six inches away.

"Lester Sharp. Nice to meet you."

To Lester's utter horror, Simon punched him in the shoulder. "Pleasure's all yours, pal." He laughed at his own joke in a wheezy, body-shaking fit. Lester raised his eyebrows and smiled politely. He looked up and saw the flight attendant smiling at him awkwardly as she passed by and took her seat at the rear of the plane.

"Funeral, huh?"

Lester snapped his head to the side and looked at Simon. "Beg your pardon?"

"Sorry." Simon held his hands up with the palms facing Lester. "I travel a lot. Talk to people, you know? And ten bucks says I know that look anywhere. You're a man on his way to a funeral. Awful sorry for your loss, partner."

Lester didn't know whether to thank him or punch him. "Are you serious?"

Simon set his hands in his lap as the plane started to taxi and sniffed through one nostril. "Yeah, it's a gift, I guess. I'm in sales, so I know people. Mom always said I could read people better than a book." He shrugged. "Never was much for reading. Cars, by the way."

Lester could not even blink. He stared at the man and fought the urge to shake his head. "What?"

Simon furrowed his brow and leaned forward. "What's that? Plane's moving, friend. You asked what I did?"

Lester was speechless.

"I'm in the car business." Simon leaned back. "Thanks for asking. Great business, but it keeps me running around the clock. I'm a bit of an entrepreneur, too. I'm on my way out to Montana to scope out some property for a new lot. Bank says it's a risk; I say it's a gold mine. What about you?"

Lester, despite himself, replied, "I own a repair shop and parts store."

Simon's eyes opened wide. "That so? Well, I might have to look you up when I get back and do some business with you. You in Hudson?"

Lester shook his head. "Olympia."

Simon nodded. "Small world."

"Huh?"

The plane took off down the runway at a rapidly accelerated speed and then tilted upward, lifting into the air. Lester felt his stomach drop, and there was pressure against his chest. They were silent for a few moments, but then Simon continued just as Lester felt the relief of the conversation being over.

"Yeah, I used to own a repair shop. Mine was in Hudson, though. I got tired of that pretty quick and opened up my first car lot."

"Really?" Lester had no idea why he was entertaining the man. The plane was still ascending, and he wanted to vomit. His bladder felt like it was going to burst.

Simon nodded. "Yep. Quite a story, actually. I had some strange things happen, and then I lost my shop to a fire. That's when I was forced to evaluate my life, and I got determined to succeed. Focus on my goals." He fell silent, and Lester turned back to the front as the plane began to level off.

After a minute, he turned to Simon. "You had a repair shop that burned down?"

"Sure did," Simon said. "I'd had so much going on that I'd decided to get religious, and then I got a phone call from my general manager that the shop was gone."

Lester was about to shout, "No way," but the captain came over the intercom to inform them they were free to move about the cabin but to keep their seatbelts fastened when seated. The flight to Huron would be three hours, and they expected no delays. Lester heard all of this but was gawking at Simon. When the captain shut off the intercom, Lester rubbed his face and tried to relax.

"I can relate," he said.

Simon looked at him out of the corner of his eye. "Oh?"

Lester nodded. "I'm on my way to my brother's funeral, and my shop burned down a couple days ago. I've been on the phone with the insurance company about a thousand times."

Simon listened and rubbed his chin. "And did you just happen to get religion, Lester?"

Lester shrugged and felt heat in his face. "I, uh . . . I don't know if I'd call it religion, but I did return to church for the first time in a couple years."

Simon continued rubbing his chin and nodded slowly. "Thought so."

"What do you mean?"

Simon lifted his fingers from his chin and shook his head. "Well, I lost my wife right before the fire, and I didn't know how to cope with it. Very few people do, turns out. I tried all kinds of things on the advice of friends and family. Went to about ten churches, but nothing helped. Then one night, I saw an angel. Thought I did, anyway. It was incredible. He came to my house and told me God had plans for me. The next day, I about ran to the nearest church. I got really involved, too. I felt so good, like I'd got a new life. Then the fire happened, and I didn't know what to do."

Lester was too stunned to say anything when Simon paused. The events of the past week began to play through his mind.

"Well, I went and found a therapist, and she helped me make sense of things."

"How so?

"Turns out the mind has a way of coping with things that can do more harm than good. It can conjure up images and sounds that seem like real life, which is what my 'angel' experience was." He made air quotes when he said *angel*. "As I found out, the brain will even manipulate our perception of time and trick our memory. What I've told you is the order of events the way they really happened. At the time, I thought I saw the angel before my wife died. Back then, it was all one day for me. I saw this angel, or whatever, my wife died; and then my shop burned down."

"That's not how it happened?"

Simon shook his head. "Not at all. The therapist was able to help me sort things out. Once I got my memory working right, I left that church and never went back. Know the funny thing?"

Lester shrugged and shook his head.

"My wife died five years before all that happened." Simon leaned forward and spoke in hushed tones. "I served two years for arson. Know why? I started that fire, but I didn't know I did. I'd finally let my mind realize my wife had died, and I subconsciously went and burned my business to the ground. Know when I figured it out?"

Lester's heart was racing. His mind was filled with doubt. "When?" he asked, timidly.

"When I showed up for my wife's funeral, five years after she was buried."

"Would you care for a drink, sir?"

Lester snapped his head to the left and gasped. The male flight attendant who had welcomed him aboard was standing behind a drink cart, looking at him with his head leaned back and eyes wide.

"Everything alright, sir?"

Lester swallowed a lump in his throat. "Fine. Can I get a coffee, please? I'm pretty tired."

"Absolutely. Cream and sugar?"

Lester shook his head.

He rubbed his eyes and took slow, calming breaths as the flight attendant poured the coffee. He handed it to Lester with a napkin and a bag of assorted nuts. Lester pulled down the tray on the back of the seat in front of him, took the items from the attendant, and set them on the tray. The attendant told him to enjoy and then pulled the cart up the aisle to the next row of passengers. Lester was about to raise his hand and call to the attendant to remind him to ask Simon if he wanted a drink, but Simon tapped his forearm.

"It's fine. I don't need anything."

Just looking at the hot coffee in the small, paper cup reminded Lester how full his bladder was. He looked at Simon, who had settled back in his seat with his eyes closed. Lester turned to the front and held the cup between both hands, telling himself to stay calm. He was not hallucinating, he told himself repeatedly. The strange man at the police station, the barista with the unnaturally deep voice, and the situation at the restaurant with Wayne were real. They had to be. Draven, the glimpse, Dillon—all of that had to be real.

"Kind of funny how similar our stories are, isn't it, Lester?"

Lester turned his head as Simon spoke, and by the time the man had said, "Lester," he saw that Simon had turned his head, as well. They looked into one another's eyes, and Lester noticed the man's eye color for the first time. Dark, nearly black, but ringed with electricity.

Lester gasped and jumped, nearly spilling his coffee. He slapped his hands down on the tray, scrambled to settle the shifting items, and nearly half of the coffee splashed out of the cup. He quickly grabbed the napkin and began to clean it up.

"Hey, are you okay?" Simon asked.

Lester nodded several times. "Fine I'm fine." He dropped the napkin and took deep breaths. "I'm just really tired, and I need to use the restroom."

Simon touched his forearm, and Lester felt a surge of electricity. "Hey, it's okay, Lester. You've been through a lot. Listen, I'm sorry for telling you my story. I probably shouldn't have done that."

Lester shook his head and snatched his arm away from Simon. "No, it's fine. Really. You were just talking."

"Hey, go ahead and use the restroom. I'll clean this up for you."

Lester stared at the spilled coffee, then into Simon's eyes. They were blue. Just blue. He nodded and unbuckled his seat belt. He thanked Simon and then rushed into the open lavatory.

After using the restroom, Lester stayed inside and leaned over the sink, splashing water on his face. He did so several times and then leaned on the counter to look in the streaked mirror. His face appeared distorted in the scratched up, compressed surface of the mirror, but he focused on his eyes. They were bloodshot and swollen.

When is the last time I slept more than an hour?

The events of the past week ran through his mind in a lightning fast collage of images. Draven appearing in his shop. Lester kicking the stranger out. Steam from a burned cup of coffee frozen in the air. Wayne dead on the floor. The police station. The body of the inmate. The red shirts of the members of The Midnight Cry. The dead woman and her stillborn child. Her attacker's mutilated stomach. Hungry people digging for snakes in the side of a mountain. Decapitated bodies less than twenty yards from their executioners.

Dillon.

A patrol of armored vehicles frozen in a moment of time, headed for an explosion. Lester was there again, pounding on the window, screaming for Dillon. Then he was in the dark outside his house, looking back over time and space through memory to the abandoned Iraqi road. To the truck. The soldiers were still there. Dillon was gone.

"The truth is there's nothing to transport." Harold's words ran through his mind as Lester once again saw himself in the mirror. *"They didn't recover Dillon's body."*

He slammed his fists on the small counter and growled. "Get it together." He steadied himself with a deep breath. There was a knock on the door to the lavatory. He pulled a paper towel from the dispenser mounted to the counter and used it to wipe his face. He held onto it as he opened the door and walked out. A woman with a small child offered him a weak, pursed-lipped smile as he passed.

When he got back to his seat, Lester noticed that there was a full, fresh cup of coffee with packets of cream and sugar next to it. The seat next to his was empty. There was no sign of any spill. Lester put his hand on the back of his seat and looked around. The attendant came forward and looked at him with an awkward smile.

"Is everything alright, sir?"

Lester pointed at the cup. "You brought me a fresh cup of coffee?"

The attendant glanced at the cup. "Yes, sir. You asked for it before you went to the restroom. Is that okay?"

Lester swallowed. "You didn't already bring my drink? Before?"

The attendant shook his head. "I don't believe so, no. Are you feeling alright, sir?"

Lester shook his head. "I said no cream and sugar. Why did you bring me cream and sugar?"

"You actually asked for both, sir."

Lester closed his eyes and rubbed his forehead. "Whatever. Uh, where's the man sitting next to me? Is he in the other restroom? I don't want to get comfortable and then have to get up when he gets back." When he opened his eyes, the attendant was staring at him with his mouth open.

"Sir?"

Lester pointed at the seat. "The guy I've been sitting next to the whole flight. Asian guy. Really big? Wearing a suit?"

The attendant shook his head. "Sir, there's no one in that seat. You're sitting alone."

Lester clenched his jaw. "Look, man, I don't need this. The plane was packed when I got on, and that guy was the only person with an empty seat next to him." He pointed. "Where is he?"

The attendant held up his hands and patted the air in front of him. Lester noticed a man about six rows up with a leather jacket and a mustache getting to his feet, watching him.

"Sir, please calm down," the attendant said. "I'm not sure what's happening, but I can assure you that you have been sitting alone this entire flight. You were talking to yourself when I came by with the drink cart, but you stopped to ask me for a coffee with cream and sugar. Then you went to the bathroom."

Lester was shaking his head, but the attendant continued. "And this is not a full flight, sir. There are empty seats everywhere."

Lester opened his mouth to argue, but then he looked up. Scanning from the back to the front, he saw the heads of many people sticking up over the headrests of seats, but numerous seats were empty. The man in the leather jacket had made his way up the aisle and walked up to them. He stopped beside the attendant.

"Is there a problem, sir?" the man asked. He was staring right through Lester.

Air marshal, Lester thought.

He nodded and held up his hands. "Everything is fine. Listen, I'm really sorry," he said to the attendant. "I recently lost my brother to an IED in Iraq, and I've got a lot of other things going on. I haven't slept, and my mind's playing tricks on me."

The attendant and air marshal exchanged concerned glances between themselves and toward Lester. Finally, the attendant looked down with his head toward the marshal and nodded. The marshal hesitated at first but then returned up the aisle to his seat.

"I'm sorry for your loss, sir."

Lester shook his head. "Sorry for my behavior."

The attendant waved his hand. "No worries. I can't imagine how I'd feel. Can I get you anything?"

Lester nodded. "Actually, would you mind taking that coffee away? I think I should try and catch a couple hours of sleep before we land."

The attendant smiled. "Absolutely."

Lester thanked him and then waited for the attendant to walk past before returning to his seat. Just as he was about to sit down, he looked into the seat next to him and nearly fainted when he saw what was in it.

A long, dark brown dreadlock, cut from someone's scalp.

CHAPTER FIFTEEN

Khufia

THE PRISONER SAT IN THE darkness of the building that had become his private prison, thinking about the eyes of the monster that had appeared two nights before. No one had come to him since then, and the prisoner was glad. Although he wished the old man or someone else would bring him food, he was thankful that no one was going to be harmed by visiting him.

He wondered about many things. How was the old man now? Was he still alive? Where had that man come from? Why had he seen the man in a vision from the past? Why had his own body looked different in the vision? How come Yusef and the others did not know who the man was? What was a watcher, and why had the man called him one? Why had that man been able to hurt him in ways the others could not?

He paused on that thought. Had paused there many times in the past two days and nights. He had begun to realize that there was something unique about him, something powerful. Something that made him heal quickly and understand languages he did not know. He was no ordinary man; that was becoming obvious. Was he a sorcerer, like they claimed? And what of this new adversary? Why had he looked like that in the vision? Was he a man or a demon?

He heard whispering and the shuffling of feet on the sand outside the building, and his muscles tensed. He prepared for another assault from the masked men, but then he relaxed. They never bothered sneaking around. They came in when they wanted to, and they certainly made no effort to quiet their voices. These voices, however, were beginning to surround the building. There were splashing noises, liquid being tossed against the walls.

The prisoner closed his eyes and took a deep breath. He felt a sense of calm, followed by an urging from deep in the recesses of his mind. Something, someone, was calling to him. He opened his eyes, and time seemed to slow. Though it was dark in the building, and only cracks in the floor and a few places in the walls allowed moonlight to peek through, it was suddenly as bright as daylight to him. And then he saw what he knew was not possible to see.

He turned his head to the left and right, scanning the walls, and looked right through them. As he moved his head, the walls seemed to become transparent, allowing him to see men rushing about, holding cans and shaking them toward the building. Liquid splashed out of the cans and spilled along the walls. The prisoner continued his scan. Wherever he focused, there was an oval-shaped sight portal projected on the wall.

He saw one of the men reach into a pocket and produce a small, thin stick. The man walked up to the wall and dragged the tiny stick downward, scraping it on the wall until it burst into flame. He tossed the stick to the ground and scampered back. Flames leapt up and began to crawl up the wall. The prisoner looked to the right and saw another man doing the same thing there. The men began to shout and hoot as smoke entered the building. The prisoner was blinded by the bright flood of light from the flames. He squeezed his eyes shut, then blinked several times. When he opened his eyes, he could no longer see through the walls, but smoke was filling the room.

He tugged at his chains and imagined being able to break them, but that was impossible, especially considering the agony in his bruised body. His heart was pounding, and he started coughing as the smoke surrounded him. The door burst open, and two of Yusef's men rushed in. One of them was fumbling with keys as he entered and ran to the prisoner. He unlocked the chains, and then the men pulled him up and dragged him outside.

He still heard men shouting; but when he turned toward the sound, he realized they were not shouting in excitement. Yusef and the rest of his men were scolding a group of men holding cans. Yusef attacked one of them, hitting him repeatedly until the man fell to the ground in a heap. Yusef then launched a back-handed attack on the man who had been standing next to him.

"You fools," he shouted. "You would burn the village to the ground for one infidel?"

The prisoner quickly scanned the area, but he did not see the monster of a man anywhere in the crowd.

"He is a sorcerer, Yusef," one of the men said.

Yusef turned to face the man. "He will die when I say he dies, but not before I root out all of the traitors to Allah in this village. And the building is metal, you idiots. All you would have done is caught a few shrubs on fire and spread it to the houses. How can you be so stupid?"

The man stood firmly and resolute with his jaw lifted. "You cannot kill him, Yusef. Your men tried, but the sorcerer lives. He survives your fists and your bullets. You keep him alive because you cannot kill him."

"And you think this is the way, Ahmed?"

The man nodded. "He cannot rise without a body, so we must burn his body until it is gone."

"No!" The man holding the prisoner on his left side shouted. "This is madness, Yusef." He eased the prisoner to the ground and walked toward the crowd. The other man, who had been holding the prisoner's right side, followed him.

"He is right, Yusef," the second man said. "We are not animals. This is not the way of Allah."

Yusef turned to face them. He pointed to the first man who had spoken. "You want me to let him go, Tahiil?" He then pointed to the second man. "You think you know the way of Allah better than me, Diric?"

Diric held his hands out with the palms facing up. "I think you have lost your way. Look at what is happening to this village, brother."

Yusef nodded. "You think I have lost my way. Is that it? And you, Tahiil? Has Yusef lost his way?"

Tahiil was quiet.

"Answer me!" Yusef shouted.

"I think we have all lost our way," Tahiil said.

Yusef held his hands in the air beside him and then clasped them together in front of his waist. "Then let me help you find yours." Before anyone could react, he unslung his rifle from his shoulder and fired a volley of bullets into Tahiil's chest. There were screams as Tahiil's body rocked back and forth. Blood sprayed into the air before he hit the ground. Yusef wasted no time, turning his rifle toward Diric and firing another volley. Diric suffered the same fate.

After Diric hit the ground with a thud in front of the prisoner, Yusef nodded and slung his rifle back over his shoulder. "Now, Ahmed," he said, turning back to the man who had been involved in starting the fire. "You were saying?"

Ahmed shrank back and shook his head, looking at the ground.

The prisoner looked away and saw a group of bystanders who had walked up and stopped twenty feet away. Hiding in the midst of them, he spotted her. She had been cleaned up, but she wore the same frightened expression. Yara. She looked directly at the prisoner. Their eyes met, and he sensed something. *Understanding?* She was afraid, shrinking away, but there was also a maturity in her face that should not have been on the face of such a young girl. He tried to probe her eyes, searching for something. Then he saw Ibrahim. The old man was beside her. He reached down, took her hand, and led her away. Ibrahim's eyes met his as the man slipped into the shadows.

The prisoner's thoughts were cut short by a volley of bullets entering his chest, and he fell back to the dirt, back into shadows of his own.

Ibrahim tucked Yara close to him with his hands covering her ears. He felt her body shaking and heard her sobbing against his stomach. The gunfire echoed through the night, and he shut his eyes as if it would stop the sound. Images of the prisoner being ripped apart by the bullets assaulted his mind, so he squeezed his eyes tighter shut and clenched his teeth. He felt tears streaming down his cheeks, and then Yara screamed.

He snapped his eyes open, scooped her into his arms, and ran as fast as his weary legs would let him. He could not go home, for they would find him there. He could not go to Nasteexo, for that would endanger her. There was nowhere to run, but on he ran. He made it to the fields and was forced to slow down because of the ridges made by the mounds of dirt concealing the seeds that would likely never produce any plants. He stumbled several times over the darkened ridges, made darker still by the fact that the moon seemed oddly absent from the chilly night sky.

Panic began to set in. He stopped and, with no choice, set Yara on the ground. He knelt before her and looked into her eyes—puffy eyes he could barely see.

"We must hide, Yara." He panted, his shoulders heaving. "The village has gone mad. They will come for us." Yara said nothing. "Do you understand?"

She was silent, unmoving, but then she nodded.

He nodded as well and braced himself to rise, but he felt pressure on his shoulder. Like a hand. He froze, not daring to turn and find out to whom the hand belonged. He looked into Yara's face. She had not looked up. She had not looked left or right, and her expression had not changed. Then she smiled. It was an odd sight. Shadows crossed her face, but there was light reflecting in her eyes. Not moonlight; pure, white light.

A warm breeze brushed past his ear, and the pressure on his shoulder warmed as well. It brought him comfort, and his mind was at ease. There was a sound on the breeze, a whisper, and he listened. The rest of the world was silent.

Go to the church. You will be safe there. The angel is unharmed, but you must take the girl to him.

He opened his eyes wide and gasped. He nearly sprang to his feet, but the pressure on his shoulder urged him to stay. *To rest,* he thought. And then it was gone, and the world came alive once more. Crickets and cicadas playing their nocturnal songs, the breeze no longer warm. No longer whispering.

He rose to his feet and took his granddaughter's hand. "Come, Yara."

Town of Rhodes, Southeastern United States

Lester's cab pulled up to the funeral home, and he was surprised to see how small it was. It was a tan, brick building between a late model home and a gas station. Across the street was a Mexican food restaurant. The cab pulled up to the curb where several cars and trucks had been parked, and Lester handed the driver a twenty dollar bill before getting out. He held his suitcase with one hand and shielded his eyes with the other. Even then, he was still squinting. It was his first time in Huron, and so far, it was not impressive.

He glanced to his right and saw the city skyline in the distance. To the left were more gas stations, shops, and a business lot with a fence around it with a sign that said it was for lease. Lester shook his head and looked back to the funeral home. He knew he was late because of the amount of cars parked out front and along the side of the building that led to the rear parking lot. He assumed the lot was full and rolled his eyes at the thought of the amount of people inside.

He felt foolish bringing a suitcase in, but he had not had time to stop at the hotel he'd booked. He was about to head inside when his phone buzzed. He let go of the suitcase handle and pulled his phone out of his pocket. It was a text from Quinn asking if he had made it and was okay. Lester swiped the notification away and put the phone away. He breathed, focused, trying not to think about the dreadlock in the front pouch of his suitcase.

On the inside, he was blasted in the face with ice cold air and was relieved to know that people in Huron were apparently not immune to the oppressive heat. Lester was greeted by a short, chubby man, who was bald except for the white, slicked hair on the sides of his head. The man's wrinkled hands were nearly swallowed by the sleeves of the jacket that had probably fit him well in his youth. He motioned for Lester to go to the left. Lester nodded and thanked him once he saw a black sign with white letters that spelled out: VIEWING. SHARP.

He set his suitcase next to the coat rack by the door—with the greeter's approval—and started toward the chapel. He heard a toilet being flushed as he walked past the men's restroom, and then the door opened. A tall man with Curt Cobain hair and a scraggly beard stepped out. Jeremy. Lester's cousin. Lester fought the urge to roll his eyes and was about to say, "Hey, Jeremy," when the man wrapped him in a bear hug and lifted him off the ground.

"Lester!" Jeremy squeezed and shook Lester before setting him down, then stood looking him up and down with a smile. "Boy, look at you. Cleaned up real good, didn't you? How long's it been?"

"Two weeks," Lester said. "You came in the shop and asked me for a part for your pickup."

"Did I?" Jeremy furrowed his brow and scratched his head.

Lester nodded. "You did. I got it for you, remember? Driver's side mirror to replace the one you busted when you were driving home drunk last month?"

Jeremy thought for a minute and then slapped Lester's shoulder and smiled. "Oh, yeah. You know, those side views are expensive."

Lester made a "hmm" sound. "Good thing you didn't pay me for it."

"Yeah, money's real tight these days," Jeremy said, shaking his head and looking down. "Barely made it down here with Sheila's tip money. That ran out, of course, but I had to get here to pay my respects."

Lester braced himself for the inevitable.

Jeremey shoved his hands in his pockets and looked down. "Don't suppose you could help us get back? I got an interview in a couple days, and I could pay you back once I get my first paycheck."

"Don't you have to get the job first?" Lester asked.

Jeremy looked over Lester's head and nodded. "Good point. I'll just pay you back when I get it, Cuz."

Lester had already reached into his back pocket and retrieved his wallet. He took out two twenty dollar bills, handed them to Jeremy, and walked away while his cousin was still acting surprised and fumbling his way through a thank you.

The viewing room had no windows or overhead lights but was lit by the soft glow from several standing lamps along the walls. The walls themselves were cream-colored, and many people either stood near or leaned against them, some in conversation while others silently reflected. At the front of the square room, on a wooden stand, was a casket draped by the American flag.

Lester exchanged nods with family members he hadn't seen in a while, waved at the friends and family who acknowledged his presence, and walked directly to the casket. He saw his parents to the right of it. Harold was glaring at him. His mother, her skeleton figure covered in a black dress, was pretending to look at a floral arrangement nearby, fawning over a dried-up leaf and feverishly running her hand through thinning red hair. Lester did not turn his head all the way to look at them but saw them out of the corner of his eye and kept walking.

When he arrived at the casket, he stopped and felt his shoulders being weighed down by the truth. Anger and sadness joined forces to pull his head and eyes to the floor, and he was reaching out without realizing it. He knew the casket was empty, but that only enraged him more. He wanted to throw the flag to the side, rip the lid off, and shout to all of them that it was a lie. That Dillon wasn't dead; he was missing. Lester wished he could go back to that abandoned road for just one more second, to stop that moment from happening.

"Do you just have to be late for everything?"

Lester closed his eyes and shook his head. He recognized his father's voice right away, but he did not look at him. "My flight just got in. I flew in from Hudson, you know."

Harold tapped him on the shoulder. "Hey. A whole bunch of these people flew or drove in from the same place. They managed to get here in time to pay proper respects."

Lester did look up then. He kept his mouth closed but rubbed the front of his teeth with his tongue. Breath steamed out of his nostrils, which he did not stop from flaring. Harold had gotten older, Lester noticed. His glasses were thicker, and they pressed into the man's pink flesh so that the skin around his temples bulged. White and silver hair fell over his gnarled ears, though the thick hair on top was slicked back.

"Drove here in cars I've kept running, old man," Lester said after steadying his breathing. "Half of them mooching off me is the reason I have to spend so much time at work. Bunch of vampires." He ignored Harold's gaping mouth and continued. "And what do they know about proper respects? Ask any of them right now when's the last time they talked to Dillon. Better yet, ask them what his middle name was or what was his favorite color."

"You too good to take care of family, that it?" Harold asked.

Lester scoffed. "Too good to *be* in this family."

Harold turned red. "I got a mind to take my belt off and treat you like a little boy, since you want to act like one."

Lester faced the casket again, shaking his head. "Yeah. You go ahead and try that, old man." He took a deep breath and pointed at the casket. "Why are are we having a dog and pony show? There's no body in there."

"Well, just what are we supposed to do?" Harold asked. "They didn't recover your brother's body. Need I remind you that he was blown up in *your* war?"

Lester snapped his head to the right and stared into his father's eyes. "It's not my war, you coward. Get away from me."

In his peripheral, he saw his mother, Carol, approaching. She was walking quickly and stormed up to him, shoving a bony finger in his face. She had one hand planted on her hip.

"Don't you dare talk to your father like that again," she said.

Lester gently pushed her hand down and away with the back of his forearm. "Father? Now you two want to be parents?" He rolled his eyes and turned away. "Hey, Mom." He didn't mean it to be as sarcastic as it sounded, but he had no intention of apologizing either.

"Oh, you're just gonna come in here and be childish, huh? Don't you 'Hey, Mom' me, young man."

Lester turned on his heels. "Don't you 'young man' me. Are you kidding me? I'm here for my brother's funeral. You two can fuss at me after this is over; but for the last time, I did not convince Dillon to join the army. He was a grown man, and he made his own choices. Blame Bin Laden and those towers getting knocked down, not me."

Carol slapped him across the face, and he turned to the side with the force. The sound echoed throughout the room; and when he looked up, everyone was silent and staring at them. From a group of three women, one walked forward. She was struggling to stay balanced on her heels, but Lester knew it wasn't from lack of wear. This was his aunt Donna, and she was rarely far from a cocktail.

"I wish you three would keep your voices down and act civil this once," she said when she was close enough to whisper. Most of the onlookers had resumed their conversations, but a few still gawked.

"Go get another gin and tonic, Donna," Lester said and waved his hand at her.

"Watch your mouth, boy," Harold said.

"Or what, old man?" Lester took a step forward, bumping into his mother. "Come on. Hit me. Try it because I promise you this, coward: those days are over." He seethed, air steaming out of his nostrils. His jaw trembled, and his eyes burned. "Lift one hand," he said through clenched teeth, "and it'll be the last."

"Folks, I'm going to have to ask you to lower your voices or step outside," someone said from the side. Lester turned and saw a middle-aged woman with jet black hair in a business suit. She was wearing a name tag that said Beverly Haas. She was standing with her legs close together and her hands clasped in front of her waist.

Lester wiped his eyes and shook his head. "No need for that. I'm clearly the problem here, so I'll just go outside."

"Got that right," Harold said. Lester started to walk toward the exit, ignoring the comment. "You planning on coming to the funeral?"

Lester spun on his heels and took one giant step toward his father. He grabbed him by the front of his button down shirt and put his face an inch away from Harold's. "You listen, and I mean listen good, Harold. Out of the people standing here, there's only one person that should be at this funeral, and it's me. I'm the one he talked to. I'm the one who listened to him crying on the phone after his first firefight. I'm the one who gave up sleep to talk him down after seeing all the dead bodies. What do you even know about your son in the past five years?"

Harold shoved Lester away. Tears rimmed his eyes. "That's your fault. You took him from us! Your brother is dead because of you."

Lester didn't think before he had his fist in the air, but it was stopped before it could connect with his father's trembling jaw. A gruff voice told him to calm down, and then he was being pulled from both sides with his arms restrained by strong hands. He struggled to get free, to launch the attack on his father he knew he would regret. Knew he wanted to unleash.

He looked left and right, saw that one of the men was Jeremy. The other was his younger cousin, Dewey. Dewey was taller than Jeremy and wider. Lester hadn't seen him in a couple of years but had heard he was a displaced lathe operator back East. He and Jeremy shoved Lester through the doorway of the viewing room, then down the hall, and finally out the main door to the outside. They thrust him forward and let go of his arms.

"What's wrong with you, Les?" Dewey asked, yelling.

Lester turned around and straightened his shirt. "Get a job, Dewey. You, too, Jeremy, and quit mooching off people." He turned and walked toward the curb. He was about to pull his phone out of his pocket to call a cab when he was filled with regret. He stopped, looked up, and closed his eyes. After a moment to collect his thoughts, he turned around and walked back.

"I'm sorry," he said.

Dewey and Jeremy both looked at him sternly with their arms folded. After a moment, they started laughing and hunched over. Before long, they both had hands on their knees and were laughing out loud. Lester looked around, eyed them curiously, and held his hands up. They carried on for about ten seconds, and then stood up. Their laughter subsided with sighs that left them smiling.

"Shoot, man," Jeremy said. "I'd have hit the old man, too."

Dewey nodded. "Yep, but we couldn't let you do that."

"Course not, man. Not at your brother's funeral."

Dewey tapped Jeremy on the shoulder. "You do need to get a job."

Jeremy touched his chest with the fingertips of both hands. "Me? Man, what about you? At least I got an interview this week. Son, the last time you had an interview was in the county jail." He put his hand on Dewey's shoulder. "Little Cuz, we call that an interrogation."

Dewey slapped his hand away and laughed. "Shut up, moron. Where's this 'interview' of yours?" He made air quotes with his fingers. "Somewhere real high class, I bet. Chuck's Chicken Shack?"

Jeremy shook his head. "Nope, Burger World." They both laughed, and Jeremy mimicked a fast food drive-thru employee. He held one hand to his ear, pretending he was wearing a headset. "Can I take your order?"

"You got the job!" Dewey yelled through a burst of laughter.

Lester watched all of this with wide eyes, shaking his head. "Are you two yahoos done?"

His cousins were slapping each other on the back and wiping their eyes, but they looked at him and nodded. "Yeah. That was good," Jeremy said.

"So, other than the triumphant victory of a grown man with two kids getting a job flipping fries part-time, anything new?"

They both looked at him, then to each other, and back to Lester. "Nope," they said in unison.

Lester ran his fingers through his hair. "Look, boys. I'm tired, and I don't feel like calling a cab. Can y'all give me a ride?"

"Sure," Dewey said and waved Lester over. "Come on."

Lester walked over and let Dewey put his arm around his shoulders while Jeremy hurried inside to get Lester's suitcase, yelling over his shoulder that he was doing so.

"This is embarrassing," Dewey said, leaning his head down toward Lester's ear, "but I'm kind of short right now. Think you can spot me ten for gas?" Lester rolled his eyes and was about to respond when he heard the door to the funeral home open and then the sound of the rollers of his suitcase against the concrete sidewalk.

"Asked you for gas money, didn't he?" Jeremy asked as he came up beside them. The three of them walked down the sidewalk, Jeremy pulling Lester's suitcase and Dewey's arm around Lester's shoulders.

"You know he did," Lester said.

"Should've called a cab," Jeremy said.

"Would've been cheaper," Dewey said, and they all laughed.

CHAPTER SIXTEEN

Khufia

THE PRISONER WOKE TO A brilliant light radiating in front of him. He moved his arms to shield his eyes, but the bite of the braces against his wrists and the sharp click of his chains reminded him where he was. He kept his head low but did his best to look forward. The source of the light was in the middle of the room, beaming out from a solitary figure. The prisoner's eyes gradually adjusted to the light, and he looked up. At the same time, the light began to fade.

After a few moments, he was looking at a tall, incredibly muscular man with blond hair and golden eyes. The man was neither smiling nor frowning. Simply there. He wore a robe that was girded about the waist with a sword belt. From the side of the belt hung a long sword in a bejeweled scabbard. The man kept his hands at his side.

"Why are you in these chains, Draven?"

The prisoner did not respond, for he was mesmerized by the melodic voice of the man. His words seemed to ride an invisible wind but also held the power of thunder.

The man tilted his head. "How has this fate befallen you?"

The prisoner leaned back. "Who are you?"

This brought a smile to the man's face, a not-unpleasant sight, which revealed teeth too white and perfect to be real. He took a long, slow breath, and exhaled it with a great heave of his chest and patience etched on his face.

"Your task was simple, Draven," the man said. "How could you be so careless?"

The prisoner shook his head. "Why are you calling me that?"

"It is your name." The man's tone was somewhere between a statement and a question and sounded smug.

"Who are you? Where did you come from? And how do you know my name?"

The man took a step forward and peered down at the prisoner. "All you had to do was show the human the things he needed to see. Then return and report. Simple."

"I don't know what you're talking about. What human? What things?"

The man squatted, making sure to angle the sword so that it stuck out behind him, rather than jab into the floor. "But you have grown weak, as I warned you would happen. Weak because you crave to be with the humans. Long to speak with them and heal their wounds, but that is not your place."

The prisoner growled. "If you know who I am, stop playing games, and get me out of here."

The man stood and shook his head. "No. There is a great battle coming, and there is no room for such weakness. Though it pains me to see you this way, it is time for you to learn this lesson once and for all, Draven."

"Who are you?"

"You really don't know, do you?"

The prisoner shook his head. "I don't know who I am, or where I am, or what's going on."

The man blasted a short puff of air through his nostrils. "I cannot reveal anything to you. There is one in this place who can restore you, but she must do so of her own volition so that she can be free of her burden. And there is another who must conquer his trial of faith. My orders are to leave you here that all of this may come to pass."

The prisoner looked up. "Yara? The girl? And Ibrahim? The old man?"

Light began to form behind the man. "I may not say anything further."

"Wait." The prisoner tried to stand, but the light was instantly so bright that it blinded him and so intense that it forced him to hunch down and turn his face away.

"Your time of restoration draws near, Draven." The man's voice spoke through the light. "But you will be faced with a choice, one that will have a great impact on what is to come. Dark forces are gathering. The war is upon us."

The prisoner shouted. "What war? What dark forces?"

The light blinked out. Gone in an instant.

The prisoner was alone in the darkness, the name "Draven" echoing through his mind.

Huron, near Rhodes

Lester sat on a tall stool facing the bar in the hotel lounge. Behind the counter, against the wall, light sparkled off the glass of myriad colored liquor bottles. In front of him, a few stools down, was a beer tap with several local and national brand logos on the pull levers of the taps. He gave a nod to the bartender, a man wearing a white, button down shirt and slacks. The bartender returned the nod with a two-fingered wave. Lester turned back to look at the bottles and swallowed, trying to drown out the sound of laughter of the other patrons sparsely scattered about the smoky lounge.

He closed his eyes and tried to push away the thoughts that had been swarming his mind since he'd gotten in the truck with Dewey and Jeremy. Although it had been good to catch up with his cousins on the ride to the hotel, the fight with his parents, the empty casket of his brother, and the encounter on the plane waited to haunt him once he was alone. After checking in, he'd gone to the bar—not to drink, but to avoid being alone. Alone meant time to think. Time to think meant memories. Haunting memories. Memories that kept him awake, kept him on the abandoned road outside Abu Ghraib.

"What can I get for you, sir?"

Lester looked from the bottles to the bartender, who was now standing in front of him and to the left. "Uh, I, uh. What?" He swallowed and then let his mouth droop open.

"Can I get you something to drink?" The bartender leaned his head forward and raised his eyebrows.

"Oh," Lester said. "Sorry. Can I get a . . ." His voice trailed off as he scanned the bottles. "A, um . . . how about a . . . "

"Are you alright, sir?"

Lester shook his head and then looked at the bartender. "Yeah." He nodded. "Of course."

The bartender bit his bottom lip and nodded. "Okay. How about I get you a water; and if you think of what you want, just wave."

"Perfect." Lester offered a thin-lipped smile.

The bartender walked over to the beer tap, grabbed a glass from under the counter, and filled it with a plain, black tap. He set the full water glass in front of Lester with a small, square napkin and told him to enjoy. Lester thanked him and grabbed the glass with his fingertips.

He took a sip of the water and set it down, unsatisfied, and caught a glimpse of someone leaning against the bar out of the corner of his eye. He glanced to his right and saw a short, olive-skinned man in a denim jacket. He scrunched his eyes, wondering how bad a person's circulation had to be to wear a jacket in Huron.

The man raised his hand and called out to the bartender, "Excuse me!" He looked at Lester and gave him a curt smile. "How you doing?"

"Hey," Lester said.

He looked back to the bartender. "Hey, buddy."

Lester tried to avoid staring, but he was clearly failing, which became obvious when he folded his arms on the bar and leaned toward him.

"Sorry. I tend to get a bit impatient when people aren't listening, even when I'm trying everything I can to get their attention. I get that from my boss." He unfolded his arms and stood up. "I focus on what I want and pursue it, you know? That means I stay distraction-free."

"Nothing wrong with that." Lester looked away and took another sip of his water. He was relieved to see the bartender walking over.

"Yes, sir?" The bartender set his hand on the bar with a slap.

"How you doing? I called in an order."

"Name?"

"Gregory."

"Yep. I think it just came up. Be right back, okay?"

"Thanks."

Lester fought the urge to look at him when the bartender walked away, but he saw him sliding toward him. He turned his head and saw that he was facing him with one elbow propped on the bar.

"What about you?"

"Huh?"

"Are you distracted?"

Lester snorted. "Do I know you?"

He shook his head and smiled. "Nope. Name's Gregory."

"So I heard."

"Well, now you know me, but you didn't answer my question."

Lester clenched his jaw and took a breath, exhaling through his nostrils. "I'm just trying to drink my water. Okay?"

Gregory smiled. "Exactly." He pointed at Lester's glass. "It's a hotel restaurant; so either you're staying here, or you're really pathetic. You look like a smart guy, so I'll give you the benefit of the doubt and say you're the former. And since there's bottled water in the rooms and a drinking fountain in the lobby, I'm going out on a limb and guessing you're thinking about ordering something else." He shrugged. "Either that, or you've got something on your mind."

Lester took another sip and made an exaggerated effort to wipe his lip. "And if it's both?"

The bartender approached from the left and set a plastic bag on the bar. "Here you go, sir." He held up the receipt that was attached to the bag and inspected it. "Looks like you paid online, so you're all set."

Gregory pulled the bag toward himself and handed the bartender a twenty dollar bill. "Thank you. Sorry for being rude when I called you over earlier. Sometimes, I lash out when I'm frustrated. And then sometimes, I make rash decisions, but I like to make good on my mistakes."

The bartender took the money carefully and looked at Gregory with one eyebrow raised. "Um, yeah. No problem. Have a good one." He looked at Lester and tilted his chin upward. "Still good?"

Lester looked at his water, then over at Gregory. He shrugged and cocked his head toward the bar.

"I'm fine," Lester said. The bartender told him okay and walked to the end of the bar where an elderly couple sat. Lester looked back at Gregory.

"Is it?" he asked.

"What?"

"Is it both?"

Lester snickered. "Why am I talking to you, again?"

Gregory shrugged. "Why not?"

"Because I don't know you."

Gregory shrugged again. "I told you my name. Not my fault you didn't reciprocate."

Lester tapped the bar with his fingertips. "What color are your eyes?"

"Come again?"

He turned and looked at Gregory, whose eyes were not the electrified onyx color he expected. They were ocean blue and rimmed with an almost golden color. "Nevermind," he said and turned back to the front.

"Okay," Gregory said. "So, is it both?"

Lester looked straight ahead and sighed. "I don't know, honestly." He did not look at him when he responded.

"Well, man, if that's the case, there's nothing behind that bar that'll help you clear your head. And I think you'll find that anything in those bottles you drink will only make those memories you're running from get bigger."

Lester's eyes opened wide. He put both hands down on the bar and turned as fast as he could. But he was gone. So was the food. He looked around and then, not seeing the stranger, stood up and stepped away from the bar. He was about to walk away when the bartender came back, holding a coffee cup with a plastic lid.

"You know where he went?"

"Who?" Lester asked.

The bartender pointed at the spot where Gregory had been standing. "That guy. I forgot part of his order, and I was trying to get it out here before he took off." He looked around. "What? Did he vanish?"

Lester held up his hands and shook his head, slowly.

The bartender's shoulders slumped, and he groaned. "Well, that's that, I guess. Hey, do you want this? Doesn't look like you put much of a dent in that water."

Lester didn't respond at first, but then he shrugged and gave a half-hearted nod.

The bartender held up his hand as if waiting for Lester to come forward; but when he didn't walk over, the bartender let his hand drop to his side with a slap against his leg. "Okay. I'll just set it here, man. Are you sure you're alright?"

Lester swallowed and nodded. The bartender shook his head and walked away, mumbling something about his shift ending soon. Once the bartender walked away, Lester took measured steps up to the bar. He looked around again and then picked up the cup. The aroma coming through the lid was familiar, so he brought it to his nose for closer inspection.

Chai tea.

Quinn pressed the off button on the television remote and then tossed it on the coffee table in front of the couch where she sat. She crossed her legs and then started tapping her knee with her fingertips.

She resisted for almost thirty seconds before picking up her phone and checking her messages. The message she'd sent Lester was there with no response beneath it.

"Stop looking at it, Quinn," she said to herself and laid the phone in her lap.

She resumed tapping her knee and started bouncing her foot. That lasted for a few seconds, and then she held her hands up in front of her face and yelled. She buried her face in her hands and growled. Dropped her hands in to her lap with a slap. Stood.

"This is crazy," she said and put her hands on her hips. "You're a young woman with the whole world in front of you. Why are you sitting here stressing out over a guy who broke your heart and can't even return a text message?"

She rubbed her forehead.

"I'm calling his mom." She bent down and snatched the phone up. As she started going through her contacts, she talked to herself. "You're completely out of your mind, Quinn. Certified lunatic." She found the number for Lester's mother and pressed the call button. She continued talking to herself as she raised the phone to her ear. "Just randomly call your ex-fiancé's mother; that's not weird at all."

"Hello?" The voice of Carol Sharp was clear, and she sounded surprised.

"Oh," Quinn said, stammering. "Mrs. Sharp? Sorry. This is Quinn." She paused, waited for a response, but there was none. "Quinn Griffin?"

"I know who you are, Quinn," Carol said. Her voice was flat and sounded tired.

"Oh, right. Of course." Quinn tried to force a smile, then wondered why she was worrying about smiling on the phone. "How are you?"

Carol sighed. "I'm fine. How are you?"

"Good!" Quinn bit down on her lip, instantly regretting sounding so excited. "I'm . . . sorry it's been so long."

"Oh, no need to apologize. It would have been awkward, us trying to talk with the way things turned out between you and Lester."

"Well, it's nice to hear your voice, Carol. And I want you to know how sorry I am about Dillon. I wish I could be there to—"

"What can I do for you, Quinn?"

Quinn closed her eyes and turned her face to the ceiling. She took a deep breath before responding.

"I wanted to extend my condolences, and I was wondering if Lester had made it safely. Will he be staying with you until the funeral is over?"

Carol huffed. "Yes, he's here. No, he will not be staying with Harold and me."

A shuffling sound came through, as if Carol had dropped the phone. There was an angry exchange of voices on the other end, and Quinn pulled the phone away from her ear. When the noise had settled, she put it back against her ear and furrowed her eyebrows.

"Quinn?" A man's voice. Harold. Lester's father.

"Yes?" She hated how timid her voice was, but Harold Sharp had always had that effect on her.

"Lester's not here. Frankly, I don't care where he is, and I'd prefer if you didn't call. Lester made his choices, and none of those were to be a part of this family."

Quinn's mouth opened in shock as she listened.

"And last I checked, you and him aren't together anymore, so I'm not really understanding why we'd need to speak at all. Now, we don't have a problem with you, but we'd like to be left alone. Goodbye, Quinn."

The phone went silent.

Quinn pulled it away from her ear and stared at the blinking *Call Ended* displayed on the screen. She stood that way for a long time, tears welling in her eyes, and then she went to her list of recent calls and dialed her mother's number. It was going to be a long night.

CHAPTER SEVENTEEN

LESTER STOOD IN THE CORNER of the vestibule of the funeral home, away from the few stragglers who hadn't gone to their seats yet. He rubbed his shoulder, which had been aching since not long after he had woken up. The funeral director had just walked away, which was a distraction from the accusing stares in the waiting area, but now he was acutely aware of them He checked his phone and cleared some notifications. A text message from Dave asking about the status of the insurance claim and their jobs. An email from the insurance adjuster asking to schedule an appointment. Nothing new from Quinn, thankfully.

It was strange to see family members who lived so close to him but hadn't talked to him in such a long time. No one visited him, but he also made no effort to see them. He felt an odd mixture of sadness and guilt. He tried his best to ignore it by focusing on the picture of Dillon on a tripod stand with information about his life and a placard next to it. The picture was old, one from before Dillon joined the military, which Lester tried not to look at because it made him angry. He glanced through the double doors and saw the American flag draped over the casket; and only a few minutes ago, he had thanked the funeral detail from a nearby military installation for coming to render honors to their fallen brother. Brothers by fire, not blood.

The door opened, and a large man with a long beard and a ponytail walked through. He was wearing a black, leather vest that perfectly matched his riding leathers, and the helmet in his right hand removed all doubt that he had just gotten off a motorcycle.

Leroy Sharp. Lester's uncle. Better known as Rhino. The man's propensity for fighting and preferred method of attack had given him the name years ago. Everyone cut off their hushed conversations and hurried out of the vestibule when they saw him. Rhino laughed. He pretended to lunge at Dewey, who had been not-so-discreetly asking another cousin for gas money. Dewey jumped back, then shot an angry look at Rhino before quickly stepping away.

"How 'bout it, boy?" Rhino said in his rich, deep voice. He walked over and scooped Lester up into a bear hug, squeezing him until Lester could barely breathe.

"Hey, Rhino," Lester said when he was back on the ground and freed from the big man's embrace. He absently rubbed at his shoulder again.

"What're you doing out here all by yourself?" Rhino tapped him on the right shoulder as he talked.

Lester was thankful he hadn't hit his left, but the "tap" from Rhino hurt almost as much as the aching. "You know why."

Rhino stroked his beard with a gloved hand. "Don't make any sense, boy. I know a bunch moved out this way when jobs got scarce back East, but ain't there still a lot of family your way?"

Lester nodded and put his hands in his pockets. "Just because they're nearby doesn't mean they want to talk to me."

Rhino scoffed. "Ah, shut up. I know my brother's an idiot, and half the family done took his side; but you're just as wrong for cutting everybody off the past couple years."

"Can we not do this right now, Rhino?"

The big man shrugged. "Just call 'em how I see 'em."

"I know. It's just—"

Rhino waved his free hand in front of his face. "Forget it. You talked to that girl of yours, Quinn?"

Lester rolled his eyes. "Come on, man. It's been two years since we broke up."

"I know, and that's a two-year-old tail-whipping I owe you. Boy, how'd you manage to mess that up?" He looked up and waved at someone, then looked back to Lester.

"It's complicated," Lester said, again rubbing his shoulder.

Rhino scowled. "No, Lester. No, it's not. Wasn't no breakup either, boy. You did that girl wrong." He looked up. "They're about to start." He walked off without further comment

Lester waited until Rhino had found his seat before entering the chapel. It was a small room with wooden pews in rows of five on both sides and a large center aisle that led to Dillon's casket, which was perpendicular to the aisle. Behind the casket was a raised platform and a small podium. Lester took his seat near the front in a seat marked with his name as a man he had not met stood behind the podium and began to pray.

Everyone had turned away or looked down when Lester had entered, which was fine with him. Clearly, Harold and Carol had been busy after he'd left yesterday, convincing everyone that Lester was the prodigal son and the cause of their stress for the last few years. They were the innocent victims of his soulless campaign to ruin them. As he sat down, he tried his best to ignore it all—even the canned prayer from the man who obviously worked for the funeral home—and fixated on the casket.

The flag covering it had been ironed so that there were no creases from folds, which Lester thought was a bit much, but he dismissed that thought with another: *Why have an empty casket and go through the trouble and expense when they could just as easily have a memorial?* The stars on the flag made him think of the American flag patch on Dillon's shoulder, the one he was wearing in the armored vehicle the day he died. The blue field that was covered in white stars was darker than Dillon's eyes, but it reminded Lester of them all the same.

The pain in his shoulder was becoming unbearable, and it felt like it might be going numb. He began rubbing it again as another of his uncles, Teddy, walked up to the podium and unfolded a piece of paper taken out of his suit jacket. Lester had to take short breaths, and he tried to keep them quiet as Teddy read through the eulogy. He didn't want to hear about Dillon's life in that moment, especially from people who had barely talked to his brother in the past five years, so he let his mind wander.

He thought about stealing cookie dough while his mother was baking on Christmas Eves and Thanksgivings. He thought about chasing Dillon down the street in a game of tag and never being able to reach him. Dillon was the athletic one, had always been good at sports. The star running back for Olympia High School, Dillon had led them to a state championship in his senior year. They'd celebrated with ice cream and friends. Quinn had been there.

Lester suppressed a groan and rolled his eyes. He remembered Quinn's text message from the day before and mentally berated himself for not responding. Of course, he wasn't sure if he should be upset with himself. What did he hope to accomplish by re-establishing communication with her? Was he in a place where he could even have a friend? Someone he'd been more than friends with before?

He pushed the thoughts away, feeling guilty for thinking about something other than Dillon. As he focused back on the eulogy, he heard everyone laughing softly. He had missed it, but he knew Teddy had probably just talked about Dillon's facial expressions. Dillon was always making faces that made everyone laugh. Lester thought of one and was about to join in the laughter, when he felt a shooting pain so sharp in his shoulder that he clutched it and gasped out loud.

He glanced around and saw that many people were staring at him with angry faces. He held up his hand and mouthed, "Sorry." Just as he had settled back in the pew, and they were no longer staring, he felt another shooting pain and yelled. He immediately heard a murmuring in the chapel, and his father stood up from the pew two rows in front of him. Harold stomped down the aisle toward Lester. When he was within hand's reach, he bent down and put his finger close to his face.

"I don't know what your problem is, Lester, but you will not make this moment about you. Quit making a scene."

Lester grimaced and felt sweat around his collar and on his forehead. "Who's standing up and talking right now, Harold?" He clutched his shoulder.

Without warning, Harold was pushed back by gloved hands, and Lester saw Rhino's hulking frame in the next moment.

"Harold, go sit down. You make me sick the way you treat this boy."

"Back off, Leroy," Harold said as he straightened his suit jacket.

"No, you back off." He shoved Harold again, this time with one hand. "This is your son's funeral, you selfish piece of trash. Y'all want to kill each other, do it later. But right now, I'm not gonna put up with either one of you disrespecting the memory of my nephew. Now sit, or I'll put you in a casket right next to your boy up there." He pointed to the casket.

Lester barely heard the exchange. He was beginning to see through a cloudy, transparent blackness, and the pain in his shoulder had forced him to his side. Sweat was pouring from his skin profusely, and he was wheezing. He managed to force himself upright again, and he saw his uncle's eyebrows furrowed together.

"Lester? What's wrong?"

He could not respond except for grunts. He saw Harold shove past Rhino and kneel down.

"Lester? What are you doing? What's happening?"

Lester felt the worst shooting pain yet and screamed. He fell out of the pew at Rhino's feet and balled his body up. The voices around him became muffled, and he saw feet and legs coming toward him through the black cloud. The room felt like it was spinning, and he squeezed his eyes shut.

He heard his father shouting for someone to call an ambulance, and then he heard nothing.

Khufia

Morane stalked through the village, slipping through the shadows of the huts and watching the people go about their business. It was late, and they would all soon be slumbering. Morane wished he had free reign to carry out the desires of his heart and cut all of them down in their sleep, but that was not possible. He took comfort in the fact that the human was out of commission for the time being. His torture of Lester Sharp was temporarily on hold, but the pleasure at seeing the man at complete odds with his family and then falling to a heart attack from the stress was pure delight.

Something more pressing was at hand, for the moment. Morane was keenly aware that Draven was beginning to notice he was not like the other humans. He suspected that the watcher may even begin to suspect that he was not human at all. In any case, his memory would return, eventually, and their centuries-long battle would resume soon enough. He did not despise that truth, but he wished to take advantage of the situation for just a little while longer and see how much damage he could inflict on his enemy in his current state.

He stopped and leaned against one of the more well-built huts as he contemplated these things. He wanted Lester and the potential influence he would have over the man to be silenced forever, but his hatred for Draven outweighed that at the moment. Never, in thousands of years, had the demon had an advantage over the watcher. He wanted to hurt him beyond repair, to damage his psyche on an immortal level. Draven had seen enough death and devastation to last for eternity, but he was built to withstand the horror of it. In his current state, he was weak, almost human, and Morane wanted him to stay that weak.

Now there was a new problem. Draven had been visited, but not by the old man. Ibrahim was missing. Draven could find him easily, but he dismissed the thought. Orac had been in the village. Morane felt the presence of the archangel. Traces of his holiness permeated the village. The scent sickened Morane.

He pushed himself off the wall of the hut and clenched his fists. He had no way of knowing if Draven's commander would remain or leave for some other matter in other parts of the world. In either case, the damage had likely been done, and Draven would be restored soon. He stretched his neck and felt it pop, and then he resumed his calculated stalking through the unsuspecting village.

It was time to visit Yusef.

PART THREE

NO ONE HAS EVER TRULY been alone. Many feel the weight of loneliness, the burden of solitude, which is only felt in the intangible senses of the mind. Perception rules the heart, enslaving thought. Perception stands in the midst of a multitude but sends the hollow cry of loneliness to the soul in need of companionship.

Alone becomes normal, accepted as the deserved fate of the depressed, distraught, and discouraged. The despondent wanderers wilting in the clutches of loneliness soon fade into a shell of an existence, simply existing from day to day in the mundane remnants of life worth living.

Alone is a wasteland.

There is no communication in the wilds of the lonely. No joy or hope to be had. Sunlight turns to darkness. Warmth turns cold. The hand of help is not ignored; it is never seen. The door of escape is hidden in woeful cyclones of sorrow. Broken feet trod unbeaten paths no map has ever marked.

But no one has ever truly been alone.

Even in the desert, there is life surrounding the deserted. Even on the highest peak, the wind touches the stranded. Alone is not a place or a person, but a perception. All walk in the presence of life. All walk through the creation, ignorant or aware of the Creator, and only those not enslaved by their own deceived minds see His footsteps beside them.

I walked in ignorance for years, feeling the weight of my perceived solitude. Blinded by the darkness of self-inflicted sorrow. But I was never in darkness, never isolated. As I cursed the creation with my angry steps, I failed to acknowledge the One who had given me the path I walked and the feet with which I walked. I hurt because I was alone, blaming that same Creator for abandoning me.

Until my eyes were opened. Then I saw the prints of His blessed feet beside, before, and behind me. I realized that my path was not unbeaten. It had been cleared by the hand of mercy and marked by the hand of love. All the years I had spent speaking into the void were lies, for my words had not gone into an abyss of my own making but into the ears of a loving Father and ever-present Savior. He had heard every word and recorded it.

I was not alone. And I never will be.

- Lester Sharp

CHAPTER EIGHTEEN

Huron

LESTER HEARD HIS NAME BEING called from a distant place he could not see. There was an echo, and he wondered how he had ended up in a cave. It was a woman's voice, and she called his name again. He tried to open his eyes, but his eyelids were so heavy. And dry. They felt gritty. He squeezed them and tried to shake his head. The woman continued calling to him, and the voice grew closer. Not a cave. It was a room, and it was warm.

A hospital.

He finally got his eyes open and blinked several times. Blurred streaks of colors began to merge together, slowly coming into focus. He tried to take a deep breath, but the air tasted strange. It was almost stale, and he realized it was coming through a tube in his nose. He felt it then, the intrusion of plastic in his nostrils. To his left, standing over him, was a short woman of Indian descent. She wore a white lab coat, could not have been more than five feet tall, and had raven black hair.

"Mr. Sharp?" she said in a heavy accent.

He managed a nod and exhaled. "Where am I?"

"You're in the Huron Emergency Center, sir," the doctor said. Her voice was strong and melodic. He would have expected a tiny voice from such a small woman, but she clearly carried herself well and commanded a strong presence. "My name is Doctor Mehta. You've suffered a mild heart attack, Mr. Sharp."

Lester tried to smile. "Didn't feel very mild."

"I'm sure it didn't." She flipped a page on the chart she held and studied it. "You're doing much better, and your levels are back to normal, but a man having a heart attack at your age is quite concerning."

Lester frowned. "I've been under a lot of stress lately."

Doctor Mehta made a "hmm" sound and flipped the page back down. "I'm sorry to hear that, Mr. Sharp. Be that as it may, stress is not usually the only factor in such cases. I need to run more tests before I can let you go." Lester opened his mouth to protest, but she held up her hand. "I promise not to hold you longer than I need to, Mr. Sharp, but your well-being is my first concern."

Lester had raised up on his pillow but settled back down. He nodded. "Alright. How long will these tests take?" He wanted to get out of the bed, rip the tube from his nose and the IV from his arm, shove the doctor out of his way, and run to the graveyard where his brother's empty casket was now in the ground.

"No more than a day, hopefully."

Lester closed his eyes and bit back a nasty remark. "Okay." He opened his eyes and gave the doctor a weak smile. "Thank you, doctor."

"I'll be back around to check on you soon, Mr. Sharp. Try to get some rest."

She left the room before he could say anything else, and Lester took the opportunity to absorb his surroundings. The room was small and well-lit. Despite the overhead lights in the room being turned off, the sunlight shining through the large window to the right brought in soft, natural light and warmth. Beneath the window was a cheaply made, wooden chair with a seventies-era pattern on the vinyl cushion. He couldn't imagine sitting in it, but he doubted anyone had done so since he had been there. Directly to his right was the standard hospital rigging of monitors, oxygen, and IV stand all hooked to the numerous wires and cords connected to him. There was a television mounted on the wall above the closet to his front, and he assumed his clothes were in there.

He thought about tearing out the IV himself, unstrapping the Velcro heart monitor around his bicep, and yanking out the oxygen tube. He was feeling much better, and the pain in his shoulder was gone. Getting to his clothes would be easy. He knew there would be an argument with the doctors and nurses when he tried to leave, but Lester wanted nothing more than to get to the gravesite and pay his respects to Dillon. He knew the casket was empty, but the symbolism of the moment was important to him. For Lester, he'd already let Dillon down when he'd stood there, helpless, on that abandoned road during the glimpse.

"Finally awake, huh?"

Lester turned to the wide, glass doorway and saw a heavy-set woman with pale skin and dirty blonde hair pulled into a lazy ponytail enter the room. She wore a set of pink scrubs with hearts of various colors and sizes on it. She sauntered up to the bed, stopped, and put one hand on her hips. She had a beautiful and inviting smile with the whitest teeth Lester had ever seen.

"Thought you were gonna sleep all day," she said as if she'd known him all his life. "How're you feeling?"

Lester tried to shrug. "Okay, I guess." He cleared his throat, which suddenly felt dry. "How long have I been asleep?"

She cocked her head to the side and looked up. "Um, I'd say a good six hours. They said you were out when the ambulance brought you in, and that was late morning. It's about supper time right now. You hungry?"

Lester shook his head. "No. Is anyone waiting to see me?"

The nurse—her name tag said her name was Sheila—tried to hide a worried look and gave him a practiced smile, one she had probably used hundreds of times when delivering bad news to patients. She shook her head.

"You haven't had any visitors yet," she said. She snapped her fingers and spun around. "Oh, but your phone went off a couple times. I turned the ringer down, so it wouldn't disturb you." She walked over to a tray cart and pushed it over to him. She slid it next to the bed so that the tray was over his stomach and then handed him his phone, which was next to a pitcher of water. "There you go. Need anything else?"

"No, I'm fine. Did I need surgery?"

"No, sir. They gave you some blood thinners, injected them so they'd work fast, and you pretty much recovered on your own. They said it was a very minor attack, which is good."

"Felt major."

Sheila folded her arms. "I bet. You sure you're not hungry?"

Lester nodded. "I'm fine. Thanks, though."

"No problem. I'll check on you after a while."

He thanked her as she turned and left the room, and then he tapped the screen on his phone to bring up his notifications. There was another message from Dave. To Lester's relief, it wasn't asking about the shop. Dave wanted to know how the funeral had gone. There were two missed calls from Quinn and a text message asking him to call her.

He was strangely devoid of emotions when he read the text. He should have been excited or nervous, but he just stared at the phone indifferently. After a minute of inner debate, he pressed the call button and put the phone to his ear. It rang once before he heard her voice on the other end.

"Lester?"

"Hey, Quinn."

He heard her suck in air, and there was a crumpling noise as she repositioned the phone. "What happened? Where have you been all day?"

He pulled the phone away and stared at the screen to make sure he was talking to the right person. When he put it back to his ear, he spoke hesitantly.

"Why are you so concerned, Quinn? We haven't talked in two years."

"Does that mean I'm supposed to just hate you?"

"Do you?"

She snorted. "No, Les. Stop it. Look, I feel bad for what you're going through, and I cared about Dillon, too. You know that."

Lester suddenly felt hot. "Did you?"

"What?"

He pushed himself up to a sitting position with his free hand and felt a tug on the IV in his arm. "Did you really care about my brother? Huh? Because I'm pretty sure he didn't hear from you in the past two years. Matter of fact, neither did I."

"Les, calm down." Her breathing was heavy in the phone.

"Calm down?" Lester rolled his eyes and shook his head. He knew he should, but he couldn't control himself. "You know, it's real funny how everyone wants to talk about me being the reason I haven't been in touch with anyone for the past few years, but I'm pretty sure you and everyone else has my number. Case in point, you've been bugging me for the past two days."

"Bugging you?"

"Yeah, driving me nuts with these text messages like you really care." He growled. "What do you want from me, Quinn? I randomly bump into you after two years, and suddenly you're interested in talking to me again?"

"Les, I don't know what's going on, but this is crazy. You left me at the altar and disappeared. You didn't return my phone calls for six months, and now you want to say that I didn't try to get in touch with you?"

"Here we go," Lester said. "Let's bring up the past again."

"Again?" Quinn was nearly shouting now. "We never brought it up or talked about it, you jerk. You left me and didn't bother to give me an explanation. You know how embarrassing that was? And I try, after all this time, with no explanation from the guy who broke my heart, to show you kindness and be your friend when you really need a friend; and this is how you treat me."

"I don't need friends." Lester sat forward and let the pillow behind his back fall. "I don't need my family, you, or anyone else. None of you bothered to show up to this hospital. None of you really care."

"Hospital?"

"Just stop," Lester said, ignoring her. "All you want is me to say I'm sorry for what I did. Well, fine. I'm sorry, okay? How's that? Feel better? I'm a horrible person, which is why God decided to give me a heart attack at my own brother's funeral in the middle of a war with my dirtbag of a father."

Quinn fumbled with the phone, and Lester had to pull it away from his ear for a moment. "Heart attack? Les, where are you?"

He scoffed. "In the middle of a joke. God's telling it, and I'm the punchline. I should have never set foot back in that church. My life's been nothing but miserable since I pulled that stupid shirt out of my drawer. As soon as I get home, I'm burning it and all ties to that life."

There was a brief silence, and then Quinn's voice came through timidly. "All ties?"

Lester hesitated, trembling with anger and seething. "All."

The phone went silent. He pulled it down and looked at the screen. The words *Call Ended* were flashing in red. He tossed the phone on the tray and laid back, wondering what he had just done. Wondering if he cared.

Quinn sat on the edge of her couch, staring at her phone. Her thumb hovered over the button to redial Lester. She set the phone down on the coffee table next to her opened Bible and then picked it up again. Lester's number was still on the screen, and she thought about dialing it again. She wanted to hate him. Wanted to love him.

She cleared his number and searched through her recent calls for her mother's number and was about to call her but then set the phone down again. She picked up her Bible and set it in her lap. She started to read where she had let off in the book of Matthew. She read Matthew five, verse forty-four: "But I say unto you, Love your enemies, bless them that curse you, do good to them that hate you, and pray for them which despitefully use you, and persecute you."

She stopped reading, propped her elbows on the Bible, and dropped her chin into her open palms. "What are you doing, Quinn?"

She let out a deep breath, moved her elbows, closed the Bible, and set it on the coffee table. She sat back and pressed herself into the soft cushions and let her head fall back. The verse rolled around in her mind, jumbling together with Lester's words.

"I don't need you."

Khufia

Ibrahim sat on the dirt inside the scorched walls of his son's church. He had marveled at first that the building remained. While most of the buildings in the village were simple huts made of materials that would have burned instantly, the church had been constructed of mud bricks and other less-flammable material. The damage was final, but the building had not been completely disintegrated by the fire.

The effort made him think of Guleed. Always putting in more effort than anyone else. Yara was lying on her side in the dirt, asleep. He watched her upper body rise and fall rhythmically with her breathing. She reminded him of her mother, Nala. It had brought him so much joy when his daughter-in-law had been blessed with child, and the day Yara had been born was still fresh in his mind as one of the greatest days of his life.

That memory was painful then, soured by the image of Yara appearing near his hut, covered in the blood of her mother. Fear distorted the memory so much that he forced it away. His home was likely destroyed. Yusef would find them and slaughter them, probably in front of the entire village. He would die a coward, and the prisoner would suffer a similar fate. Yusef would find a way to kill the stranger.

The angel.

The whisper on the breeze had called the prisoner an angel. There had been light in Yara's eyes, an unseen hand on his shoulder. The voice had brought him comfort and assurance. They were safe at the church. He partially believed that. No one would return to that place. Even the scattered huts of the few who did not live in the relative safety of the village were empty, abandoned after the decimation of the church. Perhaps, he thought, he would keep Yara there for a few days, and then they would find a way to escape. Away from Khufia. Away from the country. They could find passage on a ship and go to Europe or America. They would be refugees, probably rejected and hated, but they would be alive.

Yara sat bolt upright and screamed. Ibrahim ignored the protests of his frail and cracking bones as he sprang to his feet and rushed to her side. He dropped down to his knees in front of her and grabbed her by the shoulders, calling out her name. Yara turned away from him and screamed louder. Ibrahim said her name again and made shushing sounds, but she continued to scream. She flailed her hands in the air and brought her knees to her chest.

"Yara, what is it?"

He said it several times to no avail, but then the girl stopped screaming and froze in place. Her head turned to face him, and her eyes were wide open. They looked through him, past him. He shook his head and was about to ask her what was going on when she reached out and grabbed his wrists. Her hands were cold, deathly cold.

He was no longer in the burned church. He was no longer on his knees. His eyes darted left and right. He spun in a circle. He looked down. Yara was there, covering her face with her hands. He looked up again and saw Nasteexo. She was in her house, and so were they.

Yusef's men filled Nasteexo's home. She was surrounded by the masked men. They were questioning her, asking where Ibrahim and the girl were. Her face was fixed, stern and strong. Her eyes were resolute. She glared at Yusef and told him she did not know where her brother was.

The tallest of the men, Yasir, slapped her across the cheek. She yelped and fell to the floor.

"What are you doing, Yasir?"

Yusef stepped forward, knelt down, and reached a hand toward her. She slapped the hand away and stood on her own, rubbing her face. Her eyes smoldered with anger, boring a hole through her attacker. Yusef held up his hands and stepped back.

"We do not wish to harm you, Nasteexo." Yusef spoke calmly, a twinge of frustration riding the edge of his voice.

"That is difficult to believe right now," she said, pulling her hand from her face and directing her anger toward Yusef.

He patted the air in front of him with his hands. "Yasir gets excited. He does not like being lied to."

She smiled. "He apparently does not like the truth either because that is what I am giving you."

Ibrahim watched all of this in amazement. Yara was clutching his leg, trembling. He patted her on the head and took the temporary pause in the stalemate between Nasteexo and Yusef to look around again. Yasir was to Nasteexo's left. He did not know the man to the right or behind her. Tahiil and Diric had been killed. These must be their replacements. He turned around, expecting to see the new Al-Shabaab

thugs Yusef had brought in from the city, but the other half of the
room was empty.

Almost.

As he scanned the darkness, he caught a flicker of light in a corner. He looked past it, then snapped his head back to confirm what
he thought he had just seen. The corner of the room was as black as
midnight on a moonless night. Onyx black, but it was shifting. A tiny,
almost undetectable flash of electricity surged in that onyx pool of
shadow, and then Ibrahim was sure his mind had abandoned him and
left him insane. His heart pounded, and he shook all over at what he
saw next.

White, glistening, fangs.

Ibrahim yelled and tried to scramble backward. He ended up falling
on his back because he was no longer standing. He had been on his
knees in the dirt. He looked up and saw the night sky and the edge of
the scorched walls of the church. Shifting to his side so that he could
push himself up, he saw the dirt floor and the remnants of what had
been a pulpit, draped in shadow. He rose to his hands and knees and
crawled to Yara. She was huddled into herself, covering her face with
her hands.

"Yara," he said when he was close enough to touch her. "Is what we
saw happening now?"

She rocked back and forth, whimpering, but did not respond. He
gently touched her head. "Please, Yara. Is Nasteexo in danger? Did that
already happen?"

She nodded but kept her face covered.

Fear crawled up and down his spine like spiders as he remembered the darkness, the electricity, and the fangs.

"You saw what was in the dark?"

She nodded and then looked up, letting her hands slide from her face to her lap. She looked into his eyes. Her bottom lip was quivering. "Taken."

It was the first word the girl had spoken in days, and the shock of hearing her speak kept Ibrahim from understanding what she meant, at first. But then it became clear.

"Yusef has taken Nasteexo?"

Yara nodded.

He swallowed down the biggest lump he had ever felt in his throat. "I know you are afraid, Yara. So am I. But we must go back to the village. The man who saved you? We must find a way to help him. Do you understand?"

She took a deep breath and let it out slowly. "Angel?"

He smiled and caressed her cheek. "Yes, my love. He is an angel, and we are going to save him so that he can save us."

He stood and then reached down to help her to her feet. For the first time, his fear did not cripple Ibrahim. He saw only his sister in his mind as he led Yara out of the church and back into the darkness.

The prisoner tugged violently at his chains and shouted. The sound echoed off the metal walls, coming back as laughter, mocking him. He could not die. He could not be free. The visit from the tall man who had emerged from the strange light was fresh on his mind.

Why had the man not simply helped him? Why had he spoken in mysteries, rather than plain speech?

"Your time of restoration draws near, Draven."

Was his name really Draven?

And what of the war and dark forces? What lesson was he supposed to learn? Hearing the man tell him that he was not human came as no surprise. Though he did not know who or what he was, the prisoner was sure that a human could not survive being shot, stoned, and beaten as many times as he had. Nor could a human see in the darkness or through walls.

He tugged at the chains again. The braces cut into his wrists. There were other things the man had said afflicting his mind. Who was the "she" that would restore him? Who was the one going through a trial of faith? The prisoner pulled against the chains, feeling weaker each time.

Morane stood outside the shipping crate, listening to the sound of the chains rattling and being pulled. He had feared that Draven would have been freed when he returned from overseeing Yusef's men taking the old man's sister. They would arrive soon and then use her to force Ibrahim out of hiding.

Draven's only remaining link to humanity was the old man. With him out of the picture, Draven would remain hopeless and lost to his true self long enough for Morane to finish with Lester. The demon was growing tired of waiting.

The chains rattled again. There was a loud knocking as they were pulled on hard, but not hard enough. Morane grinned and slipped into the spirit realm. He took flight and began speeding his way to Huron.

CHAPTER NINETEEN

Huron

LESTER DROPPED HIS PHONE INTO his lap and flopped his head back on the pillow. On the opposite wall from the bed, the small television was broadcasting a basketball game, but Lester didn't know who was playing. Didn't care either. He thought he felt a vibration, and he quickly snatched up his phone to see if anyone had texted him.

Nothing.

He had been awake for a couple of hours, and his phone was still silent. Not long after Quinn hung up on him, he'd texted Dave back with a simple message: "Things are crazy. Back in a couple days." Dave had replied with a message of encouragement, which annoyed Lester, so he'd just cleared it and not responded.

As he dropped the phone back to the thin, white blanket, an elderly man in a shirt and tie walked in. He carried a Bible under his arm, and he was smiling from ear to ear. Lester sighed. The man walked up to Lester's side, bringing the smell of aftershave with him.

"Hey there," the man said. He managed to hold his smile as he spoke, and he had the kind of voice that could make him a fortune as a voice actor for Western audiobooks.

Lester looked back to the game he wasn't watching. "Hey." Out of the corner of his eye, he saw the man turn to look at the T.V. and then back to Lester.

"Basketball fan?"

"Nope." Lester made the "p" sound pop as he spoke, doing his best to sound indifferent and annoyed.

The man cleared his throat. "Eh, me either. Don't watch much at all these days. I'm Gene, by the way. Gene Close. I'm the chaplain here."

Lester gave him a sideways glance and saw the man's hand extended. He sniffed dramatically and looked back to the game. "Kind of all preached out, Gene. If it's all the same."

It, apparently, was not. Gene grabbed a chair from beside the glass entrance and dragged it over, making a loud scraping noise. He started talking again as he sat down.

"Works out pretty good. Wasn't planning on any preaching. What's your name, friend?"

Lester took a deep breath and made a show of exhaling loudly. "Lester, and I'm here because of a heart attack." He looked over at the now-seated Gene and smirked. "Thought I'd save you some questions and just give you the rundown up front."

Gene pressed his lips together and jutted them out at the same time he shrugged. "Fair enough. Pretty young for a heart attack."

Lester felt his heartbeat increase and heat pulsing through his face. "Yeah, I guess that's what happens when your brother gets blown up by some terrorist trash in a God-forsaken country, and then you run into your ex-fiancée that you left at the altar, and your business burns to the ground just a few hours later. Oh, and then the knock-down, drag-out with your father at the funeral. Don't forget about that. Kind of weighs a man down."

Gene was silent for a while and offered no response, other than a slow nod. When Lester started to shake his head and was about to turn away, the chaplain cleared his throat.

"I'm very sorry to hear that, Lester." He wiped the corner of his eye with a thumb. "Sounds like you've been through quite a lot. Now this." He looked down and shook his head. "Do you know the Lord, Lester?"

Lester tossed his hands in the air and let them fall into his lap. "You know, I thought I did, Gene. I really did. I had this crazy experience a few nights ago that brought me to the realization that I needed to turn back to God, and I was all in. Brought my neighbor to church and everything. Hasn't exactly worked out in my favor."

Gene's face was calm and stoic. "Turn back to God?"

"That's what I said."

"Do you mind me asking when you first met Him?"

Lester sighed. He didn't want to respond but decided there was no harm. "When I was a teenager. Trusted Christ, baptized, all that jazz."

"What happened?"

"Life, man." Lester looked at the game. A player was down on the court but waving away the trainers. Lester focused on the man when he tried to stand on his own and fell, clutching his knee. He turned back toward Gene. "Just got in the way."

Gene nodded. "It has a way of doing that. And you say you turned back and hit nothing but hard times since?"

"That's the long and short, all wrapped up nice. So, you can go find someone else who actually wants to hear it."

Gene leaned forward in his chair. "Lester, I'm just a chaplain in a hospital. There's not much I can do for you, but I'd like to pray with you."

Lester fought the urge to punch the man in the face. "Is that what you do?" he asked. "Walk in, get the patients to pour their hearts out, pray with them, and move on? What, got a tight schedule to keep?" He scoffed. "That help you feel better about yourself, does it, Gene? Take that back to your congregation and tell them how you're 'ministering' to people?" He made air quotes when he said the word *ministering*.

Gene smiled softly. "No, Lester. That's not it at all."

"You think you coming in here and praying with people actually makes a difference?"

Gene nodded. "Yes, I do."

"Unbelievable." Lester formed a fist and slammed it down on the bed. "That's your idea of helping people? What a joke, man." He knew he was getting loud, but he didn't care. "Tell you what, Gene. How about you pray and see if that stops the roadside bomb from blowing up my brother and his men. Then when you're done with that one, pray my livelihood doesn't get burned up, and then pray my past into something I don't have to be ashamed of. If you could toss in a Christmas with my folks without getting slapped by my own mother or cussed out by my so-called God-fearing father, that'd be swell."

He swallowed a lump in his throat and swiped at his eyes with the back of his hand as the same nurse from before rushed in. She came in so quickly that she almost slid, and she stopped with her feet spread and her arms out to the sides.

"Mr. Sharp!"

"What?" he shouted at her and then immediately settled back with his mouth tightly shut. He was breathing heavily, and Gene was rising from his chair.

The nurse stomped up to the foot of the bed with her hands on her hips. "I don't know what's going on in here, but I need you to calm down." She looked over at Gene. "You alright, Gene?" The old man nodded.

"He was just leaving," Lester said and resumed watching the game. He felt a gentle hand on his shoulder and looked up. The old man was standing over him with red, watery eyes.

"I *will* pray for you, Lester. I wish I could do more." Lester looked away with a shake of his head.

When he was gone, Sheila walked over and stood at the right of the bed. She checked the monitors behind and beside him. Some of the wires had come loose during his outburst, so she adjusted them. Lester was aware that she was sneaking glances at him as she worked. When she was finished, she stood up and sighed.

"I don't know what your problem is," she said. Lester turned his head to look at her, curious. "I don't know what kind of miserable life a person is living to shout at Gene Close, so you must really be going through it. But you need to know something. One, don't you ever talk to that old man like that again, or I'll fix it so you don't have to worry about talking to anyone at all."

Lester's eyes opened wide, and he leaned back.

Sheila continued, "You can report that. I don't care because, two: that man stayed with my son for hours at a time when he was in the hospital after an accident. Gene Close loves people, and he's dedicated his life to praying for others ever since he lost his wife to cancer. You may not put a whole lot of stock in prayer, Mr. Sharp; and, truth be told, neither do I. But it meant the world to me for him to care that much; and if you ask Mr. Close, the only thing that got him through the death of his wife is prayer."

Lester opened his mouth, but she held up her hand and looked down. "Just thought you should know."

She left without another word. Lester grabbed the remote from beside his head and turned the game off. He picked up his phone and checked it.

No calls. No messages.

Quinn didn't know how long she had been pacing in her living room, but she was aware that she was talking to herself. She was half-tempted to fly out to wherever he was and hit him squarely in the jaw. Half. The rest of her was conflicted between trying again and never speaking to him again. Her mind was a jumbled mess, a broken montage of conversations.

Laina's voice saying, *"Have you forgiven him for what he did to you?"* and *"You really need to pray for him."*

Harold Sharp saying, *"Frankly, I don't care where he is, and I'd prefer if you didn't call. Lester made his choices . . ."*

And Lester's voice, on a continuous loop: *"I'm burning it and all ties to that life."*

She stopped pacing and pushed her fists against her forehead. She took some deep breaths, groaned, and slammed her fists down into her legs. She walked over to the coffee table, where she'd left her phone, and picked it up. She unlocked it and pulled up Lester's name in her contacts list. She was about to dial, but then she started pacing again, holding the phone at her side.

"This is not your problem, Quinn," she said to herself, looking at the wall as she paced one way, then at her kitchen as she turned and paced in a different direction. "Leave him alone, girl."

She rubbed her eyes between the thumb and forefinger of one hand. Stopped. Squeezed the bridge of her nose. Let out a groan.

She had the phone up to her face again without realizing it, staring at the same picture she'd had in her phone for a few years.

"Why are you fooling yourself?" She shook her head and laughed. "Call that man."

She continued to mumble words of encouragement and mockery of herself as she pressed the dial button. Before there was time for it to ring even once, she had pressed the *End Call* button. Panicked, she pressed it several times and gasped.

"Oh, you've got to be kidding me." She held it up one more time and was about to call when she remembered when she'd taken the picture.

The night Lester proposed. It was the perfect night. Dinner at their favorite burger place. A movie—comedy, of course, because they used to love spending time together and laughing. Lester had proposed outside the theater, dropping to one knee as if he was tying his shoe; but when she looked down, he was holding a ring and smiling. *Yes* had been an automatic response. The picture she'd taken was so that she could have a picture of her fiancé to replace the one of him as her boyfriend.

She looked up and saw herself in a mirror on the living room wall. The same mirror she had looked into on her last night as a single woman the day before the wedding. The same mirror she had looked at two days later after returning from the hotel room she'd stayed in to avoid returning to the home of her single life.

"Goodbye, Lester."

She felt a tear trickle down her cheek as she deleted the number from her phone.

CHAPTER TWENTY

LESTER STARED INTO THE EMPTINESS and darkness of his hospital room, his thoughts thousands of miles away. One of those thoughts was on an abandoned road, one that had become familiar and terrifying in the past week, one he never wanted to see again. One he wished he could return to. But that road was empty, except for the haunting memory that would forever cripple him.

Another thought was not so far away, yet just as distant. It was in a church building, staring back at him with green-speckled eyes. It was his past and present combined into an unattainable beauty that mocked his future. It walked away from him, and he wondered if it was forever. The memory had also crippled him, but he longed for that pain, a pain that also healed.

Lester shook his head and rubbed his eyes. He knew he should sleep, but he also knew that sleep would not come. If it did, he knew what was waiting for him in the land of dreams: a wasteland of nightmares. The visions burned into his mind's eye waited there. Death and poverty, hunger and pain—all beckoning to him, calling from the shadows of the forgotten corners of the world. And Draven would be there.

A foreboding sense of dread and worry washed over him at the thought of the unlikely angel. Lester growled the thoughts away and slammed both fists down on the bed. The motion brought pain in his chest he hadn't felt before, and he realized the medication was wearing off. It was the first time he had felt pain since he awoke, and he began to think the tests the doctor would be performing in the morning may be necessary after all.

"Not a chance," he said to the darkness.

He picked up his phone and checked his messages. Nothing. No family. Nothing from Dave. He thought about the chaplain, Gene Close, and sighed. None of that guilt compared to the thought of Dillon's casket at the gravesite, the one he had not visited. The scene from the funeral played in his mind. He tried to push it away to no avail.

Heart attack or no heart attack, Lester decided he was going to that grave if it killed him.

Khufia

Ibrahim heard laughter and rushed Yara off the path. They were less than a hundred meters from the heart of the village. He held Yara's hand and led her to the back of a nearby hut where they crouched down and peered around the corner. Dawn had not arrived, bringing the promise of light with it, so he had to rely on senses other than his sight to make out the shapes of a group that appeared on the path coming from Khufiana.

They looked like nothing but shadows to Ibrahim, but their laughter and conversation gave them away. Four shadows dragging another shadow that appeared to be hunched over and bound. He felt the familiar cold numbing him from the inside. Fear freezing him in place. Yara was at his side, her arms wrapped around his frail leg. He exhaled with a shudder and patted her on the head.

The men led the woman into a large hut made of a mixture of mud bricks and thatch. She was resisting them, but a strike to the back of the head ended her struggle as quickly as it had begun. They shoved her inside, laughing. Ibrahim gripped the wall he hid behind and clenched his teeth.

The voice in his head reminded him of his task. His anger reminded him of his duty as a brother. Sensibility told him he would only get them all killed if he tried heroics. He remembered the night Yusef had nearly caught him coming from visiting the prisoner, and his past reminded him who he was.

When the door to the hut was closed, he grasped Yara's hand and led her back onto the path, toward the angel.

Olympia

Quinn smiled and let out a satisfied sigh. She stared at her phone and nodded. A great sense of relief and empowerment flowed through her. Lester's number, his email, and all other means of contacting him were gone. He had no social media—the man was virtually a recluse—other than the accounts for his shop. She unfollowed them, assuring herself that she had followed them only in case she needed the shop's services. Finished, she sat back on the couch.

She was about to set the phone down when she felt a rush of panic. Pulling the phone closer to her face, she began to frantically search through her contacts. It was gone. Lester's parents' phone numbers: gone. Even Dillon's old cell phone, gone.

"Oh, no," she said as she searched. "What did I do?"

She paused, closed her eyes, and took a deep breath. "It's fine, Quinn. All you have to do is go through your call log. The name will be gone, but the calls and texts to his number will still be there."

She opened her eyes with a sigh of relief, until she remembered that she had spent the last ten minutes deleting her call history and the text thread with Lester's number. She shook her head and sat forward with a yell. If his number was gone, there was nothing in her house to help her contact him because she had thrown away everything with information about him.

She stopped and looked straight ahead. *Do I still love him?*

Quinn stood and screamed. "Yes. Okay?" She made a fist and punched herself in the leg. "I give up!"

She relaxed her fist and found herself smiling. There was a mirror on the wall opposite her, and she saw her smile in the reflection. For some reason, she blushed and had to look away. She rolled her eyes and waved her hand at nothing.

"Oh, no, Lester Sharp. You're not cutting ties with me." She shook her head, ran her fingers through her hair, and turned in a semicircle.

"Okay," she said, "what am I doing?" She slid her phone into her back pocket. "Keys. Where are my keys?" She looked around, turned another semicircle, and then tossed her hands up. "Girl, what is wrong with you?"

She searched the living room and found her keys on a small table near the front door. She then continued to search for her keys for the next several minutes until she realized they were in her hands. She ran out the door, nearly forgetting to lock it, and got in her car. As she backed out of her parking space, she sneaked a glance at herself in the mirror.

She was still smiling.

CHAPTER TWENTY-ONE

LESTER TIGHTENED HIS BELT AND then straightened out his shirt, not bothering to tuck it into his slacks. Finding the clothes was easy—they were in the small closet just as he had suspected. Much easier than removing his own IV, which had caused blood to spurt all over the bed and his arm.

He made sure he had his phone and wallet, looked around the room one more time with his heart beating faster than it would have been if he had just finished a marathon, and then headed for the door. He kept his head down as he walked and lengthened his stride. He didn't know where he was or where anything was on that floor, so he had to look around when he stepped in to the hallway.

He immediately heard Sheila shouting his name, telling him to go back to his room and get in his bed. He looked up and saw her behind a low counter. She was standing, and a rolling chair slid across the polished tile behind her. Another nurse, much older, was sitting in a chair next to her and staring at Lester with wide eyes and open mouth.

Lester held his hand up with the palm toward Sheila and started talking to her as he approached the nurse's station. "Listen, I know what I'm doing. Just sit back down. Please, just let me get out of here, and I'll be out of your hair."

She folded her arms and tilted her head to the side. "Uh, no. Not happening." She kept her arms folded but pointed with one hand back toward his room. "In the bed, Mr. Sharp."

He shook his head. "Look, I've got no problem with you or this place, but my brother died. I had a heart attack at his funeral." He laughed and stepped back. "His funeral! What kind of person has a heart attack at his brother's funeral?" He held his arms out to his sides. "I wasn't there when they put his casket in the ground. I didn't see them giving him his honors. I haven't paid my respects to my own brother." He let his hands fall to his sides and slap his legs.

Sheila looked down and swiped at her eyes. When she looked up, they were red. "I'm very sorry to hear that, sir. I really am, but I don't want you to be in a casket next to him."

"It'd be better than this life," he said. "There's nothing for me to mess up in the grave." He bit down on his lip and turned his head to the side. After gathering himself, he looked back to the nurse. "Just let me go say goodbye to my brother. He was the one person in the world who still loved me."

He saw someone walking toward him out the corner of his eye and turned. It was a male doctor. He was very tall and had the darkest skin Lester had ever seen. His eyes were somewhere between black and blue. He carried a clipboard in front of him, blocking his name tag. Lester took a wary step back.

"Sir, I'm going to have to ask you to return to your room," the doctor said when he was next to the nurse's counter.

"I'm going to have to ignore that request, doctor," Lester said. He folded his arms, attempting bravado but also swallowed a lump in his throat when he saw the doctor's onyx eyes. "Look, give me a waiver or whatever you need me to sign that clears you up from any obligation to me, but I'm not staying here."

The doctor stared at Lester, looking down at him sternly. After a few moments, he held up his hand to silence Sheila's protest. She immediately stopped talking, and the doctor turned toward her with his hand still up. "Get Mr. Sharp a waiver. He is refusing further treatment and accepting all liability." He turned back to Lester and let his hand rest on the top of the counter. "You do realize, Mr. Sharp, that you are responsible for whatever happens next?"

Lester furrowed his brow, disturbed by the wording. "I. Yes?"

"You will not be able to hold the hospital, or anyone but yourself, responsible. You've made your choice."

Lester nodded.

"This is ridiculous," Sheila said. The other nurse—Patty, according to her name tag—was still just staring with her mouth open. She turned her head back and forth between the speakers, following the conversation.

"Nurse, please," the doctor said in a calm voice. "Mr. Sharp is not in prison. If he wishes to put his life at risk, we are not capable of restraining him."

"Are we even going to try and stop him?" Sheila asked. "You just walked up and said to give him a waiver. That's not exactly responsible. Also, who are you? I haven't seen you around here, and I wasn't informed that any new doctors would be arriving this evening."

The doctor turned and leaned forward so quickly that Sheila gasped and took a step back. When it was clear that he was not backing down, she took another step back, turned to a filing cabinet, and opened it. She went through a few files, glancing back and forth between the drawer and the doctor, until she finally pulled out a sheet of paper.

She closed the drawer and then walked over to the counter, keeping her sight fixed on the doctor, who hadn't moved.

She slid the paper toward Lester and said, "This states that you assume all liability and are waiving treatment."

Lester took a pen from a cup on the counter and proceeded to fill out the form. It was basic, asking for his name and personal information, all below a block of words that he didn't bother to read. He kept his eye on the doctor, who was still staring at Sheila and leaning toward her. When Lester had finished the form, he slid it back to her and stepped away from the counter.

"Take care of yourself," he said. When there was no response, he hurried away toward the elevator. He could not walk fast enough, and he forced himself not to look back.

Morane slowly turned his head away from the nurse with a smile. He watched the doors to the elevator close and allowed a smile to stretch across his fabricated face. He felt the fear of the nurse and delighted in it but decided he had more important matters to attend to than a woman who had already forsaken her faith on the day of her son's death. Lester was the target. He and his newfound compassion for others.

It was time to turn up the storm heading toward Lester Sharp.

Khufia

The prisoner had developed a rhythm. Every time the foreign name came to his mind, he tugged at his chains. His anger had grown with each tug so that the walls began to pop and creak. He felt his strength increasing.

The cryptic words of the strange man echoed in his mind. *"All you had to do was show the human the things he needed to see."*

The violent popping of the loop holding the chains echoed off the walls of his prison.

"Why are you in these chains, Draven?" He yanked on the chains, again and again. Harder and harder. Teeth clenched. *"But you have grown weak, as I warned you would happen. Weak because you crave to be with the humans."*

And then he knew.

The prisoner was not weak, as the visitor had said. He was strong, stronger than the chains, stronger than Yusef or any of his men. Some mistake had brought him to this prison, a mistake he could not fix from a cage. He did not know what the mistake was, but he was resolved not to die in that place of misery. The name no longer came to mind. Only the sound of the chains stretching, popping.

Breaking.

He paused and looked from left to right. There was still no light, the windows being covered, but he saw everything as if the room had been lit by a candle. Each of the chains had a link that was stretched and nearly broken.

"Why are you in these chains, Draven?"

The prisoner flexed and readied himself for one last, exhausted tug. He felt blood pouring from his wrists. The door swung open. Dim light briefly flooded into the room but was then blocked by the tall silhouette of a man. The silhouette became solid and entered the room, its heavy feet stomping across the wooden floor. The prisoner relaxed his arms but tensed his face, ready to shout as his eyes adjusted and he saw the man for who he was.

The guard hit him with a massive fist, knocking the prisoner's face to the side. Before he could look back, a boot landed squarely in the center of his chest. His body reeled back as air burst from his lungs. He looked up and saw the weakened link. It was beginning to split.

Two more punches to his head stole his vision, thrusting him back in darkness. The words of the visitor became distant, a hollow echo drifting away into the black. And then there was another man in the room, kicking and punching the prisoner with fury.

The prisoner felt his consciousness slipping and was ready to yield to it when he heard a shout from the doorway. The assault stopped. He looked up. He saw nothing but darkness at first and felt nothing but the pumping of blood in his temples, but then the light found its way through. Two figures were in the doorway. One was slender and the shape of a man. The other was small and less than half the other's height. The taller shadow spoke.

"Leave him alone."

The guards turned away from the prisoner and stalked to the door as sunlight broke through.

Olympia

Quinn barely had the car in park before she was out of it and rushing across the church parking lot. The panic that had found its way into her mind on the drive over had her heart racing, and she didn't need to run in order to breathe hard.

You're being irrational, she told herself as she fumbled with her keys at the door. She tried to shove the wrong key into the lock, managed to find the correct one, and then yanked the door open. The alarm started beeping immediately, but she was so fixated on her mission that she nearly ignored it. She forced herself to pause and think as she stood in front of the keypad and then punched in the code with shaky fingers.

He gave up on you.

She tried not to listen to the confusing thoughts as she jogged through the foyer, around the corner, and down the hallway to her office.

That was a long time ago.

She unlocked the door to her office and rushed inside. She left the door open and threw her keys on top of the desk as she circled it.

She spent the next five minutes frantically thumbing through folders in her filing cabinet and an old-fashioned rolodex of membership cards. Lester's information was nowhere to be found. She stopped and put one hand on her hip. She used the back of her other hand to wipe sweat from her forehead and paused with her hand still touching her head.

"Think."

She took a deep breath and tried to do just that. Frustration nearly got the best of her, until she remembered that she had been updating their records over the last few months, putting every physical file into digital format. All of the physical files were put in boxes and then storage in the attic once a digital file was created. She didn't think she had made it all the way to S in the system, but it seemed worth a try.

She rushed over to her computer and logged in, not bothering to sit in her chair. Hunched over her desk with her face as close to the screen as she could get without it turning blurry, she pulled up the directory. She scrolled through the entire list. She did a command search. Nothing. Lester's name was nowhere. She stood and put both hands on her hips.

You know what happened.

Quinn groaned as she remembered. A secret she had not told anyone. Her first act of vengeance on Lester after taking the job as assistant to the pastor. She had thrown Lester's file away and removed any trace of him ever being a member of the church.

"Oh, Quinn." She felt her shoulders slump as she dropped down into the seat waiting behind her.

CHAPTER TWENTY-TWO

LESTER PEERED THROUGH THE FRONT seats of the taxi, out the windshield and into the last remnant of daylight. The driver flipped on his headlights as the cemetery came into view. As they got closer, he realized how secluded it was and shook his head at the idea of his brother being in such a place. It was more akin to a horror movie than a cemetery where the body of a war hero should be.

As the driver of the taxi drove through the iron gate entrance to the graveyard, Lester had another thought. He realized that it didn't really matter if it was fitting for his brother's body because Dillon's body was not there. He balled his fists as he imagined an empty casket going in the ground. He stared through the rear passenger window. The barren branches of tall oak trees swayed in the wind that had picked up on the drive over, casting skittering shadows over the headstones.

"That's twenty-two even."

Lester turned away from the window and looked at the cab driver, who had turned in his seat and was staring at Lester with no compassion. He started to ask, "What," but then it registered that the driver wanted money for the ride.

"I need to get back."

The driver frowned. "Look, pal, I'll drive you to Timbuktu if you want, but every time you get out of this car, I need the green. I've been taken too many times."

Lester nodded. "Okay." He took the money from his wallet and handed it to the driver before getting out of the cab.

A cold wind blasted into him as soon as he stood. He had to push hard with both hands to shut the cab door, and his shirt and pants clung to him, pressed by the force of the wind. When they had pulled into the graveyard, he had absently noticed a tractor at the edge of a field, but now he focused on it. Parked in a field, in the only spot without clustered trees, it seemed like a metal monster. Though Lester knew it was inanimate, and that Dillon wasn't really buried there, the machine loomed in the sudden darkness like a silent assassin making no effort to hide his evil deed.

As he walked, he saw the fresh mound that could only be Dillon's grave. There would likely be additional work in the next day or so to dress the site and make it look nice, though Lester wondered how they defined "nice" in such a macabre place. Other than a few headstones of a traditional, rounded top or rectangular shape, the headstones were almost all like something from a horror movie.

Some of them were little houses with statues and idols placed in them. Some were shaped like children, men and women, or Mary in a pose with the child Jesus at her feet. Lester cringed as he approached the mound, thankful to see a standard headstone marking his brother's resting place. The most ominous grave markers were the gargoyles. Shaped like winged demons with faces like animals derived from mythology and legend, they accurately served their purpose of warding off unwelcome visitors. Lester stayed appropriately clear of all of them and followed the gravel trail to Dillon's grave.

When he finally arrived at the mound, he realized how dark and cold it was. He had been hugging himself without realizing it, but now he was forced to unwrap his arms from his chest in order to pull his phone out and use its flashlight app. He marveled at the quickness with which the night had descended. A particularly forceful gust of icy wind assaulted him from the side, and he bent his body into it to try and ward off the cold, to no avail. He managed to get his phone out and the flashlight turned on. He cast the light over the headstone and read the words:

DILLON EVAN SHARP

A LOVING SON AND FRIEND

1990-2018

"THANK YOU FOR YOUR SERVICE"

Although he was reading it, it wasn't real to Lester. None of it seemed right. It all seemed manufactured. He knew a part of that came from the grave being nothing more than a memorial, but something seemed out of place. He looked around at the trees, the moonless night that provided him with no light. Everything was silhouetted by the distant lights of the taxi, and the storm that had picked up as if on cue was too uncanny.

Lester pushed those thoughts from his mind, remembering why he was there. He took a deep breath and put his phone away. He opened his mouth to speak several times, but no words came. The events of the past week played through his mind like a movie reel on an endless loop. He tried his best to keep his thoughts away from that abandoned road, but they wanted to run there. It was as if his unconscious mind was trying to tell him something about that scene, about that part of the glimpse. He shook his head to clear it away. *It's just your mind playing tricks on you.*

"Hey, bro," he said. His words were immediately swept away in the increasing intensity of the wind. "Sorry I'm late." He chuckled and then had to suppress tears. "I don't know if I can deal with any of this without you, man. You were always my rock." He shoved his hands into his pockets and looked at the ground. "I messed everything up. The shop's gone; Mom and Dad hate me; the whole family turned their backs on me; and now Quinn's back in the picture."

He looked up and focused on the words on the headstone. "I've already messed that up, and there's not even something there to mess up, you know? Man, I wish you were here. I've got all these people without jobs depending on me, and you wouldn't believe what happened to me a few nights ago." He laughed. "I don't know. Maybe you do. You were there."

Lester snatched a hand from his pocket and put it to his face as tears streamed. They came without sympathy or apology. His shoulders shook, and the sounds of his sobbing attached themselves to the icy fingers of the wind, joining to the moaning call echoing across the graveyard. He felt heavy raindrops splashing on his head, and thunder cracked from not so far away. He continued to cry but looked up. Lightning was flashing, streaking across the sky and leaving blue and white ghost wisps in the cryptic air. He ignored it and fell to his knees.

"I couldn't save you, bro!" he shouted into the wind. The moaning had reached a crescendo. He heard branches cracking nearby. The sound of one dropping to the ground behind him startled Lester, but he kept his eyes focused on Dillon's name, etched in stone.

A bolt of lightning impacted in the field near the tractor, sending an explosion of dirt and light into the air. The rain had nearly soaked him, and Lester heard screaming. It was his name being called from the entrance to the cemetery. He didn't care.

"I love you, Dillon." He reached out with ice cold, trembling hands and touched his fingertips to the dark stone of his brother's grave.

Quinn pulled out her phone and called Pastor Greene, talking to and scolding herself for the impulsive actions she had taken. It took several rings, but he finally answered. His *hello* came after an extended yawn.

"Pastor Greene?"

There was a heavy sigh in the ear piece. "Yes, Quinn. Did you realize you called me? Or . . . are you sleep dialing?" His questions showed his irritation.

"No, no, it's me."

"I know it's you, Quinn."

"What?"

There were muffled voices on the other end, and Quinn scrunched her face. She tried to listen but heard only pieces, like "who," "Quinn," and "time of night?"

"Quinn, what's going on? I've got you on speaker phone, just so you know."

"Oh," she said. "Okay. I'm sorry to bother you—"

"But," Greene interrupted, clearly not in the mood.

She inhaled through her nose, slowly. "I did something bad." She turned and sat on the edge of her desk. There was no reply, so she continued. "I deleted Lester's number."

There was a chuckle and then the sound of someone being slapped. Greene yelled, "Ouch," and then told his wife to stop hitting him.

"Quinn, that's pretty normal," he said. "My wife deletes my number about once a week. Just go to your call or text history, and you'll be able to find it and restore the name to the number that matches your conversations with him."

She wanted to crawl under a rock. "Yes, sir. I thought of that."

"But you deleted those, too."

"Yes."

"Well, you weren't playing, were you?"

"No, sir."

There was another chuckle, another slap, and another exchange of words. Quinn heard Greene's wife threatening to do "a whole lot worse than slap him if he kept on" and waited patiently.

"Okay, Quinn," Greene said after a few moments. "Listen, it's late. In the morning, just get his number out of the member files, and you'll be good to go." When she didn't answer, he asked, "You deleted that, too, didn't you?"

She hesitated. "Yes, sir."

"Okay, that's a bit too far." He took a deep breath. She could hear it plainly. "Alright, I don't want to deal with this tonight. Quinn, I can understand why you did that, but it was wrong. I can't have you fooling around with member information, and you know that."

"Lester's in the hospital." She didn't have time for a lecture. Her mind was screaming at her that Lester was in trouble. "He had a heart attack, and I think something worse is going on. I need to talk to him, and I need to pray for him."

Greene didn't respond right away; but when he did, he was humble. "I've got his number in my phone. Hold on." There was some tapping and scraping sounds as he pressed buttons on his phone. He gave her the number and then said, "We'll be praying for him. Call me if you need anything else, and we'll just talk more in the morning."

"Thank you, Pastor."

"Night, Quinn."

She hung up the phone and looked at the number she'd written down. It dawned on her that she had finished writing it before Greene had given her all of the numbers because she knew it by heart. She looked up at the decorations on her office wall. There was a decorative plaque with a verse of Scripture in calligraphy burned into a piece of wood:

"For the weapons of our warfare are not carnal, but mighty through God to the pulling down of strong holds."

Quinn nodded. "Time to go to war." She set her phone down and got on her knees behind her desk, touched her forehead to the ground, and began to pray.

Khufia

The prisoner read both fear and confidence on Ibrahim's face. The old man held Yara's hand at his side and did not move when the guards started walking toward him. Warm beams of sunlight pierced the dark and radiated into the room in thin shafts. They spread throughout the room quickly as the distant ball of fire rapidly made its ascent into the silent sky behind Ibrahim.

The prisoner tried to keep his head up, but he was weary and in pain. He had not slept that night, and his arms ached from the constant tugging at the chains. His face throbbed, and his chest felt as if it were about to cave in. He glanced at the chains again. The tiny split in the weakened links now seemed microscopic and impossible to widen. Seconds before, they had seemed so fragile. Twigs in the palms of his hands. But those hands were weak, as the visitor from the light had said he was.

He heard one of the guards say, "You will regret coming here, old man."

The prisoner looked through puffy eyes. Blood dripped down his face as he watched, helplessly.

"My only regret is not coming here sooner," Ibrahim said.

The guards finished the short march to him, and the taller guard backhanded him. Ibrahim fell to the ground, and Yara screamed. The guard grabbed her by the shirt, shouted at her to be quiet, and then tossed her to the floor inside the room. He used his foot to push her out of his way and then stepped through the doorway. He reached down and picked Ibrahim up with one hand, lifted him to face level, and shook him violently. Ibrahim let out a cry that was quickly interrupted when the guard punched him in the face and then threw him away from the door.

The smaller guard cackled and stepped through the door to join in the fun. Yara was huddled into herself, her arms over her head. The prisoner saw a flash in his memory Another scene with the girl in that same position but outside, on the ground behind some brush. He had gone to her.

He remembered.

She was scared. Yusef's men were shouting and running toward her. Toward him. Shouting about the sorcerer. He had picked her up and shielded her body with his own. Bullets had entered his body, gone through him. One had struck her in the shoulder. He had reached in and taken it out.

But how?

Men shouted outside the room, and he heard a woman screaming. The prisoner's mind was chaos. Nothing made sense, but he knew Ibrahim was in great danger. He straightened his body and yanked at the chains with as much power as he could muster.

"You have grown weak."

He pulled and pulled, but the chains were heavy, like impossible anchors. He sighed and closed his eyes, letting his arms droop as low as the chains would allow. He *was* weak. An image flashed through his mind. A small man, in a different place, in a different time. He was also in chains. He was badly beaten, and it looked as if his eyes were infested with some disease that made them crust over and ooze yellowish liquid. The man looked as if he were on the verge of death.

And then it was more than a flash.

The prisoner could smell the dungeon the man was in. He could feel the chill, the damp, and he was not in chains. He was in the corner of the dungeon, observing the man. He looked behind him and heard low, rumbling laughter. The darkness behind the man in chains began to take shape. Two tiny, electric orbs sparked above a set of shimmering white fangs that had just appeared.

And then the dark shape began to speak.

"Hello, Draven." Its voice was callous and sinister.

The prisoner heard screaming in the far distance. A man and a woman. He ignored them momentarily and said, "You will not take this one, Morane."

The dark shape stepped from the shadows, becoming the solid figure of a demon, but just as dark. It laughed. "Perhaps not, but I will make every day miserable for the wretch." He turned and pointed at the man in chains. "Look at how weak the Almighty's greatest servant is. Shackled like a common thief. A play thing in my hands." He looked back and faced the prisoner. "And you, Draven, are helpless to stop me."

The prisoner shook his head. "I do not need to stop you, Morane. You misunderstand because you do not know what true strength is. You are but a thorn in this man's flesh. You may buffet him with your fists. You may cause havoc with your whispers in his ears, but you cannot take away what resides inside of him. In fact, the more you attack him, the more powerful the presence of the Almighty becomes within him." He smiled. "You, Morane, are but a play thing in the hands of the Creator."

The man in chains lifted his head and began to sing. It was not a song, just him lifting his voice in praise. Morane threw his head back and roared with his fists balled beside him. A moment later, with the man in chains still singing, the demon cut off his roar and fixed his eyes on the prisoner.

On Draven.

He opened his eyes and bolted upright. He felt a surge of energy pulse through him. Yara was in front of him. Her hands were on his head, and her eyes were wide with terror. She yelled and stumbled backward. The screams of the woman outside had turned into words. Pleas for help, for mercy. Whoever she was, her cries were to God. The voices of many men were shouting and laughing, attempting to drown out her cries.

He looked at Yara. She was frozen with fear.

"Do not fear me, Yara," he said.

He flexed his arms and gave the chains one last tug. They fell from the walls as easily as if he were pulling threads from a worn-out cloth. The thud echoed through the room. The chains hit the floor and kicked up dust.

The watcher stood.

CHAPTER TWENTY-THREE

Andersonville County

LESTER LIFTED HIS HEAD IN a panic and stood. He didn't know how long he had been on his knees with his head to the ground, but something had definitely changed. He looked around and saw that a tree had been struck by lightning and was now on fire. There was a massive hole in the ground in front of the tree, and smoke hissed into the night, despite the thick sheets of rain.

He was shivering and chilled to the bone. He pivoted to face the entrance of the cemetery. The cab was gone. He remembered hearing someone screaming his name, but he didn't know how long ago that had been. All he knew was that he was alone on a country road with no idea of where to go. Lightning flashed above him, followed by a roar of thunder. He jumped at the sound, but the light illuminated the road enough for him to see that he was in thick woods.

He held up his hands and leaned his head back to face the sky. He was instantly pummeled with rain in his eyes and mouth, but it barely bothered him. He shouted as loudly as he could. There were no words, just shouting. He yelled louder and louder, forcing as much of his anger to the surface as he could manage until words formed.

"Why are You doing this to me?" He hesitated, afraid that things might get worse if he expressed his anger toward God, but then he let go with abandon. "What's wrong with You? Is this a sick joke? Do

You like seeing me suffer? I went on Your twisted tour. Your glimpse. I saw all those things. I saved Wayne, but You wouldn't let me save Dillon. Why do You hate me?"

Lester lowered his arms and face toward the ground. The only response was lightning striking the cemetery where it exploded a headstone.

He ran. He was soaked, and the rain was getting heavier. He slipped as he sloshed through great puddles but managed to stay on his feet. He got out of the cemetery as quickly as possible and headed straight for a patch of trees. He knew that running to the woods in the middle of a lightning storm was not a safe option, but he also knew that he had to find shelter. He would not survive against the elements, and it didn't look like the storm was going to let up any time soon. He felt his phone buzzing in his pocket, and he was about to answer it, but lightning hit the road, taking out a huge chunk of it and knocking him to the ground.

Lester got to his feet and ran into the woods.

Quinn heard Lester's voice and sat forward in her chair. She had already received four messages saying that the customer could not be reached and was possibly out of service range. That time, though, Lester had picked up.

At least, she thought he'd picked up. When she realized that she was listening to his voicemail message, she yanked the phone away from her ear and pressed the *End Call* button with enough force to make her worry the phone would crack.

She dialed again. "Come on, Lester. Pick up." She put the phone to her ear and listened to the ringing. His voicemail picked up again. She screamed and nearly threw the phone. She said a quick prayer under her breath and dialed again.

"Please pick up. Please."

Voicemail.

Khufia

Draven tore the braces from his wrists and let them fall to the wooden floor with a clang. He stalked forward, knelt, and looked into Yara's eyes. He placed a hand on her shoulders and felt her shivering. He smiled and placed his forehead against hers.

"Thank you, Yara." He felt her body steady beneath his hand. "Your grandfather has been praying. His prayers have been heard."

He leaned back and studied her. She was crying, clutching her hands in front of her chest, wringing them. "What about the bad men?"

Draven nodded, letting the smile fade from his face. "They are leaving."

He stood and walked past her, patting her on the head. When he stepped through the doorway, he saw Yusef, unmasked, holding Ibrahim up by the collar. The old man's feet were dangling just above the ground. Yusef's men surrounded a woman. She was on the ground with one hand raised toward Yusef. Her face was swollen, dirty, and streaked with tear stains.

"One last chance, Uncle," Yusef said. His face was only inches from Ibrahim's. The old man was barely conscious. His head wobbled and swayed. Yusef practically growled his next words. "There is only one God, and His name is?"

Ibrahim's voice croaked, barely a whisper, but he spoke with a smile on his face. He said one word: "Jesus."

Yusef shouted and moved to toss Ibrahim to the ground. The other guards rushed toward him, ready to pounce. But Ibrahim never hit the ground, and none of the guards reached him. Draven was there in less time than the blink of an eye. He moved in and out of their ranks as if they were standing still in time. He simultaneously pulled Ibrahim from Yusef's grasp and pushed Yusef to the ground. After setting Ibrahim on the ground, Draven went into a blur of movement.

He sent the first of the guards that had attacked him minutes before reeling backward, clutching his throat after a ridge hand to his jugular. The shorter man that had been with the first guard was neutralized by a palm nearly crushing his forehead. Yasir rushed at him, but Draven grabbed his fist in mid-swing and used the man's own momentum to send him tumbling through the air. He followed him and delivered a swift kick to Yasir's jaw. Draven turned and caught Yusef by the throat just as the man was about to plunge a curved knife into his shoulder.

"Look at your men," Draven said. "I put them down before you even knew I was here. That's after a week as your prisoner, being beaten, shot, and stoned. What do you think I could do at full strength?" He let go of Yusef's throat and pushed him forward.

Yusef stepped back, rubbing his neck. "What are you?"

"The end of your tyranny." Draven rolled his shoulders and cracked his neck from side to side. "Care to challenge that?"

Yusef sneered, curling his upper lip. "This is my village. I put you in chains once. I can do it again."

Draven arched an eyebrow. "Really? You think so?" He moved faster than Yusef could react. In the next moment, he had slammed into Yusef, lifting and carrying the man through the air, and dropping him to the ground from ten feet.

Yusef rolled back and forth, groaning. Draven stood over him, casting his shadow on the man's face. Yusef looked up but could not speak because the wind had been knocked out of his lungs with the fall. Draven leaned down and put his face close to Yusef's.

"You and your men will leave this place and never return. Your day of reckoning has come, but a far greater judgment awaits you. Repent, or face the fire."

Yusef waited, sucked in a huge gulp of air, and gasped for breath. When he had finally caught it again, he responded. "I am not going anywhere, sorcerer. I will kill you."

Draven smiled and let his body make the transformation into his true appearance. He stood and stretched, elated as he felt skin and sinews collapsing, being replaced by his immortal skin. He looked at his hands, solid but perfectly blended with his surroundings. He looked himself over as the transformation completed. Taller, stronger, and with every memory intact.

Yusef was hollering, terrified, and scooting away as quickly as possible. Draven took confident strides forward. "You were saying?"

Yusef hopped to his feet, turned, and ran as quickly as his bruised body would let him. Draven heard terrified shouts, and then the other men were running past him after Yusef. They turned and looked at the watcher over their shoulders as they ran but did not stop. He laughed but then remembered Ibrahim. He rushed over to the old man and found him slipping from consciousness. Draven fell to his knees and then scooped Ibrahim into his arms.

He was shocked that the old man did not seem afraid. Instead, he smiled. "I knew you were an angel," he said in a hoarse whisper.

Draven nodded. "You had faith."

Ibrahim coughed and shook his head. "No. My faith failed. I denied the Lord before those men. I failed."

It was Draven's turn to shake his head. "You had a moment of weakness, but you depended on God in the end. True strength is found only in Him."

Ibrahim coughed again, and blood splattered on his lips. "Thank you for saving my Yara." He reached up and tried to touch Draven, but his hand never reached the watcher's face. The old man's eyes closed for the last time, and his hand fell limp at his side.

"I told him he would die for his Jesus."

Draven looked up and saw a woman standing over him. Nasteexo. Ibrahim's sister. He looked down, gently placed Ibrahim's head on the ground, and placed his hand on the man's chest. He waited, remembering all the men and women he had seen die in similar ways since the fall. After a moment, he sighed and stood, towering over Nasteexo. Yara was at the edge of the shipping crate that had been his prison, huddled against the door and crying.

"He died in faith and with honor," Draven said.

She wiped at her eyes. "He was always so afraid. I never saw such strength in him."

Draven nodded. "He found true strength when he surrendered his own."

Nasteexo looked up. "You are not what I thought an angel would look like."

He smiled and was sure that she could not see it. "We are a multitude, made of many kinds. My appearance matches my purpose."

"Which is?" she asked.

"To watch over you." He pointed at Yara. "And her. But the care of the girl is in your hands now. Great things are planned for her, but only if she walks the correct path, a path you know nothing about."

She shook her head. "I cannot be her mother. I failed my brother. I failed her whole family."

Draven touched her chin, lifting her head. "You are her family." He let his hand go back to his side and stepped past her. She called out to him, and he turned.

"Where are you going?"

He exhaled, thinking. "To war."

He looked back at Yara one last time and then let himself slip into the spirit realm. He heard Nasteexo gasp but did not look at her. There was a strange presence as soon as he was immersed into the world of the spirits. Something that was out of place. He saw a flicker. Not light, but shadow. At first, he thought it was Morane, but then he smelled and sensed a different kind of being. He could not place it, so he shrugged it off.

Weak from so many beatings, Draven fixed his mind on Morane. It was time to end it.

CHAPTER TWENTY-FOUR

Andersonville County

RAZOR-SHARP, ICICLE RAIN ASSAULTED LESTER from every angle. His face was freezing but felt like it was on fire. He kept his eyes squinted with one arm across his forehead as he ran through ankle-deep water. His feet stuck in the ground, like the attaching and detaching of suction cups with every plunge into the malleable clay. It was harder to yank his foot out with each step. His legs burned, and his body was getting stiff from the dramatic drop in temperature.

He came into a small clearing, just wide enough for him to see farther ahead than the ground in front of him. The water was rising, and the trees seemed taller. Ancient. Looming. The darkness was nearly impenetrable, and even when the ground was solid enough for him to run without getting stuck, the weight of the water around him forced him to drag his feet through. Coerced by the elements to a painfully slow walk similar to hiking through thick snow, he was defenseless when a lightning bolt struck a tree to his right.

The blast sent him airborne and showered him with piercing pieces of wooden shrapnel. He tried to shield his face, but too many of the massive slivers got through. One hit him and lodged itself just below his eye. His scream was drowned out by the sudden roar of thunder and cascading rain. He felt as if he flew forever, but his flight was cut short when something solid and unforgiving slammed into his back.

His body bowed backward in a crescent, and then he tumbled to the ground. Thankfully, he landed on a bed of roots that had risen out of the ground, so he was not immersed in the steadily rising flood.

He writhed back and forth on the protruding roots and groaned, clutching his ribs. He was nearly in shock from the combination of cold and pain mixed with terror, so he almost missed the sensation of something buzzing in his pocket. He rolled toward the tree, grabbed the stump of a long-ago broken branch and pulled himself up. He stood precariously on a root nearly as wide as his thigh and leaned over with his hand against the tree. The pain was unbearable, and the vibration of the phone amplified the cacophony of his senses. He felt his body jerk and spasm as he wretched. He was glad that the noise of the wind and rain covered the sound.

The rain inexplicably decreased in that moment, enough for him to see the blood mixed with his bile. He reached his free hand to his side. He took a deep breath and regretted it as sharp pain from his ribs nearly buckled his knees. His phone went off again, and he managed to get it out of his pocket and shield it from the rain with his head and chest. In the darkness, the screen of his phone was like the light of a tower on the shores of an ocean. He looked at the display.

Quinn.

All the world was a blur of color and chaos. Villages, mountains, oceans, and cities all a stream. Lives coming new and dying. Draven's vision continually shifted from the spiritual plane to the physical, allowing him to keep his bearings without focusing on any particular event. The world rested in some places, cried out for help in others. Violence like volcanic eruptions. Sorrows like salve sealing brokenness.

The watcher tried to force the memories of witnessing man's unending war for precedence to the corners of his clouded mind. Blood shed for money. Money shed for blood. Always feeding. Always hungry.

Practically numb to it for centuries, Draven was acutely pierced by the pain of it again after having his memories restored so abruptly. He flew past it all in the span of a breath beneath a foreboding sky painted with the orchestrated destruction of a storm. Sensing Lester's presence, Draven allowed his vision to shift to the physical plane. With his sight restored, he was able to see for miles and control it. In the distance, running through sheets of icy rain and violent wind, he could see Lester. He was more than in trouble. The man was going to die. Thunder roared through the night. Lightning filled the onyx tapestry of the heavens.

Draven pushed on as fast as he could and shifted his vision to the spiritual plane. He scanned frantically until he saw the demon. Nearly as black as the sky, Morane stood in a swirl of electric radiance. His arms were raised, weaving in and out of one another in a stunningly poetic, chillingly evil dance. Lightning sparked from his fingertips, and he swung his hand out, sending bolts of electricity toward Lester.

The lightning hit a tree just before the man was about to run past it. The ancient oak exploded with brilliant light, and the blast radius engulfed Lester. He was thrown through the air and landed on the opposite side of the clearing he had just entered. The heavy rain cascaded over him, immediately quenching the thread of fire that had begun to sew its way from his legs to his torso. He rolled back and forth on the ground, and Draven heard his screams of pain.

Then he heard Morane's haunting laughter.

Draven closed the distance to Morane in a fraction of a second. Using the demon's elation over Lester's plight as a distraction, Draven came down like a stake in the ground, flipping his body at the last moment to drive his foot into Morane's back. Morane fell and tumbled forward. The properties of the spirit realm made such things unpredictable. Though it was solid enough for immortal beings to walk on, it was also not fully tangible. Morane's body slid nearly a hundred feet away. To Draven's sight, it seemed like only a few feet.

Morane was lying on his side, groaning. He turned so that he could look at Draven, who was now standing firmly on the plane, using his command of the wind to send rain in swirls around the burning tree. It was out and smoldering, and Draven focused on calming the storm. He heard Morane laughing, so he lowered his hands and looked at the demon.

Still laughing, Morane slowly got to his feet and then faced Draven squarely. "Did you enjoy your vacation, watcher?"

Draven stretched his neck. He slid one foot out and brought it slightly back as he crouched, then raised his hands into loose fists and snarled.

"The time for talk has ended, demon."

Morane flashed his impossibly white teeth and growled as he stalked forward.

"Quinn?"

Lester strained to hear, but her reply was broken up. He heard bits and pieces of a word that sounded like his name. It came again, a little clearer this time, and he repeated her name. He pressed the phone against his ear as hard as he could and cupped his hand over the other ear.

"Lester!"

It was Quinn's frantic voice. He was about to explain to her what was happening, but he was cut off. He pulled the phone down, looked at the screen, and saw the blinking words telling him the call had ended. He immediately tried to call her back, but it would not go through. The signal bar at the top was gone, replaced with the symbol of a tower with a line through it. He clenched his teeth and growled. He tried to call again. And again. He finally gave up, screamed into the howling wind, and shoved the phone back in his pocket. He stood up, clutching his ribs, and looked around. There was nowhere to go.

He closed his eyes, breathed as deeply as he could without causing himself shooting pain, and then opened his eyes again. Lost and alone, he ran.

Quinn slammed her phone on the desk after trying to call Lester back for the fifth time. The same message telling her "the cellular subscriber is out of cellular range" made it clear that she was not going to get through. She put one arm across her chest, propped the other on her forearm, and pressed the fingertips of her propped arm into her forehead.

She stood in that position for several minutes, trying to figure out how there could be a loss of signal in a hospital room. Sometimes, there was interference from equipment, but it seemed odd. She also didn't understand why he was shouting her name into the phone or why it sounded like he was in the middle of a storm. Although she had heard him for only about two seconds, there was no mistaking the wind roaring in the background. She didn't pay much attention to news, and she didn't know much about Huron or the central part of the country, but she thought it was strange for there to be a storm in a place known for drought and heat.

She picked her phone up and opened the weather app. She typed *Huron* into the search bar and waited for the results. At first, everything seemed normal. The forecast was for the high eighties and low nineties with sunny skies. Then she saw the alert.

STORM ALERT FOR HURON AND ANDERSONVILLE COUNTY:

THUNDERSTORM. LIGHTNING STRIKES REPORTED. FLASH FLOODING.

Quinn clicked on the report and read the brief, poorly written flash article that stated an unexpected storm had struck the southern part of Andersonville County, a rural area several miles outside of Huron. She stared at it, not understanding. Where had the storm come from, and why would Lester be in the middle of it? The lack of signal, the sound of wind and rain, thunder in the background—it added up, but it made no sense.

She had a thought and backed out of the weather app. She opened a search bar and typed in Dillon's name, soldier, and funeral services. Surprisingly, the announcement for both Hudson and Huron came up. She clicked on the first link in the search results and hastily read through the key points of the announcements. And there it was.

Sharp will be laid to rest, with full military honors, in the Hudson State Cemetery. The cemetery is located outside of

Huron, Texas, in Andersonville County. The onsite service is at 11 a.m. on Tuesday, November 14.

Quinn set the phone down as the dots connected in her mind. Lester was nowhere near a hospital, but he might soon need one.

The demon came straight on and led with an obvious punch. Draven stood his ground and easily blocked it. Morane yelled and launched a series of strikes. Draven was forced back as he blocked and countered each of them. His own punches were deflected. Morane was powerful and quick. Kicks were added by both combatants.

One slipped through Draven's defenses, and he had to step back to avoid another. There was a slight pause in the fighting, and he held his stomach with his hand. He had grown accustomed to pain over the past week, but Morane inflicted far more damage when he hit than did Yusef's men. Draven knew he had to mount an offense and keep momentum on his side to keep Morane off balance.

He rushed in and launched his own series of attacks. They came together in a clash of fist, elbow, and knee strikes, both landing hit after hit on his opponent. They began to circle and move back and forth while striking, blocking, and countering in a blur. Draven pressed as much as he was pressed, felt the sting on his knuckles as much as he felt the sting on his head and body. The fury increased, and Morane began to electrify his strikes. Draven added the force of the wind to his own.

It became obvious to Draven that he was at a disadvantage. He realized that if the two of them continued to attack each other with elemental powers, the Earth would be slammed by the storm they were creating. He deflected a punch and took a slight step back to sneak a glance at Lester. The man was running through a flood of water, and even the watcher had difficulty seeing him through the heavy rain. He saw a building not far from Lester and felt a glimmer of hope.

It was dashed away by a kick to the face, then another. Draven stumbled back and reached up to his face. His vision blurred, and he could not see the next kick, the one that sent him flying. He did not go far, but he knew it was long enough for Morane to follow his descent and deliver a devastating attack. He hit the ground and bounced, just as Morane had. He bounced several more times until he came to a stop on his back. He sat up as quickly as he could. Far away, Morane's hands were raised, but the demon was facing away from Draven.

Lightning was gathered in between his hands, and Draven saw Lester running up the stairs to the building. Draven got to his feet and tried to run forward but stumbled. It was then that he realized he was not truly recovered from the abuse he had endured. He felt weak; his body was wracked with pain; and his legs were unstable. He looked up and saw that Morane was poised to launch, waiting for the moment Lester entered the building to send his lightning bolt.

Draven drew on all the strength he could and stood once again. He yelled Lester's name with all of the force he could gather into his nearly collapsed lungs, sending the wind with the sound of his voice and willing it to penetrate the storm. Beyond the spiritual realm, at the edge of the top step to the building, Lester paused and looked around. Draven felt his adrenaline surge, and he sprinted forward. The distraction didn't last long.

Lester ran into the building Morane sent the lightning. Draven didn't attack the demon. Instead, he kept running and slipped into the physical realm. He turned and braced himself as he descended toward the building. As soon as he turned, he took the force of the electricity in his body. He screamed as pure energy pulsed through him, holding him above the ground in an agonizing grip. He clenched his jaws and fists, but nothing could diminish the intense pain.

After what seemed like hours but was probably less than a second, he hit the ground, splashing through a foot of water. The lightning danced along the water and surged once more through his body, this time amplified. Draven managed to look around. The building had not been hit, but the lightning had surged far and wide enough to strike some trees at the roots and set them ablaze. Held by the impossibly strong electric current, he had no choice but to slip back into the spiritual realm.

He was freed from the deadly current, but Morane was waiting for him. The demon hit him from every angle, sending blow after blow to his head, stomach, chest, and then his back when the watcher fell forward. He was prone then and felt Morane's powerful foot striking his back repeatedly. It stopped only long enough for him to be picked up and thrown through the air.

CHAPTER TWENTY-FIVE

LESTER COULD BARELY LIFT HIS feet, but he forced himself to push through the wind and rain. He had seen a rooftop on the other side of the wide clearing he was now in, and that had given him the motivation to keep his burning legs churning through the heavy water. He was colder than he had ever been, and his fingers were numb. His teeth chattered incessantly, but he felt relief and hope wash over him stronger than the rain water when he came out of a cluster of trees and saw the front of a building.

He could not make out any details in the whitewash of the rain; but he knew there was shelter in front of him, and that was all that mattered. A sense of overwhelming dread came over his mind as soon as he touched the edge of the steps to the front door, but the storm was too strong to pause and contemplate emotions. He had to get inside. He hoped the door was open because he didn't want to have to bust it down and risk leaving the inside vulnerable to the elements.

At the top of the steps he reached out for the door handle, but he stopped when he heard something. He turned his head and strained to hear above the violent pounding of the rain and the howling wind. Not howling, he thought. Shouting. Someone was shouting. Someone far away, yet oddly close. The sound came only once, a single word: his name. Lester had been running for a while, so his heart rate was already elevated, but the sound of his name being shouted through the most sudden and intense storm he had ever seen made it pound.

As if his name was some sort of cue, the rain decreased slightly; but the sky grew eerily dark, and lightning surged high in the heavens. Lester could not afford to ponder the source of the shout. He turned back to the building, grabbed the door knob, and twisted. It turned easily in his hand, but the door did not immediately open. Lester made sure the knob was turned as far as it could go and and held it that way as he slammed his shoulder into the door. It swung inwardly, the sudden motion nearly knocking him down, and he stumbled through the doorway.

The wind followed him in full force, and he quickly turned and used his body weight to get the door shut. He pressed his back against it and surveyed the inside. It was a small building with rotting wood floors, ceilings, and walls. It was caked in thick dust and void of furniture. Lester thought about walking around to see what the rest of the building looked like, but the sudden quiet and lack of elements assaulting him reminded him of something.

The voice. It had sounded familiar.

Something exploded outside, and the force of it collided with the building. Lester was thrown to the floor. He felt cold and rain come in, and he crawled back to the door and forced it shut once more. As he was pushing it, he saw a surge of electricity fading from the flood water outside. Moreover, he got just a glimpse of a man in the darkness, in the water.

Only, the man wasn't actually in the water. And he wasn't actually a man. At least not human. Lester saw only what looked like a shadow, but it was a shadow made of light and shifting elements. Before he could take a full look, the man was gone, and necessity forced Lester to get the door shut.

He ran to a window and looked out. Despite the heavy rain, the explosion and surge of electricity had caused several trees to catch on fire, but the flames were quickly doused. He tried to look to where he had seen the creature of light, and he saw him again. But he was not alone. Another figure, this one taller, bigger, and dark, was stalking toward the creature of light. He saw the dark figure lash out at the other, and the creature of light fell over.

Lester moved as far away from the window as he could, scooting backwards on his rear end. When he was against the far wall, he reached into his pocket and pulled out his phone. He was breathing hard, and his heart was racing; but he managed to dial Quinn's number. The signal did not go through. He tried again. And again. Five times. Nothing. On the sixth try, he heard Quinn's voice, although broken up.

"Lester?" The worry in her voice was clear.

"Quinn, listen to me." He held up his hand while talking, as if she could see him. "I need you to pray."

"Lester, what is going on?"

He waved his hand in the air. "No questions. Please, Quinn. Pray." He sighed. "I know I've made a mess of everything, and I'm sorry." He was nearly shouting. Even in the building, the sound of the storm was too loud for normal voice inflections. "Right now, I just need you to pray. I'm in a lot of trouble, and I don't even know where I am."

"Lester, you can't expect me to listen to something like that and not ask questions."

He nodded. "I know, but you'll just have to trust me. I wouldn't trust me if I were you, but I'm begging you. Please pray."

There was no response. He said Quinn's name. Said it again. Nothing. He pulled the phone away and looked at it. The signal had been lost. All he could do was hope that she'd forgiven him enough to pray.

It was the only hope he had left.

Morane watched Draven sliding across the translucent black ground and smiled. He rolled his neck and then shook his head to clear the fogginess. Even weak, the watcher was powerful. Morane was about to call out to Draven to surrender when the watcher stood up. Even though Draven could barely get up and stood swaying when he did, the sight of his unyielding adversary infuriated Morane. He snarled and started to take a step forward.

Draven leapt into the air and let out a battle cry that caused the demon to pause. His eyes opened wide, and he wondered how the creature was still going. In the spiritual plane, Draven looked more solid then he did on Earth, where his body blended with his surroundings and allowed him to hide from human sight in the blink of an eye. High above Morane and poised to strike, radiating light, Draven looked like a falling star. Morane was so stunned by the sight that he offered no defense.

He was struck in his powerful jaw and knocked to the ground. He had a rush of panic, fear that Draven might win again, might banish him to the underworld once more; but the follow-up attack he anticipated did not come. He pushed himself up and turned to look at Draven, who was standing over him and swaying. His mouth was open, and the light emanating from him had dimmed to a faint glow.

Morane spun himself around, kicking his legs out as he turned and swept Draven's legs. The watcher fell backward and landed hard. Morane was on top of him, pummeling him with alternating punches to the temples and jaw. He then changed the direction of his attack and wrapped his powerful hands around Draven's throat. There was little resistance as he flexed his arms and tightened his grip. Draven made gurgling noises and slapped at Morane's arms, but that subsided after a moment. The watcher's eyes closed.

Morane stood, grabbing Draven's hand as he did. He was too filled with battle lust to smile, too consumed by his anger to enjoy the moment; but his hatred for the human was ever present. He started to drag Draven across the plane. His chest heaved, and he heard his own labored breaths. With little effort, he casually tossed a lightning bolt through the plane in the direction of the building the human had run into, not bothering to see where it landed.

The human would die; that was unmistakable. Dragging his archnemesis, Morane could only think of how sweet it would be to deliver one of Heaven's host into chains of darkness. That thought restored his smile.

Lester was huddled in a corner of the small building, clutching his knees to his chest with his forehead down on his kneecaps. His eyes were closed, but he could hear that the rain had slowed and the wind was no longer howling. That brought relief, but not nearly enough. His mind was a battlefield of warring thoughts.

Flashes of images and memories of the past week slammed into one another and blinked out of existence, only to be replaced by another set of competing images. He rocked back and forth and wished the glimpse had never happened. He began to wish that he had never seen the things he had, that he was still the same person. He wanted to be the same Lester, the same callous man without concern for others and their struggles.

"Do you hear that, God?" He lifted his head and shouted. "I don't care. I don't want to be a part of this!"

A violent explosion shook the building, and he had to shield his eyes as brilliant light exploded outside, filling the window. Immediately, the building was on fire, and smoke entered the room. He got to his feet and turned to run out of the back of the building but saw smoke in that direction, too. He didn't understand how both sides of the building had caught fire so quickly, but then he heard a creaking sound above him. He looked up and saw that the roof was on fire. The building had taken a direct bolt of lightning but had not been instantly leveled, and Lester knew why.

He dropped to his knees and called out to God. "Lord, forgive me. I don't want to doubt You. I don't want to be angry. I'm just scared, and I don't understand why any of this is happening. Please, have mercy on me."

He looked up. The roof was about to collapse, but when he looked around, he knew there was nowhere to go. The entire building was consumed with flames, except for a small circle around him. He bowed his head and squeezed his eyes shut.

"Please, Quinn. Pray. Pray." Lester opened his eyes and coughed as the smoke began to overwhelm him. Between coughs, he called out to God. "I'm not the man I was. Please let me prove it. Give me a chance."

Quinn held her phone at her waist, staring at the black screen. Lester's broken up words reverberated in her mind, asking her—*telling* her—to pray. She didn't bother fighting the tears streaming down her face. She wanted to scream and throw the phone. She had no idea what Lester was doing or where he was, but an anger she could not understand filled her. An image of her mother's disappointed look—along with a hundred wedding guests—assaulted her memory.

She sank to the floor, letting her back slide down her desk. On the ground, she shoved her head into her hands and pressed it to her knees. She sat up straight, angrily running her fingers through her hair, and slammed her back against the desk. It was solid and didn't budge. The back of her head hit, and she unconsciously closed her eyes from the sharp pain. When she opened her eyes again, she was looking up at the wall at the back of her office. Hanging there was a painting of Calvary. It was a hill at sunset with three crosses rising into the sky.

She studied it and felt a new stream of tears. Her heart sank, and she cried out to God. She told Him how sorry she was for never forgiving Lester and then lying about it to everyone. She wept and prayed, her eyes on the cross.

She wiped her face and pulled herself to her feet. Shaking her head at her own stubbornness, she went into her recent calls and redialed her mother. It rang several times, and Quinn began to cry again while she waited, but her mother's groggy voice could finally be heard.

"Hello?"

Quinn didn't give her mother time to talk. "Mom? I need you to wake up and listen."

"What?"

"Mom! Listen."

"Okay, Quinn. I'm listening, but—"

"Lester is in serious trouble, Mom. I don't know what's going on, but I think his life could be in danger."

"Quinn, what are you—"

"Mom!" Quinn steadied herself. "No questions. Pray, Mom. I know you don't like him, and I'm not so sure I do right now either, but this man needs someone to pray for him."

"Of course, I'll pray, Quinn. I don't hate the man, but—"

"No. Don't. Just pray." Quinn's mind raced. "And start a prayer chain, Mom. Call Gloria, and tell her to pray and start calling everybody. Now!"

She hung up before her mother could respond. She stammered through a prayer for Lester as she opened up a social media app on her phone. She frantically typed:

URGENT!!!!

IMMEDIATE PRAYER REQUEST

FOR LESTER SHARP! LIFE IN DANGER.

PRAY NOW!!!

She copied the message and sent it out on every social media app she had, all while praying. She fell to her knees and dropped the phone in a fit of sobs.

"God, please help him. I'm sorry. I forgive him. Please save him."

CHAPTER TWENTY-SIX

DRAVEN FELT HIMSELF BEING DRAGGED and heard someone talking. Disoriented and in darkness, panic washed over him, but it quickly subsided when he opened his eyes and saw Morane. He was facing away from him, dragging Draven across the spirit realm. Draven quickly scanned his surroundings and saw that they were no longer near Lester.

Space and time were, to a degree, suspended in the spirit realm. Draven could tell that not much time had passed, but a great deal of ground had been covered. He lifted his head, tucked his chin to his chest, and saw a whirlpool of red light in the distance. The air around it glowed in a dim crimson, and winged creatures with furry, canine faces flew in swooping circles around it. He did his best to twist his body around and managed to get his head turned at enough of an angle to see the building Lester had gone toward. They were far from it, but Draven's eyes saw it in full detail as if it were only a hundred yards away. The building was on fire, and he knew that Lester was in there.

He turned back around when he heard Morane's voice.

"Don't worry, watcher. Everything will be fine. The human will die, but they all do. You know this; you've seen it a thousand times." The demon continued to effortlessly drag Draven along, never looking back. Draven looked ahead to the whirlpool and recognized it for what it was: an entrance to Hades.

Morane was still talking. "And you will have rest in the company of the fallen ones. Of course, not true rest. You will be bound in darkness, tortured, haunted by the screams of the damned; that much is true. But you won't have to witness the depravity of this world any longer. After a few decades, you'll thank me."

While Morane was talking, Draven heard another voice. A whisper. Barely discernible over the screams coming from the whirlpool, which grew louder every foot closer they got. Morane was saying something about his own release being dependent on eliminating the human and Draven simply being in the wrong place at the wrong time. Draven stopped listening to the demon and strained to hear the whisper.

More than one voice.

He closed his eyes and concentrated. The voices were not whispers, he realized. They were simply distant, overpowered by the cacophony of noises surrounding him. He cleared his mind and forced the screams away, forced the sound of his body being dragged and the voice of Morane away. One by one, words began to filter to him—words of prayer, he realized. They were frantic and coming from all over the world. He heard a name. The rest were competing words, words a watcher was not capable of discerning. Understanding the prayers of saints was not within the power of an angel, but the name being uttered was clear.

Lester.

Draven felt a calling. Sensed himself being urged to attend to the recipient of answered prayer. He pulled against Morane, drawing his feet toward his chest. Morane was not looking at him, so the change in momentum caught him off-guard and gave Draven the break he needed to then kick out with both feet. Morane had been forced to turn when Draven had pulled his feet in, and his side was now exposed to Draven's kicking feet. Draven landed a clean blow to Morane's ribs, causing him to stumble and flee. It was not a powerful kick because Draven was in an awkward position, and Morane was only slightly phased by it, but it gave Draven room to get to his feet.

As soon as Draven stood, Morane was on him, fists leading. Draven spun backward around the first punch and continued to spin until he was facing Morane's back. He launched a fury of punches into the demon's dark flesh. Morane cringed and tried to twist away, but Draven went with him and continued to drive his fists into the thick hide.

The screams behind him intensified but so did the prayers, now loud and resonating. He heard them both and focused on the calling, the holy urging within every fiber. Morane managed to throw himself into a forward roll, stand, and turn to face Draven. Draven stalked forward, undaunted, and launched another attack. This time it was fists, feet, elbows, and knees going into Morane's head and body, but Morane began to counter. They went back and forth, but the building was now in Draven's line of sight. It was farther away than he thought, but he caught a glimpse of Lester through the window, shadowed in flames.

Draven intensified the number of strikes he threw, and soon Morane had to step back with the force of each one. He alternated between head and body shots, keeping the demon off-balance. He landed a solid punch to Morane's gut. Morane bent down, and Draven punched him on the side of his head. Morane nearly fell, but Draven stepped in and grabbed him by the head and waist. He yelled and pulled with all of his strength, strength he did not realize he possessed. Morane was airborne in the next moment, soaring above Draven's head and extended arms. He watched in amazement as the demon was thrown nearly out of sight, and he marveled at how far he had just thrown him.

Draven snarled and took a step forward, but then he remembered the building and the fire. He called on the elements of wind and rain and sent them flooding toward the building. He turned just enough to see the water hit and distinguish the flames in a rush before thrusting himself in the air with a yell. His vision slipped between the spiritual and physical realms to help him get his bearings as he rocketed toward the fallen demon. The events of the past week came to his mind, and he was temporarily mesmerized by his own power. Morane had flown beyond the fiery whirlpool, across hundreds of miles.

As he approached, he saw that Morane had gotten to his feet and was mustering a lightning strike. The skies were filled with electricity, sparking and dancing through the night. Draven led with the wind, sending a heavy gust into Morane that forced him to pause the strike he was preparing to unleash; then Draven came in hard. He shifted his body into a spear and collided with Morane with such force that both of them continued with the momentum. He willed himself forward, wanting only to get Morane as far away from Lester as possible. He shut out every thought, closed his eyes, and pushed with the last of his strength.

Cold, razor-sharp water hit his face. He opened his eyes and immediately regretted it. Salt water cut into his skin and eyes as he and Morane were immersed into the heart of the Atlantic. The sudden shock of it overwhelmed him, and he suddenly felt weightless and calm. He was in darkness, floating. He no longer had a grip on Morane, nor did he have a grip on reality. It was peaceful, dark, and cold.

Draven shook his head and flailed with his hands and feet. He was in water. Unlike a human, he did not need to hold his breath; but the shock of suddenly waking up in the ocean overwhelmed him, and he swallowed some of the salt water. He looked around. It was mostly darkness, but he could make out Morane's drifting body in the distance to his left. Far below him, he saw a large gate on the ocean floor next to a coral mound and knew exactly where he was. He focused and swam toward Morane, grabbed the unconscious demon, and then speared them both toward the ocean bottom.

Once there, he held Morane with one hand and lifted the bars with the other. They came up with a swirling cloud of dirt that filled the water around him. He allowed it to clear before looking down into the pit the bars had covered. He was hundreds of feet below the surface, but the pitch-black pit he was looking into descended thousands of feet. He heard screams coming up from the pit, clear despite the water. With a snarl, he pulled Morane along with him and descended into the darkness.

Lester kept his knees tucked to his chest tightly, his arms wrapped around them, and his head pressed into the top of his thighs. He could feel the intense heat of the flames on his back, and he could not stop coughing. Every breath was acidic, smoke-filled, and burned. He rocked back and forth, praying.

He heard the cracking of the floor over the roar of the flames, and the entire building shook as it began to collapse in on itself. He prayed through every sound, through the pain, begging God to spare him. The flames were on him then. His clothes caught fire, and he began to scream. The smoke threatened to choke him out and asphyxiate him before the pain of being burned alive caused him to pass out. He hoped for neither as he prayed but knew it was inevitable.

He heard a loud crash above him. Still screaming in agony, he lifted his head and saw the ceiling coming down. He balled himself up and wrapped his arms around his head. Flames jumped onto him the moment his face connected with the collapsing floor, catching his hair and arms on fire as chunks of the ceiling fell all around him. For a brief flash, he thought of Quinn and felt regret, but that thought was dashed by the worst pain he had ever felt in his life. He screamed and writhed as the flames consumed him, and the words from Pastor Greene's sermon echoed in his mind, "I shall come forth as gold."

Heavy, freezing water dropped in on him with intensity he had never known. Instinctively, he moved his arms and looked up and was nearly drowned. The water cascaded like a mighty waterfall, collided with the burning, falling floor, and extinguished the flames with a hissing sound that made him think of the steam engines on an old train. He had to shield himself from the onslaught of water and was forced to roll onto his stomach.

Steam rose all around him, and he breathed it in, which proved too much for his exhausted, smoke-saturated lungs. He tried to rise but collapsed in a wave of dizziness. His face splashed through water and smacked against the hot, wet wood of the floor. His thoughts slipped into darkness.

Lester sat up and gasped for air. He pushed himself up and stumbled to his feet. He spun back and forth, looking all around and sucking in huge gulps of fresh air. He paused when he realized that the air was not filled with steam or smoke. The building was dark. No fire. No smoke. No steam rising from smoldering wood. It was completely out, although the floor and walls were nearly destroyed, and water dripped from the ceiling. He completed a circle and inspected the room.

He lifted one of his arms to check his burns. His arm shone silver in the beam of moonlight cast on it through the hole in the roof. There were no burn marks. Not even singed hair, and he felt no pain. He looked at the other arm and saw similar results. He patted himself up and down, felt his face, and ran his fingers through his hair. He was unharmed but soaking wet. He slowly lowered his arms and turned to the window. Cautiously, he walked over and peered through. The night was clear, and the flood water had receded. He looked over his shoulder, giving the building one last glance; and he realized that it was not a house, as he had thought. He was not sure what to make of it, nor did he want to stay and investigate.

Lester pulled open the door, which was dangling from the top hinge at an angle, and then he walked down the steps while looking around. The treetops were gone from many of the trees, and there were scorch marks along the ground. Everything was wet, but the night sky was clear. He walked away from the building, looking left and right as he went, and saw that what he thought was a small clearing was actually a very large and open area that had been purposely cleared.

To his right was a wide, concrete parking area. It was all but covered in grass and weeds, and the concrete was cracked in so many places that he doubted any cars had parked there in years. He stood in silence, staring at the parking lot, and saw a road leading to it. The road led to the highway, and he saw the lights of cars in the distance. For some reason, that made him laugh, and he shook his head. He turned around to look at the building again and was humbled by what he saw.

The moon cast enough light on the siding for him to be able to see that it had once been painted in brilliant white. Now what remained was dingy and scorched from the fire. A once carefully laid path of gravel with plants lining either side led to the steps, and the remnant of an old sign was to the right of the steps. There were only a few letters intact on the sign, but it looked as if they had once spelled The Church at Harmond Grove.

Lester sighed and lowered his head.

Not sure what else to do, he walked over to the steps, pulled out his phone, and sat down with a tiny splash. The phone was dead, killed by the fire and then the rain water. He marveled that the phone was not a melted ball of plastic after enduring such heat.

Nearly burned alive.

Pastor Greene's sermon came to mind. He did not understand why he had endured what he had, but he knew he was not the same. His faith had wavered in the heart of the storm, but he had found it again, rekindled in the same flames that had nearly killed him.

He thought of the three Hebrew princes in the book of Daniel. They had refused to worship a pagan king or his image, so they had been thrown into a furnace. They came out unharmed. Not even their clothes had been singed. The pagan king, Nebuchadnezzar, had announced that there was a fourth man in the flames that had the appearance of the Son of God.

Lester had seen something outside the building, two inhuman figures battling in the midst of the storm. No hallucination. They were real. He did not think either of them was the Son of God. Jesus would not need to engage in combat; a simple word spoken, and His enemies would fall. But there was no doubt it had something to do with him.

The storm had been too sudden, too intense, to be coincidence. It brought more questions, ones he could not answer. What he did know was that he had not been alone.

He had felt the flames burning him, but there were no marks on him. He had been praying, even as the flames promised to end his time on Earth. He looked up at the moon, the miraculously clear sky, and smiled. He tossed his phone into the remnants of the flower bed next to the steps. He lifted both hands high, closed his eyes, and worshipped the One who had been in the fire with him.

Quinn looked at the weather report for Huron and Andersonville County on her phone. The forecast was for the high nineties with a lot of humidity. The moon displayed was nearly full and called for high visibility. A report ticked its way across the bottom of the screen, stating that the storm and flash flood had passed. There was no explanation, and there had been no reports of loss of life or injuries.

She checked her messages. Nothing. She looked at her call log. No missed calls. She dialed her voicemail, just to make sure. No messages. She blacked out her screen and rested her head against the back of her desk and spoke to the walls.

"Where are you, Lester?"

It was going to be a long night.

Draven secured the thick chains around Morane's waist and locked them in place on the stone wall that the demon's back was pressed against. He looked up at the incredible height of the blackened wall, ignoring Morane's snarls of protest. Fires burned, and screams echoed behind him. The wall stretched beyond even his sight, though he knew that was an illusion. This place was hidden from mortal eyes.

He looked back down and stared into Morane's sinister, onyx eyes. They were filled with hatred and no remorse. Draven wanted nothing more than to kill the demon and end their ageless battle, but he was restrained by his sense of duty and honor. He stepped back and surveyed his work, giving the chains a slight nod.

"You think these chains will hold me?" Morane snapped his sharp teeth and struggled against the chains, which rattled with his movements.

Draven shook his head. "I know they won't. I have no doubt you'll be back on Earth, creating havoc."

Morane smiled. "I will make that wretched human's life miserable when I return."

"I'm sure you'll try," Draven said. "And I'll be there to stop you." He took a step forward and leaned in so that his face was close to Morane's. "I always am."

Morane laughed as Draven leaned back again. "You won't defeat me again, watcher. You nearly lost this time."

"I've nearly lost before, but who's the one in chains?" He turned his back to Morane.

"All the same, you will not win the battle that is coming."

Draven turned just enough to see Morane over his shoulder. His mind recalled words spoken by the visitor to his prison—Orac, he realized. The captain of the watchers had told him there was a war coming.

"What battle?" he asked Morane.

Morane only laughed in reply, a maniacal, sadistic laugh.

Draven nodded and turned away. He looked out over the chasm that divided that side of Hades from what was once a paradise. He remembered the day it had been removed but stopped himself short of reminiscing on those days. Morane's warning had startled him, and he did not want that to show through.

"The serpent may ascend," he said without looking back at the demon. "But know that all of your kind will come to bow before the Lion of Judah. Enjoy your imprisonment, traitor."

He leapt into the air and began his ascent from the underworld. As he flew upward, he heard Morane say, "Enjoy your death, fool."

He continued his ascent, beyond the flames, beyond the cavernous core of the Earth, into a vast emptiness and darkness until he was immersed in cold, briny water. He torpedoed himself through until his hands wrapped around bars above his head. He pushed upward and knew that something was out of place as he emerged onto the ocean floor, so he paused after closing the bars again.

Though he was in the darkest part of the sea, he could see as easily as if he were under the stars. Beside the gate was a figure, what he had previously thought was simply a mound of coral. He approached it, walking through the water as if it were nothing more than air. It was a man, giant in stature compared to the watcher. Most of his body was covered in coral, but his face and parts of his body that were exposed had the complexion of the ancient Greeks. The giant appeared dead, but Draven sensed life. It was no mortal creature. Few things could invoke fear in a watcher, but a distant memory screamed from the recesses of his mind, preventing him from taking another step. The identity of the giant clicked, and Draven retreated. Not for fear of the giant, but the implications of him being there, rather than locked away in Hades.

"Orion."

Orac's warning sounded like an alarm in his mind. *"Dark forces are gathering. The war is upon us."*

Draven shook his head and stepped back. Then he fled. He ascended as fast as he could, through the sea, into the freezing air of the surface world, and back to the sanctuary of the spirit realm.

And there it was. The same, unfamiliar feeling that had been there in Khufia as soon as he had entered the spirit realm. It was alien. Something was in the spirit realm that did not belong. Human, he thought. He sensed fear.

Draven remembered Orac's other warnings. His failure to report immediately to Heaven after Lester's glimpse had resulted in his captivity. He was obligated to report now. But his desire to know if Lester had survived was too strong. The rules had changed, and until he knew exactly how, he was operating on pure instinct. He would just have to face the consequences later.

In a matter of minutes, he was standing in the spirit realm, watching Lester. The man was drenched. The building behind him was almost completely decimated. Draven watched as Lester lowered his hands, folded them in his lap, and opened his eyes. He stared out into the night, never realizing that he was looking directly at Draven. The watcher fought a myriad of conflicting thoughts and emotions. The code of the watchers prevented him from making contact without permission. His sense of duty was berating him, begging him to report what he had seen at the gate to Hades. The series of events in the past week demanded he go to this man.

He knew he was about to make a compromise he might come to regret, but he stepped through the plane.

Lester lowered his arms, slowly, and folded his hands in his lap. He opened his eyes and stared straight ahead, into the night, wondering how he was going to get home but also not caring. The air seemed different. It was the kind of night on which a person should feel alone, but he did not. He felt the presence of God. His peace.

But that was not all Lester felt. He knew he was not alone, spiritually, but there was something else there. Physically there. He tilted his head and listened. There was a sound. A humming. The air in front of him grew warmer, thinner, and seemed to stretch. He blinked several times, shook his head, then rubbed his eyes. He squinted his eyes, peering into the space in front of him, and saw a figure emerge.

That was the only way he could describe it: a figure. It had a head, arms, and legs; but as it stepped through nothing to stand before him, Lester thought he was looking at a silhouette against the night. The stretching of the air collapsed behind the figure, which was still dark and seemed like nothing more than a section of the ground and sky cut out and shaped into a tall man. Then the figure took on a more solid, definite shape. It blended perfectly with its environment, better than any chameleon ever could; but as it stepped forward, the figure became three dimensional, and Lester could see eyes and a mouth.

He wanted to run, to scream, but he was frozen. No monster under his bed as a child had ever terrified him more than what was standing in front of him. He immediately thought of Quinn and never seeing her again, of all what had happened in the last week, and he wondered if it was all meaningless. And then, he noticed something as the figure turned its head. It had hair, but not just any hair. Lester had to blink several times again, sure his eyes were tricking him, but the figure had what appeared to be long, twisted hair; and though it blended with the silver of the moon and the blackness of the sky, the twists resembled dreadlocks.

"Hey, Lester." The voice sounded like it was mixed with water, and it echoed. Lester did not respond, but he felt his mouth hanging open. "You survived." The echo was not as loud this time, and the voice sounded more familiar.

"Draven?"

The figure shifted, shrank, and slimmed. The locks of water and shadow were replaced with dark brown dreadlocks. The silhouette skin transitioned into the dark skin of his guide. The figure's eyes turned from reflective ebony to ocean blue, and they settled on Lester. In seconds, he was looking at Draven—slender, dark-skinned, and seemingly human.

Lester did run then. He was up from the steps and running to his right with his heart threatening to beat its way out of his chest when a strong hand grabbed him by the wrist and pulled him back. He yelled and put his hands over his face to block the terror of what he might see next, but nothing came. Then there was a soft chuckle, and he lowered his hands, easing them to his sides. Draven was standing in front of him, suppressing laughter.

"Dude, you just gonna run?"

Lester trembled and pointed but could not form words.

"What? Never see a black man at night before?"

Lester swallowed. "It's not like that," he managed to say as his heart rate decreased and he felt a sense of irrational calm washing over him.

"Sure, man. Whatever." Draven smiled.

Lester acted before he knew what he was doing, stepping forward and wrapping his arms around Draven. He felt himself about to tear up, so he quickly backed away. He wiped at his eyes and took a step back toward the church.

"What is this? What are you?"

Draven cocked his head to the side and raised an eyebrow. "You still haven't figured that part out?"

Lester waved his hands in front of his face. "No, no. I get it. You're an angel, *or something*. But, what? Like. What?"

"Yeah, we don't all have wings, man."

Lester stood in front of Draven, blinking. There was no doubt; it was his guide. Rage suddenly welled inside of him, and he stepped forward.

"Was it you?"

Draven's forehead wrinkled. "What?"

"Has it been you all this time?" Lester felt his chest heaving as he fought to keep his breathing calm.

Draven tilted his head to the side. "What are you talking about?"

Lester shook his head. "The lawyer. The woman at the coffee shop. The salesman on the plane?" Draven arched his brow as Lester talked. "The doctor?"

Draven held his hands up. "Do I look like a doctor to you?" He let his hands go back to his sides. "What are you saying?"

"I just saw you shapeshift. Who else could it have been?" Lester did not mean to yell, but he was fighting to contain his anger.

Draven lowered his head and nodded. "Oh. I see." He looked up. "I don't know what you've been through while I was gone, Lester—and there's some things you just shouldn't know—but whoever was messing with you, it wasn't me."

Lester turned and walked away, stopped, then wheeled around and pointed at Draven. "I thought you said you'd be watching."

Draven shrugged. "And I thought I would be. Let's just say, you don't know what I've been through either."

Lester shook his head. "Dillon died. My whole world's been flipped on its head, man."

Draven nodded. "I guess you could say the same about my world. But I am sorry about your brother."

Lester sighed. And tossed his hands up. "Sorry? Why did you take me to that place? Why did I have to see my own brother about to die?"

Draven shook his head. "I don't know. Up until a week ago, I just followed orders."

Lester furrowed his eyebrows. "Up until a week ago? What does that mean?" He waved his hands in front of his face. "Forget it. I don't want to know. Look, whatever that glimpse was, it worked. Okay? It changed me, and all this craziness in the past week has changed me. I almost died tonight, but I think it was for a reason."

"I'm glad to hear that, Lester." He put his hands in his pockets and walked forward. "I'm sorry you had to go through it alone."

Lester folded his arms and shrugged. "That's just it. I didn't go through it alone. I mean, it seemed like it, but now I know that I've never been alone. I don't understand anything about what's going on, but I know the Lord is with me."

Draven smiled. "Then it was all worth it."

"All what?" Lester unfolded his arms. "Where have you been, Draven?"

Draven shook his head. "Can't tell you, dude."

"Why not?"

"Just can't."

"Are you serious?"

"Very."

Lester rolled his eyes and groaned. "Fine. Secret angel stuff. Whatever. But I need to know something." He paused and pointed at Draven. "Why do you talk like this and not all . . . you know."

"Like an angel?"

Lester nodded.

"This is more fun. Comes with the human disguise. Is that really what you want to talk about?"

Lester shook his head. "No. What just happened to me? That was you I saw, wasn't it? You were fighting something?"

Draven leaned his head back. "You saw that?"

"Uh huh. During the storm. It was like water and lightning in a battle."

Draven nodded. "Yeah, something like that. I can't believe you saw it, though. I can't tell you what happened, and I can't stay. I shouldn't even be here talking to you."

"Why?"

"There are rules to this sort of thing and I broke them."

"By talking to me?"

Draven nodded.

"So, you're in trouble?"

Draven shrugged. "I don't know. I'm not really worried about that right now. Something bigger is happening, and I need to find some answers."

"Big like what?"

"I don't know, and I can't tell you. Like I said, I shouldn't be here."

"Then why tell me that much? You know it just makes a person curious when you say stuff like, 'Something bigger is happening, and

I need to find some answers.' And if you're not supposed to be here, why are you?"

"I had to make sure you were okay."

Lester took a deep breath and exhaled. "Well, I am. I think. I don't know. It's been one of the worst weeks of my life, but it's over. So, what now? Do I just, like, call your name, and you show up?"

Draven shook his head and glanced at his feet. "No. You won't be seeing me anymore. I broke the rules, and there's going to be consequences for that. But now you know there's a lot going on that your mortal eyes don't see. Something will always be trying to destroy you, but there will always be someone fighting for you."

"You mean you?"

Draven laughed. "No, the Lord of hosts fights for you, Lester. Never forget that." He stepped back, and his body began to shift.

"Wait!" Lester called out and held his hands out toward Draven. "That's it?"

"Sorry."

"But what am I supposed to do now? I'm stuck in the middle of nowhere. I don't even have a phone."

Draven had fully shifted back into the silhouetted figure, and his voice became the watery echo once more.

"Be seeing you, Lester."

Then he was gone.

Lester stood, staring at the now empty space in front of him. As the air stabilized, a hundred questions ran together in his mind, along with a thousand worries. The ones that stood out were how to get home, what to do with his shop, and what to say to Quinn. He pushed every other thought away and focused on one. He was not alone anymore.

Moonlight was shining on the broken road that led out of the woods. He went and retrieved his phone, in case the sensitive information and his contacts could be salvaged. He slipped the phone into his pocket, then looked up at the road and headed toward it.

EPILOGUE

DRAVEN KEPT HIS EYES FIXED on Lester as he merged into the spirit realm. He knew he had said more than he should have. He should not have gone to Lester at all, and there was a touch of fear in his mind that he would soon face the consequences of his actions; but none of that mattered to him in that moment. Lester was alive. Morane had failed. In that moment, things were as they should be.

But then, they were not.

The unfamiliar feeling was there again, alerting him of an alien presence. He sensed something more tangible this time, felt a presence that could be touched. He turned and lashed out, grabbing onto something. He felt his hand grasp a taught, muscled throat. He thrust his body forward so that he was fully immersed into the realm and gripped the throat tightly. He growled as his vision shifted, and he came to a stop. He saw the man whose throat he was holding, and the familiar face made Draven release him and back away.

Barely visible, shifting in and out of the realm, was a man who seemed more shadow than human. He wore the urban camouflage of a military soldier, and he was tall. He disappeared and reappeared several times, being covered by shadow. Draven did not mistake the face. He had seen this man many times, most recently sitting in the commander's seat of an armored vehicle outside Abu Ghraib, Iraq.

Draven swallowed hard. "Dillon?"

The man's body shifted enough to be seen, and he nodded. "Help," he spoke.

And then he disappeared.

Lester was nearly dry and all the way exhausted. His feet were blistered from walking in wet socks and shoes, and the humidity in the air was amplified by the dampness of his clothes. He took one step after another, keeping his eyes fixed on the speckled lights of the city on the far away horizon. He wasn't sure how long he had been walking, but he figured it had to be more than an hour. Nor did he know how far from the city he actually was. He was not from there, and he had been in a daze on the cab ride to the cemetery.

For the first fifteen minutes or so cars and trucks had passed him at regular intervals of a minute or so, but that had turned into one car every few minutes and then to no more cars before or behind him. The moon had risen fully in the sky, but it did little to comfort him against the looming darkness. It felt almost palpable, as if the black sky was a hand closing about him. But he trudged on, intent on getting home and putting his life in order. He was not scared. Fear had left him in the fire.

The road before him lit up dimly. He glanced over his shoulder but did not stop walking. A pinprick of light appeared in the distance, like a beacon against the dark. Lester turned his head and continued walking. He had no hope that the driver of the car would be different than any of the other drivers who had passed by him without so much as a glance in the last hour. The low whine of the engine rode the almost non-existent breeze and teased his ear with hope of not walking anymore.

Against better judgment and without much hope, he stopped and turned in the direction of the oncoming vehicle. It was approaching at a somewhat more rapid speed than normal. He sighed and was about to turn back around, convinced that the driver was driving at that speed with an intent to get into the city as fast as possible. There would be no slowing down, no picking up a half-drenched hitchhiker on a nearly abandoned road in the middle of the night.

But then the car slowed. The engine became quieter, the headlights brighter. Lester felt a flicker of hope as the driver pulled to the side of the road and came to a stop. Lester squinted his eyes and lifted a hand in front of his face. He took a few cautious steps toward the car, straining to see details of it. It was red and looked like it could be either a Honda or a Toyota. He made his way to the passenger side and moved to lean into the window to talk to the driver.

Crammed into the driver's seat, taking a noisy sip of coffee, Duck stared at Lester. As soon as Lester opened his mouth to ask why and how the man was there, Duck held his free hand in front of him with his palm toward Lester.

He sighed. "Get in, Lester. We need to talk."

QUESTIONS FOR GROUP DISCUSSION AND PERSONAL REFLECTION

1. Quinn is reluctant to pray for Lester because she has not forgiven him for hurting her. What are some things that hinder your prayer life?

2. Lester finds himself facing difficulties immediately after making his decision to be more compassionate and serve the Lord. Have you dealt with this in your own life after making a decision to follow Christ?

3. Ibrahim is resolved to honor his Savior; but when he is faced with the possibility of death, he lies and even denounces Jesus Christ. This is an extreme situation. What are some more common ways Christians often betray the Lord, even without knowing it?

4. There is a letter at the beginning of all three parts of this book from Lester. How do the things he writes about connect with each of the parts?

5. Why do you think Lester was so angry in the hospital? Even toward Quinn?

6. When Quinn finally decides to pray for Lester, it comes after seeing a picture of Calvary. What is the connection to Calvary and Quinn's decision?

7. While still suffering from amnesia, Draven is visited by the commander of the watcher angels, Orac. He tells Lester there is a war coming. What war do you think he may be referring to?

8. When Draven returns to the spirit realm after speaking to Lester, he discovers that the "alien" presence he has been feeling is actually Lester's brother, Dillon. When Draven lets go of him, Dillon disappears and calls out for help. What do you think may have happened?

9. Duck is obviously more than he appears. Who do you think he really is?

TOPICS FOR FURTHER STUDY

Battling demons

Humans cannot physically battle demons. We wrestle not against flesh and blood (Ephesians 6:12). Spiritual warfare is real. We have an enemy (1 Peter 5:8). The enemy spirit is the antichrist (1 John 4:2-4). The enemy is the god of this world and has blinded unbelievers (2 Corinthians 4:4). The weapons of our warfare are prayer, fasting, and the Word of God (Ephesians 6:11-18).

Appearances of Angels and Demons

Draven's and Morane's appearances are fictions of my imagination, but it is based on the description of the "man" who appeared to Daniel when he was at the river Hiddekel (Daniel 10). Draven is not immediately rescued by other angels. This is also based on passages from the book of Daniel. Daniel prayed for help for three weeks, but the man that appears to him says he was delayed by the "prince of Persia" until Michael, "one of the chief princes," came to help him (Daniel 10).

Trials and Tribulations

Lester's situation is based loosely on the book of Job, but his story is familiar to many who have made decisions to follow Christ. As already established, the enemy is real and seeks to devour whom he may. As soon as Lester decides to follow Christ and be more compassionate, his world is turned upside down. Such trials are discouraging, but we must remember that they serve a purpose. Tribulation brings hope (Romans 5).

Suffering for Christ in Today's World

We are commanded in Scripture to remember those who are suffering for Christ. My depiction of Somalia and the suffering of Christians in that hostile country may be fiction, but the situation is all too real. Al-Shabaab is a real organization, and its members have vowed to wipe out all Christians from the nation. Many who convert to Christianity in Somalia are immediately killed, often by family members. Hebrews 13:3 says, "Remember them that are in bonds, as bound with them; and them which suffer adversity, as being yourselves also in the body." Please pray about and consider supporting organizations such as The Voice of the Martyrs and International Christian Concern.

THE JOURNEY OF FATE SERIES

ANGEL OF FATE - A SHORT STORY

FATE OF THE WATCHMAN

FATE OF THE REDEEMED

Before time froze, angels and demons battled for a man's soul.

Hidden among the rooftops of a dark city, the archangel, Orac watches as a lone vehicle travels into the night. Armed with his fiery sword and orders to protect the driver of the vehicle at all costs, Orac takes flight. He seizes on the element of surprise to defeat the demon, Talnuc, but soon discovers that the demon is not alone . . .

Lester Sharp is a workaholic, obsessed with the success of his business and oblivious to the world around him.

All of that changes when a peculiar stranger comes into his shop asking for food and help. Lester soon finds himself on an impossible journey around the world to bear witness to some of the greatest tragedies a person can know, all frozen in a single moment of time.

In this challenging and gripping novel, debut author Chad Pettit, delivers a supernatural, pulse-pounding adventure in which Lester Sharp is in for the longest second of his life and learns lessons to last a lifetime.

For more information about
Chad Pettit
&
Fate of the Redeemed
please visit:

www.chadpettit.net
www.facebook.com/ChadPettit.Writer
@pettit_chad

For more information about
AMBASSADOR INTERNATIONAL
please visit:

www.ambassador-international.com
@AmbassadorIntl
www.facebook.com/AmbassadorIntl

*If you enjoyed this book, please consider leaving us a review on
Amazon, Goodreads, or our website.*